DARK
BUSINESS

C J LAURENSON

Acknowledgements

I would like to thank everyone who has helped in any way in the writing of this book, the radical redraftings of it and the innumerable edits.

A special mention to Dr. James H.K. Grieve, Emeritus Professor at the University of Aberdeen, who answered all my questions, with kindness and good humour, and even made me laugh on occasion, which can't be bad! If I got anything right in terms of the medical details, it is entirely down to him. Any mistakes are, of course, all my own work.

Thanks also, to D.I. David Parkin, of the City of London Police, who gave me his insights into such things as interpersonal relationships within the police force and disciplinary procedures, as well as advising on other sources of information. As with the good doctor above, any accuracy in police procedures will be thanks to David's advice, and all mistakes entirely of my own making.

Special thanks must, of course, go to all those brave souls who offered to read my book and/or who made helpful suggestions and encouraging noises, including (in no particular order) Beth Gerrard, Lynda Froud, Ian Borthwick, Jane McAlinden, Jean Kinloch, Gillian Carson, Mary Blance, Colette Duggan, Anne Mackenzie, Tina Kingsman, Amanda Quail, Pamela Muir and Di Farmer. I am notoriously forgetful and disorganised, so if I've missed anyone out, please do let me know and I will amend this section.

Last, but definitely not least, grateful thanks go to Matthew, Robbie and Hannah, my three amazing, and apparently all-grown-up children (how did that happen?), who have been there for me throughout this journey, rescuing me from an astonishing array of technical problems to do with recalcitrant laptops, infuriating software and, of course, my own Ludditesque ineptitude.

1

It was closing time. Union Street was swarming with people, their voices amplified by alcohol, their progress impeded by it. Stephanie weaved and swerved, trying to keep her distance from lurching bodies, clawing hands, the fug of stale perfume and sweat. Someone grabbed her arm and she recoiled, with a gasp of terror.

'Fit's wrang wi' ye?'

A red face loomed over her, breath ripe with stale beer and cigarettes.

She pulled away, and ducked into an alleyway to wait for the bulk of the crowd to pass. She tried to control her breathing to minimise the agony of bruised muscle over cracked ribs. Her face felt tight, still swollen from the beating; she tried not to touch it, didn't want to ruin the thick make-up she'd used to hide the bruises. Don't let anyone see the damage. Blend in. Be invisible. Get away. Bus, train - didn't matter. Anywhere would do.

She emerged from the lane and crossed the main road at the lights, careful not to catch anyone's eye, keeping her distance, but constantly alert for any sign she was being followed. She headed downhill, towards the harbour, walking quickly, her small shoulder bag thudding against her tender ribs. Ahead of her, more people started pouring out of a pub. She veered off down another side road and carried on going. The narrow street was deserted, cobbles shining damp under sparse street lights. A throat-catching stench of urine lingered here, mingling with the fishy tang of the dockside, making a nauseating bouquet. But she was almost there.

She hurried on, turned the corner, and started running, blinkered, fixed on her goal. The slap-slap of her feet on the cobbles rang out in the narrow alleyway but she paid no attention. She could see the bright lights of the station now, less than fifty yards away.

Her heart was thumping in her ears. She was aware of her own noisy breathing, ragged gasps and an occasional sob of pain as her muscles screamed for her to stop. But she couldn't stop yet. She was almost there. She didn't hear the dull click of a car door opening, or the soft, whispering tread of rubber soled shoes.

A swooping shadow fell right across her path. Before she had time to turn or scream, powerful arms were around her, crushing her throat, squeezing fresh stabs of pain from broken ribs, pulling her down into the darkness.

'Hello? Fraser?'

He couldn't remember even giving her the number but he must have done; it was ex-directory. He shivered, naked apart from a damp towel tied around his waist. Water dripped off him, making a ticking sound on ice-cold quarry tiles, as his feet began to cool and ache.

'Laurie?'

'I'm sorry, bad time?'

'No, no, you're all right. Everything okay?'

'I ... it's... there's something on the beach. I can't go out there. I'm sorry...'

Fraser heard the ragged catch in her voice and knew he had no choice.

'Give me half an hour.'

As he drove, rattling past open fields, he saw that the grass had silvered under a thin covering of frost and was glad of his winter tyres. Now and then, he felt the jolt and slide of icy patches under the wheels. The turning was marked by a tall sycamore, standing alone by the side road, its branches stunted and twisted by the pitiless beating of near-constant winds. He swung the wheel and headed down the narrow lane, a rutted track of hard-frozen mud, jewelled with pockets of ice.

The road rose steadily before dropping again towards the cottage. Laurie Gray stood waiting at the gate, swamped in an oversized sweater, curly brown hair flying out behind her like a tattered flag. She was at the car door before Fraser had even put the handbrake on.

'It's on the beach,' she said, as Fraser climbed out of the car and edged around her.

'What is?'

'I don't know.'

Fraser's heart sank, but he could see the terror in her eyes and forced himself to be calm and reassuring.

'Don't worry. I'll go and see,' he said.

'Over there. I couldn't go, in case it was... I'm sure it is... at least I thought so, and now the tide's gone out and it's there...'

Fraser let his gaze follow her gestures to a spot on the beach, where a pile of seaweed lay in a small mound.

'I'll check it out. Maybe you could put the kettle on?'

Fraser touched Laurie's arm lightly as he said this. She rewarded his gesture with a cold stare, then turned and almost ran back into the cottage.

Fraser watched her go and then set off down to the small shingle beach, pulling his jacket around him in an effort to keep out the cold. As he crunched over the pebbles, he began to make out what looked like a pile of wet clothes. As he got closer, he saw long tendrils of light brown hair clinging, sodden, to the stones and, stretched out towards him, a small, white hand, its fingers curling softly in towards the palm, beckoning him to come closer. He wished he could refuse.

The girl lay, as if relaxed in sleep, but numerous welts and bruises, in various stages of healing, on every area of exposed skin, told quite another story. Her open mouth was jagged with freshly broken teeth, one eye swollen shut, the other half open, staring sightlessly towards him. Around her throat a tight ligature indicated a brutal death. Fraser realised that she had not been long in the water or she'd have looked even worse. He could see tell-tale scabs and track marks scarring her forearms, and took a deep breath, letting it out again slowly. It didn't matter how often he'd seen this, it still got to him. She looked thirty, which probably meant she was still in her teens. Painfully thin, she would doubtless have been dead soon anyway, but someone had intervened to make sure of it.

It was the same as the others; he was certain of that. But last time he'd started poking around, it had not ended well for him. He should keep his mouth shut, ignore it. But could he ignore the instincts that were, even now, gnawing away at his insides?

Laurie opened the door just as he reached the front step and ushered him into the small kitchen-cum-sitting room. Heat was belting from the Rayburn, turning the tiny room into a sauna. Fraser sat down at the table by the window and watched Laurie as she moved on silent feet, busying herself making tea. Laurie placed a steaming mug in front of him and sat down opposite. He sipped at the scalding brew, trying to avoid eye contact.

'Who is she?' she said.

The question hung between them for a moment, like a veil.

'You've been down to see her then?'

Laurie shook her head and Fraser thought he detected a faint pinkening of her cheeks, as if she were embarrassed.

'I don't understand,' said Fraser. 'How would you know, unless-'

'I heard her last night. All night. I couldn't sleep.'

Fraser stared at Laurie, mystified.

'She was here?'

'No, no, no... you don't understand. I *heard* her. I hear people sometimes. Not for a while but.... Why do you think I live out here, away from everyone?'

Laurie got up quickly from the table and walked over to the sink. She stood for a while with her back to Fraser. He watched the spasms in her shoulders that told him she was crying. There was no sound. Then she turned on the tap and stooped to splash water over her face. She patted herself dry with an old towel and half-turned towards Fraser.

'I... I'm sorry. Please don't say anything.'

'There's nothing to say,' said Fraser, even though there were several things he could have said, if he'd had a different upbringing. Laurie came back to the table and sipped at her mug of tea. It was a while before she raised those huge grey eyes to Fraser.

'This morning... I hoped it might be a piece of driftwood. I couldn't... after last night... Do you see?'

Fraser nodded. She smiled then, and seemed to be genuinely amused.

'You're a very bad liar,' she said.

Fraser waited for her to grow solemn again before he spoke.

'Laurie, this is a police matter. They'll want to speak to you about it. They'll ask when you noticed the body. Probably best you don't mention the voices.'

Laurie nodded.

'I don't suppose you ...?' she said, beseeching.

'I'm not working just now.'

'Oh. Did you leave? '

'It's complicated. I'd rather not talk about it.'

'Oh, of course. I'm sorry.'

The old American clock above the stove tick-tocked softly across the strained silence. Fraser got to his feet and gestured towards the house phone. Laurie nodded, and then sat, stiff and motionless, whilst Fraser called it in. When he ended the call, she got to her feet.

'You *will* stay?'

Fraser smiled, resigned.

'Yes, of course I will. I've told them the tide's just gone out. They'll want to get her away before it comes in again.'

'Of course...'

'It'll all be over soon. Don't worry.'

'She was very young, wasn't she?'

Fraser looked at her, wondering what he should or shouldn't tell her. Then he realised that she would need to know something if she was going to avoid talking about those voices of hers.

'I think she was, but the post-mortem will confirm it. She's fully clothed apart from a lost boot. Looks like she's been beaten badly, so probably dead before she went in the water. Might be best to say as little as possible. You were scared when you found the body and called me because I'm your nearest neighbour?'

Laurie stared at him, her forehead creased with puzzlement. Then she relaxed and smiled. She bent and shook her head as if amused by the notion.

'I get it. You don't believe me, and neither will they. You know, that girl was pleading for her life last night, and I couldn't help her. Do you have any idea how that feels?'

There was a bitter edge to those final words. Fraser knew only too well how it felt, but he said nothing. Laurie crossed to the sink and began to wash up. They stood facing away from one another. A few minutes passed. Then Fraser zipped up his jacket and turned back towards Laurie.

'Think I'll go out and wait for them.'

She said nothing and Fraser slipped quietly from the room.

The wind had dropped a little but it was still breezy, so he stayed near the house where it was relatively sheltered. He wondered who would turn up and was surprised at how nervous he felt. It was clear that some of his colleagues believed the worst, despite having known him for years. And, of course, some had been delighted by it all, notably Eric ('he's not a') Diamond, or 'Notter' for short. He hated Fraser. The feeling was mutual.

Fraser peered out, shivering, from the lee of the porch. What if the tide came in and carted off the body? He forced himself back out into the wind and marched to the top of the beach, pulling his jacket close around him. The body was still there, the tide still out. As he turned his head to check the road behind him, he noticed Laurie standing at the window. She looked pale, as if in pain. Fraser thought of going back to check on her but she turned her face towards him and waved her hands, indicating an emphatic no. Why that gesture? How did she know? He had to get a grip. He'd never had much of an imagination before. It would be infuriating to develop one now. Then he heard the faint rumble of approaching vehicles.

The first person he recognised was Doctor Tony Fields. Fraser was glad it was Tony and strode over to say hello.

'Good God, if it isn't the errant Inspector Gilchrist!'

They began to shake hands and then slipped into a man-hug.

'Good to see you, Tony,' said Fraser.

'How did you happen across this then? This where you're staying nowadays?'

'No. Neighbour's house. She asked me to come over.'

'Ah, yes...You still...?'

Fraser nodded, grimly. A sudden slap on the back made him whirl round into the laughing face of Detective Constable Harry Thomson. Fraser grinned and shook his hand too.

'What, no cuddles for me?' said Harry.

A sudden loud clearing of the throat signalled the arrival of someone a lot less welcome. Notter.

'Well, Gilchrist. Seems you're a magnet for trouble. What are we looking at?'

Fraser swallowed the words that were threatening to spill out of his mouth and took a deep breath. He gestured towards the beach.

'Young woman's body. Evidence of trauma. Looks recent. That's all I know.'

'And how did you come to find her?'

The others quietly moved away.

'I didn't. My neighbour, Laurie, did. Lives on her own. She phoned. Asked me to come over. But I'd be more than happy to go now, unless of course you can't manage?'

Notter glared at him.

'We'll need statements. You know the drill. My sergeant will be happy to assist. I believe you know each other?' Notter smirked and gestured to his car, where Casey Drummond, stood, nervously chewing her lower lip.

'Casey. Of course. You'd have to take her too.'

'She's not your property, Gilchrist.'

As Notter walked away, Fraser was suddenly aware that he was clenching his fists. So tempting... He watched as the man picked his way over the shingle in his ridiculously shiny shoes, and wholeheartedly longed for him to fall on his arse.

'Good to see you, sir,' said Casey quietly. Fraser turned to see Casey gazing after her new boss with undisguised loathing. He smiled to himself, feeling gratified.

'You can drop the 'sir'. Fraser will do now.'

'I'll try to remember that, sir.'

Fraser chuckled.

'Right. Allow me to introduce you to my neighbour. You might find her a little strange but try not to leap to conclusions.'

Casey wondered what he meant by that but Fraser did not elaborate. He turned away and headed up to the cottage, his lanky strides forcing Casey into a mad trot as she tried to keep up.

Laurie was making tea. A sketch book lay abandoned on the table; a graphite pencil stuck out at an angle, marking the page. Casey gently opened up the book and caught the pencil as it rolled out. It was a thin sketch, barely begun, of a young woman with haunted eyes. A few scribbled words were scattered at the bottom: 'crying'... 'no names'... 'Susan knows'. Casey sighed. She would never understand modern art. Suddenly, the book was snatched away from her. Laurie stood staring, her face white with rage.

'I'm sorry. I didn't mean any harm. You're very talented.'

But Laurie had stormed away to the other end of the house. Fraser and Casey exchanged surprised looks.

'Should I?' asked Casey pointing to the door.

Fraser just shook his head and gestured to a chair by the stove. Casey sat and waited. A few minutes later, Laurie reappeared, acting as if nothing had happened. Fraser helped her with the tea things and then gestured to Casey to come and join them. Laurie poured tea into three mugs and lifted the milk. Casey nodded, almost afraid to speak. Fraser waited for Laurie to finish what she was doing. Then he reached over and placed his hand gently on hers. She looked up at him.

'This is a good friend of mine, Detective Sergeant Casey Drummond. I don't think she'll mind if you call her Casey. She has to take statements from us separately, so I'll take my tea outside, if that's okay. I'll be right by the door if you need me.'

Laurie nodded, her lips pressed tightly together, in a semblance of a smile. Fraser headed outside. Casey pulled a notebook from her pocket and looked at Laurie, who was staring at the door as if she could will Fraser back in.

'So, when did you first notice the body?'

Laurie turned to her, and seemed to be struggling to understand the question. Casey waited.

'I... I get up at five every morning. It was maybe half five, quarter to six, something like that. But I didn't know what it was then.'

'So, when did you decide to go and look?'

Laurie fixed Casey with her strange, steady eyes, as if she were trying to see inside her head. Casey tried not to feel threatened but was decidedly uneasy.

'Maybe about eight? I phoned Fraser about then, I think?'

Casey was amazed to be feeling so rattled by this woman.

'And you heard nothing before that? No sounds of any kind?'

Laurie shook her head. She seemed on edge, afraid, as if she were hiding something. Avoided eye contact.

'No. Nothing.'

'So,' said Casey. 'Anything else you can tell me? Anything at all?'

'No. I told you everything. There's nothing else.'

'Okay. Well, I'll get this typed up for you to sign. Will you drop by the station or should I come back this afternoon?'

'I don't go into town much.'

'That's okay. I'll pop by later.'

'I'll be here.'

Casey was glad to get back outside.

'How did it go?' asked Fraser.

'Fine, but I'm sure there was something she wasn't telling me.'

Fraser looked as if he were about to say something, but the moment passed, and he turned away. For some reason, that bothered Casey even more.

2

Casey watched Liz Carmichael, the young admin assistant, stomp past, going to her desk. What was eating her? She was always smiling, always reasonable, but she wouldn't even look anyone in the eye. Curious, Casey followed her and stood in front of her desk until she had to acknowledge her.

'Yes?' said Liz. She was close to tears.

Casey pointed at the door. Liz frowned and stood up. Casey grabbed her arm and marched her towards the stairs.

'What's going on?' said Casey, as soon as they were out of earshot.

'It's nothing.'

Even as the words rolled from her lips, her eyes began to fill.

'Coffee break. C'mon.' said Casey and steered her down the stairs and out into the daylight, such as it was at this time of year. Liz took a few shuddering breaths and swiped at her eyes, then she hung her head, avoiding eye contact. Casey waited for her to calm down. Eventually, Liz looked up at Casey again.

'Sorry,' she said.

Casey stared into Liz's face.

'So?'

Liz leaned up against the wall and took another deep breath. She blew it out slowly and noisily.

'Notter called me in, to ask for some files. There were some guys there, having a meeting or something. Notter seemed really stressed. Anyway, one of them, this tall heavy-set guy in his fifties, said I should go and make tea. Notter started to say that it wasn't my job but the guy just shouted at him and said, "You don't mind doing that, do you, sweetheart?" So, I went and got their drinks, and the papers Notter had asked for. He said thank you, and seemed a bit embarrassed by it all. Think he's a bit scared of them, to be honest. Anyway, as I was leaving, this other guy followed me out. He came up behind me and shoved me up against the wall, in that corner by the photocopier... you know...'

'Bastard,' said Casey.

'His hands were... everywhere and he was... I can't say it,' she said, brushing a tear away. 'Anyway, then he heard someone coming along the corridor, and he stopped. He whispered, "See you soon." The way he said it... it was scary, you know?'

'You should report him.'

'I can't. It would be his word against mine. And I wasn't hurt or anything.'

'Okay, Liz, but, if we see him, will you point him out to me? Just so I know? Might be useful to have an idea who he is and what he's capable of, in case something like this happens again.'

Liz nodded and managed a smile. Casey made a mental note to keep a close eye on these guys. One hint of anything dodgy and she'd be on it, would linger around them like a bad smell.

'Now,' said Casey. 'Let's go get that coffee.'

Casey took a chair next to Liz for the next half hour, under the guise of getting her to demonstrate how to use a particular software package. It was doubtful that Liz really believed that was the reason for Casey hanging around, but she was sufficiently traumatised and grateful for the support not to question Casey's motives. Casey's eyes kept flicking towards Notter's office door. Eventually, the door opened, and three men emerged with Notter. They shook hands in the doorway. Casey was sure she detected a look of disgust on Notter's face but it was quickly masked by an all-purpose false smile. Liz leaned in to whisper.

'The tall one asked for tea, the fat one is the groper.' She slid the visitors' book towards Casey. Three names – Dougie Harrison, Robert Priestley and Jason MacDonald-Sim. Casey looked over at the men again, and realised she knew all of them.

She'd recognised Harrison straight away. He was never out of the papers, was instantly recognisable because of his less than athletic figure, and of course everyone knew he was Notter's father-in-law. Then she realised who the small, slim one was, the one that was looking as uncomfortable as Notter. He was a well-respected local architect, Robert (Bobby) Priestley. Taught from time to time at the local college. Supposed to be an okay guy, but he was keeping bad company today.

The tall one she recognised too. Always on the news. Double-barrelled name said it all, really, as far as Casey was concerned. Fraser always told her she was an inverted snob, judging people by their income and status, but she didn't care. Fraser's background was very different from hers. He'd never be subjected to the class distinction she'd endured from people like this when she was growing up. She knew she was being irrational but she hated him on sight. He was of a type. Rich, entitled, doing the sort of jobs that paid several times Casey's salary for one day's work a month – chairman of the board and suchlike. And he was always on the news, criticising the council or the government for over-spending on vital services, banging on about the need for more jobs and investments, like he gave a shit.

He also liked to attack environmental or social campaigning groups, saying they got in the way of good investments. Always against pay rises for ordinary workers, saying it would cost jobs, whilst constantly seeking tax breaks for the rich... essentially, in her eyes at least, he was an arse.

Once the men had left, Casey marched over to the office door, and knocked. She waited for Notter's usual barked response and then walked in. Notter was busy gathering papers together. He shoved them into a drawer and then looked up at her. He seemed exasperated.

'Sergeant Drummond. What can I do for you?'

His tone of voice seemed to indicate that whatever it was, the answer would probably be no.

'It's about your visitors... er, sir.'

He glared at her for a few seconds, and then sighed.

'Okay then, sergeant. Am I going to like where this is going?'

'Probably not, sir.'

Anger flashed in Notter's eyes.

'I cannot imagine why my visitors should be any of your business, Drummond. It was a private meeting.'

Casey felt her face flushing with rage and struggled to control it.

'Let's just say that, having spoken to Liz, I am making it my business. Sir.'

Notter stared at her and his lips tightened to a thin line for a few seconds before he replied. He sat down heavily and leaned forward on his desk, staring at Casey.

'Go on,' he said.

'Do you realise what that... that man...Mr Harrison... what he just did to her?' Casey felt her cheeks burning as she realised she'd almost let her anger run away with her. To her surprise, Notter looked more defeated than angry. His shoulders slumped and his head drooped. It clearly came as no surprise to him, but then it was his father-in-law; he had to know what the man was like. Then Notter seemed to stiffen and sat up straight, as if making an effort to remain in control. He looked her straight in the eye.

'Does Miss Carmichael wish to make a complaint?'

'No... no, but – '

'Then there isn't very much we can do, is there, sergeant?'

'No, sir.'

'I trust she is not physically hurt?'

'No, sir.'

'Please pass on my apologies for the behaviour of my visitor.'

Casey stared at him.

'Anything else, sergeant?'

'Why *were* they here? Sir.'

'If you must know, they were here on behalf of the Kilgarry Club. As you know, their generosity has been invaluable during these last few years, with budgets being squeezed. I hope I don't need to remind you of the importance of maintaining good relationships in *all* our local communities. That includes the wealthy as well as the poor, in case you didn't understand.'

Casey took his point, although she couldn't help thinking that if everyone paid their taxes, there might be less need for charity. She thought about Notter's father-in-law, Dougie Harrison, a nasty wee bastard by all accounts but there was nothing much anyone could do about that. As Fraser never tired of reminding her, their role was to uphold the law and that sometimes had very little to do with what she might call justice.

'Is that all, sergeant?' said Notter.

'Yes, sir. Thank you, sir.'

She turned and was just going out the door when he spoke again.

'And sergeant, could you be a little discreet? No need for this unpleasantness to become office gossip.'

She turned and stared at him. He held her gaze briefly and then turned away, reaching for his phone. Casey left the office, closing the door softly behind her. She knew he was right, that wouldn't be fair on Liz, but she also knew that concern for his secretary was not what was motivating him. It was pride, embarrassment, some misplaced sense of decorum, and she despised him for it.

3

Eddie answered the door on the second knock. He was in his bathrobe, pink-faced from the shower. A trail of wet footprints led back down the corridor behind him. He gave Fraser a crooked smile and stepped to one side.

'Great timing as per...' he muttered, before heading back towards the shower room.

Fraser smiled and went on into the sitting room-cum-kitchen. It was a modernised tenement flat in a leafy west-end street. Eddie had inherited a lump sum from his grandparents, so he'd bought it several years ago as a doer-upper, and had only needed to take out a tiny mortgage. Very grown up of him. But when Fraser and he got together, they felt like irresponsible teenagers all over again, albeit wiser versions thereof. And one huge advantage of Eddie's place was that it was an easy stagger to the pubs, to the restaurants, to anywhere in the centre really. Perfect. Fraser lifted a couple of cold beers from the fridge and unloaded a carrier bag of the same into it. He opened both bottles and then wandered back through to wait for Eddie.

Eddie appeared a couple of minutes later, lifted one of the bottles and drained half of it in a one-er.

Fraser raised his eyebrows and cocked his head to the side, waiting.

'Yeah, okay, I'm a bit behind myself. Long story.'

'A woman, I assume?' said Fraser.

A slow smile spread across Eddie's face, which answered the question.

'It was a good night. And day, come to that. And no, nothing serious. And yes, I probably will call her again... if I have the energy. So, anything new with you?'

'Matter of fact, there is. Body washed up near my neighbour's house, just down the coast a bit from my place. Doubt it's anything out of the ordinary, but... I don't know...'

'You got one of your famous feelings?'

'No. Eddie. I'll leave that to you!'

'Har-bloody-har! Speaking of which, anyone lighting your fire lately?'

'No. I'm happy on my own.'

'Bollocks! You need to get out there. Sell that wee hermitage of yours and come back to civilisation. You could crash here until you find something.'

'Yeah, sure. I'd give it a week. Probably never talk to each other again!'

Eddie pulled a face.

'You may be right... policeman in the house might cramp my style. What about that cute sergeant of yours though? Casey? She's just your type.'

Fraser felt himself colour.

'I don't have a type.'

'Yeah, sure. Never mind. I'll say nothing.'

Unfortunately, Fraser knew that Eddie was incapable keeping quiet for very long, and right now anything too personal was difficult to deal with.

Could be a long night. Maybe he should have stayed home. Fraser drank his beer, gulping down the bitter taste of his own self-loathing.

The pub was busy. A buzz of voices filled their ears every time the music stopped. Fraser waved to 'Bear', resident bass player, and an old friend, but he got no response. Fraser followed Bear's gaze and understood. An attractive young woman with long, auburn hair was making her way towards him. Bear had always had a weakness for red-heads. Fraser chuckled to himself.

Around their table, a peculiar version of musical chairs was being played out. Folks would get up to dance or go to the bar and others would slide across the gap to speak. Eventually, Jamie moved close enough for Fraser to be able to talk to her. She wrapped her arms round him in a drunken embrace and kissed him on the cheek. He gave her a quick peck back and wondered if he was likely to get any sense out of her, the state she was in.

'I was hoping to see you tonight, Jamie.' He said. 'Something I wanted to ask you.'

'Nah! I refuse to marry you!'

'Nothing like that I promise,' said Fraser, laughing.

'Awww... that's a pity... I like the strong, silent, older man type...'

'Much, much older. Behave and listen!'

'Ooooh! Masterful as well... hahaha!'

Fraser ignored her. Eddie got up and walked towards a couple at the bar, obviously old friends

23

judging by the happy hugs and smiles. Fraser turned back towards Jamie again. She was staring at him, the hint of a smile tugging at her lips.

'Well? What were you wanting to talk to me about then?' said Jamie.

'You work at the drop-in down at the harbour, don't you?'

Jamie nodded and waited for him to continue.

'I was wondering if you'd noticed someone who's maybe stopped coming around, someone who's usually there, someone missing recently?'

'Of course not.'

'What do you mean, "of course"?'

'Well, we don't exactly keep a register, do we? I mean, sometimes they don't come for a few weeks or even months, vanish off the face of the earth for a while, and then just appear again like nothing happened. Why?'

Fraser hesitated. Hell, he was only a witness, and it would be in the papers soon anyway.

'My neighbour called me, in a bit of a state. I didn't know why until I got there. Turns out a body washed up on the beach by her house. Very young. Probably a user. Thought she might have been... anyway, if you do notice... if someone says anything...'

'Phone the station? Yeah, I know... Fraser, are you okay?'

Jamie met his gaze, whilst struggling to appear sober.

Fraser tried to smile and broke off eye contact.

'Fraser?'

'Yes, yes, I'm fine. Why wouldn't I be? I've seen a few dead prostitutes in my time.'

As soon as the words were out of his mouth, he realised what an idiotic thing it was to say. He was in danger of becoming an abrasive bastard, "a tool of the state" to use Jamie's terminology.

'You can be a prize shit, sometimes,' said Jamie.

He knew he shouldn't have started this conversation.

'I'm sorry, Jamie. I didn't mean to sound flippant.'

'Another murder? That's it, isn't it? Another one, like those others you were... before the bastards...Fuck's sake!'

Jamie seemed to sober up in an instant as rage flooded through her.

Fraser felt like a complete bastard for mentioning anything about it. He saw Jamie's eyes fill with tears, even though her expression was one of pure rage. He knew better than to try to hug her.

'I think so. She washed up on the beach yesterday morning,' he said.

'I thought that you were suspended. What were *you* doing there?'

'Like I said, a neighbour asked me to come over. I was there as a friend, not a policeman.'

Jamie seemed to shrink in on herself. Her boyfriend, Dod, who'd been talking to someone else all this time, suddenly turned round. He gave Fraser a mildly disapproving look and drew Jamie in for an embrace. She kissed his cheek and struggled free again. Then she looked over at Fraser with a sad and sulky expression.

'Why did you tell me this when I can't do anything? Jesus! Makes me feel so helpless, and I fucking hate that! She'll be ignored like all the rest, now that you're off the case.'

'I'm sorry, Jamie. I thought you might know something that could help.'

'Help who? Help *them*, those fucking colleagues of yours? They don't care! And you're not working just now so why are you playing at policeman?'

That stung. Fraser pressed his lips together and closed his eyes for a second.

'Yeah, well, I kind of got dragged into it. Laurie was scared. She called me. I thought you might want to help but you know where the station is, anyway. Ask for Casey Drummond. She's one of the good guys.'

'Oh, Fraser. I'm so sorry,' said Jamie, falling on his shoulder again. 'What a bitch I am. God, I hate myself sometimes.'

'It's okay. Stupid of me to bring it up.'

'I could ask Suzy; she might know something. She's there more than I am'

'Would she speak to me, do you think?'

'She might. Best to phone her first though.'

'Of course. She a friend?'

'Sort of... sometimes go for a drink together after work, that sort of thing... but, you know, never been to her house or nothin'... so... I don't know... she's sound though. '

'Any reason why you've not been round? Or are you just not all that close?'

'Well, we were out one night and I thought we could maybe go back to her place with a bottle or something, since I knew she lived near there. West-end. Quite posh, you know? But, anyway, she said no; her man was home and he doesn't like people coming round, apparently. No idea what that's all about, but I got the feeling it was better not to ask, you know?'

'He abusive?'

Jamie burst out laughing.

'She'd not put up with that! Fuck, she'd put the shits up most blokes I know, you included, I expect. I wouldn't cross her anyway. Sound though.'

'Are you sure? No odd bruising or anything? People can be good at covering it up.'

'Nah. Not that I've noticed anyway. Forget it. She's fine.'

'So, what does *he* do? I take it he's away a lot?'

'I think so... Why all the interest? I've no idea. She talked about him getting contracts and stuff, some self-employed consultancy bollocks... sounded dead boring to me. Probably just a sad old fart who doesn't like company.'

'Ah, okay.'

'Do you want me to ask around about that girl?'

'No, Jamie. Might not be safe. Just keep your ears open. If you hear anything, let me know. Or trot along and speak to Casey.'

'You know that no-one really gives a shit about these girls, don't you? So what if they disappear? It's like they don't exist.'

'You care though, and so do I.'

'I know... it's just that nothing ever seems to happen and the papers just make it worse, like it's their own fault or something. I mean, why do they always have to say "prostitute killed"? Why not just "woman"? Never see "shiny-arsed clerk killed", do you? Bloody journalists!'

Eddie chose that precise moment to return from the bar.

'What the fuck have I done now?' he said.

'Not you. You don't count,' said Jamie.

'Not sure how to take that,' said Eddie.

Jamie ignored him and turned back to talk to Fraser again.

'Someone has to stop him. You tell Casey that, okay?'

'It's a deal,' said Fraser, although quite how he was going to do that was beyond him at that moment. Firstly, he was not a working policeman just now and secondly, Casey almost never did anything he *told* her to do, which is why he tried to avoid telling her to do anything. He would hint, suggest or cajole where appropriate, but only ordered her around in situations where there wasn't time for anything else. Casey appreciated that, and she had never let him down.

'Hello, Fraser, you away with the fairies or something?' said Jamie. 'Mine's a rum and ginger, by the way.' She waggled her empty glass in his face.

'You might want to slow down a bit there,' said Fraser.

'Awww, I just want one more. The bar'll be shutting soon anyway...'

'Okay. Just the one and then Dod can carry you home.'

Fraser got up, glad of a chance to stretch his legs, and took orders from around the table. He could just about afford it. And it was only once a week...

That night, Fraser dozed fitfully on the sofa-bed in Eddie's sitting room. His head felt woolly from the one-too-many pints he'd ended up drinking. He kept thinking about that poor girl on the beach. She didn't deserve to die like that. No-one did. And she was so very young. You think you're immortal then. He let his mind drift back to some of the more reckless episodes in his misguided youth. He found himself smiling. Nostalgia replaced anxiety, and soon he was snoring again.

4

A murmur of dissent spread through the small crowd, gathered together in the dingy meeting room. Casey and Harry watched in silence as Len Taylor got to his feet. A familiar local character, Len was a born activist, someone with strong principles allied to a deep affection for the sound of his own voice, someone who often glided very close to the line without actually crossing it. Both Casey and Harry had a sneaking admiration for him, even if he had caused them some problems in the past.

'We have to do something. They're walking all over us. Marches, demonstrations, it's all a waste of time. They'll pay no attention. And they've got the media in their pocket too, haven't they?'

There was a low chorus of agreement that rippled through the group.

Mark Mackenzie got to his feet again at the front of the room. He walked forward and took centre stage.

'Len, I know you're frustrated. We all are. But we have to stick to our principles of non-violence. Otherwise, how can we reasonably object to the bully-boy tactics of Harrison and his hired thugs?' He spoke with a gentle authority. His voice was soft and rich, with that musicality which comes from a good education and years of experience in public speaking.

Len jumped up again. He looked angry.

'You don't get it, do you? This isn't just about Oaklands, although that's a damned disgrace. It's far bigger than that. We've got people in here who've suffered first-hand, people whose lives have been destroyed by this bunch of animals. When are we going to do something about that? How are we going to sort out these bastards, when they've got everything sewn up from the police and the courts to our local council and bloody government in Edinburgh! They own the fucking media for Christ's sake, so we get no coverage, and Joe Public thinks we're just a bunch of delusional hippies! We have to take action.'

There was a roar of approval. Mark had an expression on his face that told everyone that he was half-inclined to cheer himself, but knew he had to rein it in. Casey felt a pang of sympathy for him then. She had heard rumours about the intimidation and bullying of local residents but with no physical evidence and no-one willing to act as witness, there was nothing that the police could do about it.

'Len, I think I can speak for everyone in this room when I say that I agree with almost everything you've just said. However, this group, our group, cannot and will not condone violence or criminal activity in any shape or form. I do hope you understand?'

Len stood again.

'Mark, you're a good bloke and we're all grateful for the time you have given to this movement. I do appreciate what you're saying but I can't agree. I think the time is now. We can't wait any longer, not while people are suffering. We all know about that other stuff that's going on... but nothing's being done about it. And, before you say anything, I know it's not your fault. Going the legal route requires evidence, which we don't have. Yet. But, there are a few of us who don't care about the legal route for this. We just want justice for our families and ...' His voice tailed off as he struggled to control his emotions.

Casey wondered what he meant by 'other stuff'. From the expression on Mark Mackenzie's face, she thought that he was probably wondering the same. But Len hadn't finished yet. Casey forced herself to concentrate on what was actually being said.

Len cleared his throat loudly and started to speak again.

'So, we have decided that we want to form another group. That way, we can do what we have to do without it affecting you or anyone else here. I hope we can work together on some things in the future but for now... I hope you understand?'

'Of course I do,' said Mark, sadly. 'I wish you wouldn't, but I don't think there's anything I could say that would convince you, is there? But please be careful. Also, I would like to thank you, on behalf of everyone in this room, for all your hard work. You'll be a big miss.' There was a ripple of applause at this point. Len walked over to Mark and shook his hand, slipping from that into a man-hug quite naturally.

Casey couldn't hear what they said to one another but it seemed to be very amicable, with lots of nods and smiles. They clearly liked one another even if they didn't always agree. Bit like Casey's relationships with her colleagues. Some displayed an unnervingly casual sexism that was clearly unconscious. It was hard to stay angry with them since they were completely unaware they were doing it. And there were some plus sides; now and again they treated her as if she were a lady. Not often, of course, but still... and she knew she could rely on them to back her up if she needed their support. Oddly enough, though, most of the violent drunks still wouldn't dream of hitting a woman, so it was often Casey who waded in to deal with them.

Casey watched as Len gave Mark a half-smile and a brusque nod before walking away in the direction of the exit. Half a dozen people followed him out. Mark watched them go. He looked worried, his face solemn and tense. The secretary announced the next item on the agenda, but Mark did not appear to be listening. Casey wondered what was going through his mind. Was he worried that Len would get into something crazy and discredit the entire campaign? That's what Casey would be worried about, if she were in his shoes. She looked over at Harry, saw his eyes droop and flicker. He was almost sleeping, poor sod. She elbowed him gently and he turned towards her.

'Wasn't sleepin' by the way,' he murmured.

'Of course not,' said Casey. 'That would be most unprofessional... beer?'

Harry managed a grin.

'You buyin'?' he said.

They quietly crept from the hall. Nothing much to worry about as far as they were concerned, although they might have to keep a weather eye on Len and his cronies.

It was a dreich night, damp with a promise of frost. Casey looked over the road, where Len stood talking and laughing with a small group of followers.

'Seem harmless enough,' said Harry.

'They always do,' said Casey.

'You think there's something to worry about then?'

'You know me. I always worry about these things. Good people do bad stuff sometimes.'

'Bloody hell, you're a cheery wee sod, aren't you?'

'Fuck off, Harry.'

Casey walked away and then stopped and turned to look at him.

'Well? D'you want that beer or not?' she said with a smile.

Harry grinned back and strolled after her.

'What was Fraser saying?' said Harry. 'Saw the two of you chin-wagging the other day outside that cottage. Isn't it time you got on with it, you two?'

'Give it a rest, Harry. So sick of people saying that stuff...'

'Beg pardon, miss.'

Harry mimed the doffing of an imaginary cap, and tried to look repentant.

Casey laughed.

'He wasn't really saying much. Seemed a bit brighter than last time I saw him though.'

'Been a rough year.'

'Yeah. He even suggested we go to the blues night tonight.'

'We?'

Casey coloured. It was only a white lie.

'Yeah. You and me.'

'Christ, he must be desperate! He knows I hate that stuff. Just a bloody noise.'

'Well, he asked.'

'Reckon it was you he wanted there. I'm just the excuse.'

Casey said nothing. Fraser wouldn't mind. Couldn't say he'd only asked her. Would just confirm the rumours. And it was all quite innocent. She was sure of that.

'Case?' said Harry, interrupting her reverie. 'You going then?'

'Told him I was working.'

'Of course you did. You could go now though. I won't be offended.'

'Nah. Pretty knackered. Quick drink and off home to bed I reckon.'

'And there was me thinking that I was the boring old fart...'

Casey didn't reply. She didn't trust herself. Fraser was just lonely, and probably pretty depressed. If anything were to happen between them it wouldn't mean anything. And then there was the suspension. It was obviously a set-up. Someone had beaten the guy up, someone who wanted Fraser to take the blame. But why? And why had Fingers gone along with it? And she knew, annoying though it was, that if any of them were seen spending time with Fraser, and he was later exonerated, some bloody journalist would try to make out there was a cover up. Safer for Fraser if they all kept their distance. At least, that's what she told herself. Fact was that Fraser seemed to be keeping his distance from all of them lately. Wasn't even answering his phone half the time. She hoped he was holding it together. It would be so easy for him to slip over the edge again, into oblivion…

5

Fraser was woken by a torrent of screamed expletives, as Eddie came stumbling through to the kitchen and stubbed his foot on the leg of the misplaced coffee table. They'd moved it last night so that they could open up the sofa bed. He was still groaning as he limped through to the kettle. Fraser sat up, yawning.

'Thanks for the dawn chorus,' said Fraser.

'Fuck off, Gilchrist. And it's hardly dawn. Almost eleven.'

'Shit, really?'

'Coffee?'

'Yes, please. Black. Got any painkillers?'

'Bathroom cabinet.'

The cabinet was mirrored. Fraser tried to ignore the train wreck that stared back at him and opened the door. He found a couple of paracetamol and wandered back through to the kitchen.

'You don't look too clever, matey', said Eddie cheerfully.

'Out of practice. Unlike yourself. How's the foot, by the way?'

'Ooh, harsh! Bit fractious are we, Petal?'

'What?'

'Your little treasure never showed last night.'

Bugger. He'd forgotten about that. What had possessed him to tell Eddie that Casey might come along? It was official. He was an idiot.

'She said she wouldn't be coming.'

'Ah, but you were still hoping, weren't you?'

'Fuck off.'

'Touchy. Don't worry. Our little secret, eh?'

Eddie switched on the TV and flicked through channels until he found some football. Fraser had no interest in the game but was glad of it in so far as Eddie would no doubt get so engrossed he'd forget he had a visitor. It would be a couple more hours before Fraser could safely drive. They would need breakfast first, but there was nothing in the fridge apart from a bit of milk and some beer. Fraser dug in his pockets for his wallet. He had roughly a fiver. Might get a loaf and some eggs. Possibly bacon or sausage? He got to his feet and reached for his jacket.

'I'll go and get breakfast sorted,' he said.

'Oh, aye. That'd be dandy!' said Eddie, never taking his eyes off the screen. 'Ohhhh! You absolute fucking plonker!'

Fraser shook his head and made for the door. He hoped Jamie was all right today. Probably didn't get hangovers yet. Too young for that. But he'd been a prat to talk to her about the girl. He hoped she wasn't going to poke around and ask questions. That would be stupid, possibly dangerous. Jamie knew that, knew how to handle herself. She wouldn't risk getting into anything dodgy. Still... He might have to check in with her later. Just to be sure.

After a late breakfast, Eddie and Fraser lay, stuffed and contented, on separate couches.

'So,' said Eddie. 'If there were an award for biggest prick in politics, who would you award it to?'

'What, just now or from any time in the past?'

'Biggest prick of all time. Plenty of contenders...'

'Hmmm... Hitler?'

'Stalin was probably worse... but yeah, he would be a contender.'

'Who would you nominate?'

'Maggie Thatcher. No contest.'

'Oh, come on... biggest prick of all time? Really?'

'Yeah... Oh, all right... Maybe Genghis Khan. He wasn't very subtle.'

Fraser laughed.

'We could restrict it to the U.K. if you like?'

'Nah... let's have some fun with it. How's about... Saddam Hussein, purely on the grounds of his God-awful taste in works of art!'

'Queen Victoria, for never being amused?'

'She a politician?'

'Mebbe?'

'Let's check online. Might find a few others!'

Eventually Fraser checked his watch, and decided he was probably safe to drive. He then downed another glass of water and, to use Eddie's delicate turn of phrase, buggered off back home, leaving Eddie to giggle alone, over insane video clips.

It was almost nine o'clock before Fraser remembered about Jamie. He tried Jamie's mobile a couple of times but it went straight to voice-mail. Eventually she answered. From the noise in the background, it was obvious she was in a bar.

'Fraser! Everything okay? You don't usually phone me.'

'Erm... yes, well, after last night... just thought I'd check you were okay.'

It sounded lame, even to him.

'Oh, that's so sweet. Yeah. I'm fine. Bit hung-over but apart from that... Not heard anything, by the way, but I'll keep an ear out.'

'Just don't go poking round or asking questions. Might have been what got her killed.'

'Aw, bless you, but I've been working with these girls for a while now. I do know the lines not to cross. Don't worry about me. I'll be fine. And I'll see you next Wednesday if not before!'

'Okay. But if you're worried about anything, well... you know. '

'I've got your card.'

'You do?'

'Yes, you numpty. You gave it to me last night. Don't you remember? And I thought I was the one who was drunk!'

Fraser listened to her hoarse chuckle at the other end of the line.

'Just be careful.'

'I will. And Dod's here too, so it's all good.'

'Okay. Speak soon then.'

'Okey-doke. Bye!'

The next morning, an overcast sky kept the light at half strength. It was a day of howling winds and crashing waves, of draughts that found invisible openings in Fraser's tiny cottage, a day when he was supremely thankful for his wood-burning stove and the vast supply of logs he'd sourced over the summer.

At noon, after a bowl of soup and a quick stroll along the beach to blow the dust out of his brain, Fraser dragged out his sketch pad and began to draw. He sketched Laurie's little cottage from memory, the rocky beach and the dark shape on the shore that represented a girl who arrived there unannounced just a few days ago. He began playing with the shapes, emphasising accidental lines in the sketch and downplaying the original objects, until a series of tonal patterns and shapes covered the page. It looked like nothing at all and he doubted that putting it away for a few days would make it look any better, but there might be something in there that he could use for a painting.

He flung the sketchbook to one side. He was seriously out of practice. He knew that. It frustrated him. But drawing wasn't something you could just stop and start at whim. He's got out of the habit years ago and now he was paying the price. Not that it really mattered. Although he had always loved drawing and painting and enjoyed seeing great works of art for himself, he had developed a reluctant dislike for the modern art world, one in which the traditional skills he'd always admired were being replaced by dubious reasoning, gaudy showmanship and irritating sales patter. He was old-fashioned enough to believe that there was some merit in learning how to draw accurately and in studying the techniques of the old masters. His traditionalist approach had not gone down well at art school, and he was invited to leave after three years, having flunked his end of year assessment. He had to admit he deserved it, since he was hardly ever turning up by then and when he did he paid no attention whatsoever to the advice of his lecturers. He'd had enough anyway and was glad to get out of it.

Fraser went to stick the kettle on for the umpteenth time, when a rattle at the window almost activated his colon. He looked up to see Laurie, her hair rain-plastered to her deathly white face, her mouth moving as if she were shouting something, but it was so noisy with the wind that Fraser could hear nothing. He gestured towards the door and she nodded and ducked back down out of sight.

Fraser went and unlocked the door. He ushered her into the warmth and handed her a towel. She stood in front of the stove, towelling herself roughly and shivering. Fraser saw the colour coming back into her face. He gestured to her to sit down and went to organise some hot tea. When he came back through, he saw that she'd found his sketch book. She looked up at him, smiling.

'I had no idea you drew too,' she said, warmly.

'Very out of practice, I'm afraid.'

'No, no, but you're good. You should do more.'

'Thank you,' said Fraser, embarrassed. He handed her a mug of tea.

'Lovely. Cold out there.'

'What on earth were you doing out in this?'

'I did knock but I don't think you heard me. The wind, I suppose.'

'But... what brings you here? Did you walk?'

'Yes, of course I walked, but I came along the beach. It's much faster.'

'You could have phoned.'

'Ah, but then I couldn't have given you this.'

She handed him a carrier bag. Water dripped from it onto the floor.

'Oh, sorry. Quite wet out there. But it might be sea water I suppose...'

Fraser opened the bag. Inside was a girl's jacket. It was soaking wet.

'Found it on the beach, near where the girl turned up. I think it might be hers.'

'Okay. We know who she is now, anyway, so it's probably not going to help much.'

'I think there's something in the lining of the sleeve. Right hand side. Thought it might be important. I don't know about this stuff. Anyway, I didn't want to phone you again in case you got mad. Didn't seem fair to keep bothering you. But I won't stay. I'll just warm up a little and drink my tea if that's okay and then I'll be off.'

Fraser thought about looking at it himself but he'd get read the riot act for contaminating evidence et cetera. Anyway, it wasn't his job any more. He'd phone Casey to come and collect it.

43

'Tell you what. Stay and warm up for a while and then I'll run you home. How does that sound?'

'If you're sure you don't mind?'

'No, not at all. Just have to make a quick phone call. Be right back.'

'Of course.'

Laurie seemed almost normal today. Maybe she should walk out in storms more often. It was an uncharitable thought and Fraser banished it on the way through to the bedroom and the extension phone.

Casey answered at the second ring.

'Sergeant Drummond speaking. How can I help you?'

'Hi, Casey. Sorry to bother you. Need a wee favour.'

'Depends. Tell me more.'

He could hear a smile in her voice and felt very pleased. Ridiculous. Get a grip.

'I have a surprise visitor. Laurie walked here, through this storm, to bring me a coat she found on the beach. Thought it might belong to our victim.'

'Damn. You know there'll be grumblings about evidence and trace and all that stuff?'

'Oh, yes. I also know that the coat itself is probably superfluous, having spent some time in the North Sea washing machine.'

'The coat *itself*... What are you saying?'

No flies on Casey.

'There is something hidden in a sleeve, according to Laurie.'

'It's been in the North Sea, Fraser!'

'I know, I know....'

There was silence for a moment.

'I'll try. Thing is, Notter wants us to close the case,' said Casey, at last. 'No chance of finding out who did it, he reckons, and he keeps banging on about resources.'

'Fucks sake! The guy is an arsehole. She's a prostitute so it doesn't matter. Is that it?'

'Hey! Don't get on at me... *Sir*!'

The irritation in her voice was very clear.

'Okay, I'm sorry. Would you try? Please?'

He heard a sigh at the other end.

'I'm about to take a break. I could be with you in about fifteen minutes?'

'You're an angel.'

'Don't push it!'

Fraser laughed as he replaced the receiver.

Laurie stood up abruptly when Fraser came back into the room. She stared like a frightened rabbit. Fraser smiled, half amusement, half pity. She was an odd wee thing.

'Sit down, Laurie. Casey's coming out to collect it. You can tell her exactly where and when you found it. Anyway, she'll be here in about quarter of an hour. Then I'll run you home. That okay with you?'

Laurie nodded and sat down again, looking a little awkward and embarrassed.

'It's a nice house. Cosy,' said Laurie.

'I know. Even smaller than yours, I think?'

'Oh, that wasn't what I meant...' Laurie flushed.

Fraser laughed.

'It's okay,' he said. 'Used to belong to my grand-uncle. Never married or had children. There were rumours that he might have been gay. I think he was just too shy to ask a girl out. He lived here on his own for most of his life. He left it to me. The poor old place needed a lot of work but I enjoyed doing it. And I needed something to do at the time...' Fraser's eyes misted over with emotion. Horrified, he turned away quickly and looked out of the window to the dunes and sea beyond. 'Suits me fine, anyway. I'm a bit of an old hermit nowadays.'

'It's a lovely place. This whole area is wonderful.'

'And what about you?'

Laurie looked up at Fraser, a slight frown of puzzlement creasing her forehead. He glanced down at her and caught her expression. Then he crossed to the stove and started feeding more fuel into it. She didn't answer. Obviously, she didn't understand what he was asking. He stood up straight and turned to face her, smiling with amusement.

'Well, you're clearly English,' said Fraser, smiling. 'What brings you up to this wild and breezy corner of Scotland? Can't be the weather!'

Laurie held his gaze for a moment and then turned her face away. When she eventually spoke, there was a distinct tremor in her voice, which was low and husky with emotion.

'I needed a change. There was a bit of trouble... I... it was something I...'

Now, it was Fraser's turn to feel awkward. Whatever it was, it was clearly still very raw. He wondered what on earth could have affected her so deeply for so long, and then he realised that it was absolutely none of his business.

'I'm sorry,' said Fraser. He sat down next to her and placed his hand lightly on her forearm. 'Please don't talk about it if you don't want to. I had no idea... forgive me?'

Laurie looked up at him and her sad, grey eyes softened in a smile.

'I could tell you. Maybe you would understand. But, if you didn't believe me... I...' She shook her head slowly and sighed.

Fraser waited for her to go on. Eventually, he realised she wasn't going to say any more. He was wondering whether he should offer her tea when he heard the door knob rattle and a hammering on the wood.

Casey was drenched to the hide. Fraser ushered her into the warmth, apologising for the delay.

'I can't stay.' said Casey. 'Meeting with Notter in half an hour.'

Casey looked around her.

Fraser handed her the offending item. Casey looked at Laurie.

'So you found this on the beach today?'

'Yes. It was trapped among some rocks at the far end of the beach. I don't know how long... didn't notice it before.'

'Okay. Well, thank you for that. I'll be in touch if I need some more information. Sorry, but I have to rush back,' said Casey. Then she nodded at Fraser. 'I'll see myself out.'

And then she was gone. Fraser felt a little stunned by her speed but realised it was unavoidable with Notter on the rampage. He wondered what nonsense the guy was up to now. Such an idiot. That's no way to manage a team. You need to respect everyone, not just the ones with more pips than you.

The journey back to Laurie's was a quiet and subdued affair. Fraser attempted to make conversation but quickly realised that Laurie was lost in her own thoughts. Again, he wondered what had happened to her. He could find out. But did he have that right? He should wait until she was ready to tell him. When they drew up outside Laurie's house, she sat frozen and still, unmoving for a minute or two. Fraser said nothing, afraid to stress her further. Eventually she turned towards him. There were tears in her eyes.

'If you really need to know, contact Inspector David Johnson. Ipswich. I'm sure you can find him, with your contacts. My name then was Anna Stevens. Laura was my middle name. Gray was my mother's maiden name. I always used Laurie Gray for my work in children's books. After what happened, I just kept it. Permanently. Once you know the story, you might understand.'

Fraser felt ashamed. She didn't want to tell him. He was forcing her hand somehow.

'It's okay,' said Laurie. 'It might be easier if you know. I just find it hard to say the words. Please don't feel bad about it. I know I come across as an odd fish sometimes.'

With that, she dived out of the car and rushed off into her house. She didn't look back. Fraser sat for a moment, stunned. It was as if she knew what he'd been thinking. But that was impossible. She just realised that he was curious, that's all. Wouldn't need to be psychic to figure that out. Yes, that's all it was. Good grief, her strangeness was clearly rubbing off on him. He turned the wheel and headed for home. When he looked in his rear-view mirror, he saw Laurie standing motionless at her window. He felt an odd sensation in the pit of his stomach, a lurching feeling of unease, like a haunting, as if she were casting some strange spell over him.

6

Casey signed off another form. She looked at the pile on her desk. It never seemed to get any smaller. She looked around the office. Every desk was the same. Must destroy entire forests on a weekly basis, the amount of paperwork they got through. So much for the paperless office idea. A lot of the stuff was online now but they would always need hard copies, if only for back-up.

She thought back to the previous evening and that meeting. The Oakbank Project. It had been in the news a lot but she knew very little about it. Bit of research? It was work-related, after all.

She typed "Oakbank Project" into the search bar. A long list came up. There were videos on there too but she had no desire to listen to them and she guessed her colleagues wouldn't be keen either.

After a few more clicks, she found what she was looking for – minutes from a meeting, giving a list of people involved in the project. Harrison was on that list, of course; he'd bought the land. That architect from the other day, Priestley, was mentioned in the body of the piece, as a possible designer for the development, although there were some disagreements mentioned about the number of units possible. Harrison thought there should be more. The architect disagreed and had stated his reasons as being environmental impact, as well as aesthetic considerations. Smarmy-pants of the double-barrelled name was also on that list. He was probably paid to do it. Contacts in high places. Always handy for a developer. Probably how they got those permissions in the first place. Interesting that the local planning department turned it down initially. Casey wondered why they'd changed their minds.

She looked at the other names but none of them meant anything to her. She'd run it past Harry later. He knew everyone. She pressed print and went to retrieve the print-out from the machine, which stood in the far corner of the office. She hoped it wasn't out of paper. One of those recurrent, if minor, irritations that could really mess with your head after a while.

Whilst she waited, she thought about Fraser. He was a big miss. Like Harry, he seemed to know everyone. Unlike Harry, he didn't expect everyone else to know them as well. And he could talk to people, really easily, even angry, dangerous ones. Calmed them down within minutes. Fraser also had an incredible instinct, could home in on that one small detail that meant something to a case, even if it always seemed a lot less obvious to everyone else. Casey hoped she would be able to do that too, eventually, although she had her doubts. Her strength lay in reading people, but even that hadn't been entirely successful lately. Could nearly always tell when someone was lying though and she could detect narcissism or psychopathy at a hundred paces. Had plenty of practice at home with her screwed up family. No-one knew about any of that though, not even Fraser. He was aware that she had spent a few years in care. Casey told him it was because her mother was ill, which was true enough. She didn't tell him what her life was like before that though, that her mother was sick in other ways as well.

Casey picked up the print-out and went back to her desk. She saw Notter heading her way and slid the document into a drawer before he could see it. Harrison was his father-in-law after all. He might not be happy about Casey digging into his business dealings, whatever the reasons. She looked up as Notter stopped by her desk.

'You have those statements finished?' he said.

'Yes, sir.'

'Expenses filed?'

'That too, yes, sir.'

'You went to the meeting last night. Any new information?'

'Not really, sir. There was a split in the group though, which might be a problem.'

'Report?'

'Just about to do that, sir.'

'Well, get on with it, sergeant. The march is on in a few days and we all need to be briefed. Make it a priority.'

'Yes... sir.' Casey could barely get the words out between clenched teeth.

Notter seemed to sense her anger and smirked.

'I hope you understand the situation with D.I. Gilchrist?'

'Sir?'

'I know that you are friends outside of work but it might be in your best interests to stay away from him for a while, at least until the investigation into his conduct is completed.'

Casey stared at him without answering.

'Sergeant? Well? He must not be permitted to have any part in this current investigation. Do you understand that? He is suspended from duty.'

'Yes, sir. I do understand that.'

Casey was enraged. Who did he think he was?

'And you will distance yourself from him until things are completed?'

'Even off duty?'

'You're a police officer, Drummond. As such, you are never off duty. You must always behave in a manner that is above reproach.'

'I will bear that in mind, yes, sir.'

Casey saw a flash of anger in Notter's eyes and concentrated on maintaining an impassive expression. Notter stared down at her for a few seconds, clearly not satisfied with her answer but not sure how to respond to it. In the end, he let out a "pshaw" sound that signified his frustration.

'Very well, sergeant,' he said. 'Carry on then.'

He turned and stalked off towards his office. She noticed Harry pulling faces at him behind his back and stifled a laugh. Harry winked at her and then went back to what he was doing. At least she still had Harry.

Casey turned back to the task in hand. The report from the meeting would be very thin, especially since they left early. Still, as long as people were aware of the Mark-Len situation, that was all that mattered. Even that was unlikely to be vital. Chances were, the march would be a fairly low-key affair. Most folk were reluctant to get involved in any cause that didn't directly affect them. She had some sympathy with that. There was enough crap to deal with generally without importing any.

She wondered how Fraser was and hoped he wasn't offended by her refusal to go to the pub with him and his mates. He probably recognised her excuse as just that, an excuse. It made her feel even worse. And it had been so good to see him. Even under those circumstances, with that poor girl.

He did seem a little brighter. She remembered how he was a few months ago. He wasn't looking after himself, had lost a lot of weight. She should have done more to help him, but what? He was never going to be back to normal until this damned suspension was dealt with. No wonder he was fucked up. If she'd lost a child, especially like that, she wasn't sure she would ever get over it. His mother too. He was close to her. Never talked about his father though. They clearly didn't get on at all. Happy bloody families, eh? And then that accusation, just as he was beginning to come out the other side, get that gleam back in his eye.

Cold cases. A series, he reckoned. Casey wondered what those cases were. Maybe she could carry on the work for him. Notter needn't know about it. Just until Fraser came back. If he ever did come back... No, it wouldn't do to think that way. Of course he would be back. "Good shit always floats to the surface." Wasn't that what Harry always said? She remembered Fraser's reply to it as well – "I'm afraid I do not have your familiarity with the data on the relative buoyancy of turds." She smiled at the memory and hoped he would soon be back at work. Then she pressed a few keys and began writing the report.

7

Fraser was determined to enjoy a quiet night in with a book. In some ways, he felt glad to be an outsider. Let Notter deal with it all. He'd cock it up, of course, and make sure someone else got the blame for it, largely because he had balls the size of raisins and an ego so fragile he could not admit to any mistakes. But that was a problem for other people now. After a few minutes of reading and re-reading the same few paragraphs, Fraser realised that he couldn't concentrate well enough to read and felt the silence in the cottage closing in on him, more oppressive than relaxing.

He let his eyes wander over to the manila envelope on the mantelpiece. His paperwork for the upcoming meeting with the head honchos. The thought of it made him feel weary. He missed the job but he didn't miss the arse-sniffing sycophancy that passed for office politics sometimes. He might eventually have to think about what else to do with his life, given that he might not get his job back, but, just now, he was still on full pay, had no mortgage, and knew that he could probably manage on the money he had stashed away for a couple of months if needs be.

They might stop his pay, of course. That was his main worry right now. He'd got over the first, sickening shock of the accusation and was now left with a vague unease and a barely controlled touchiness on the subject of what had been his career. To be suspended had been an awful blow, especially when it was on the word of a known villain, nicknamed "Fingers", on account of the fact that you'd be advised to count your fingers after shaking hands with him. Just a petty thief, occasional drunk and all-round pain in the arse.

Funny thing was, although Fraser had lifted him a couple of times in the past, and despite Fingers claiming to have been beaten up by him a few days before, the wee shite completely failed to recognise Fraser when they met at the station. The arrests... well, they were a while back and the guy was pissed so that could explain some of it. But the assault? Surely people weren't really buying that?

There was also some dodgy paperwork, of dubious origin, that Fraser had apparently signed but which he had no recollection of ever seeing before. He'd love to know where that came from. He felt powerless and angry and... yes, dammit... more than a little offended. How could any of them have believed that, with over twenty years of service, he'd suddenly decide to take back-handers and compromise evidence? It was maddening. And frustratingly difficult to prove himself innocent, which seemed to be what they were asking him to do.

The phone began to ring. He hoped it wasn't Laurie. There had been enough strangeness from that quarter lately.

'Hello?'

'Hi Fraser, it's Casey here. Just to let you know that I have been instructed to distance myself from you during the course of this investigation, so if I don't call round, it's not personal,'

'Are you okay? Your voice sounds funny.'

'Just tired and a bit pissed off. I'll be fine.'

'Anything I can help with?'

'No. It's okay. Well, thing is, there was a USB in that jacket Laurie handed in. I gave it to the techy guys to look at, but their report was sent to Notter instead of me. He wasn't best pleased that I'd not run it by him first. Got a lecture from him about wasting resources et cetera. Told me that if I ignored proper procedures, my career could be compromised. He's right, I suppose, since the high heid yins are always banging on about budgets. I never had to... when you were here... anyway, it was a total over-reaction. The guys get paid anyway and were glad to help, but Notter was making a point I suppose.'

'Forget about it. Probably a waste of time, anyway.'

'Not entirely. They did manage to retrieve a tiny bit of data, not that it means anything to me, just a bunch of numbers and letters. Haven't figured it out yet. Your name came up, of course. I've no idea how he knew. He just did. Maybe he's not stupid after all?'

'No. Never stupid. Erm, I don't suppose there's any chance of a copy?'

'You know better than that. I know better than that. Jeez... shouldn't be talking to you at all... anyway, as I said before, it makes no sense.'

'Are you allowed to visit out of work time? I make a decent lasagne.'

Fraser heard Casey chuckle.

'Maybe some time. But now is not good. Text me if you need anything but, if it's anything to do with work, be prepared for a no.'

'Understood. Take it easy. You've done nothing wrong so he can't touch you.'

'No? You think? Look what happened to you, Fraser.'

'That wasn't him though. It was that wee tow-rag from Peterhead.'

'Yeah. But that wee tow-rag, as you call him, didn't have anything to do with that phoney paperwork did he? That had to be somebody here. Maybe the same somebody that actually *did* beat him up. And then told him to lay the blame on you. Someone must really hate you.'

'I can't see Notter falsifying documents to be fair. He may be a petty little pen-pusher but he's not a crook. Unless, of course...'

'I know we all joke around about him being an idiot, and in a lot of ways he is, but maybe we shouldn't underestimate Notter. He's a sneaky wee bampot with a giant chip on his saggy shoulders.'

Fraser felt the impact of this and other possibilities like a blow to his solar plexus. He had told himself not to be daft, that there was no conspiracy, it was just incompetence, all some hideous mistake, someone had stuck the wrong name on a form... were they forms? He barely remembered the papers that had been shoved under his nose that day, had been so shocked he couldn't take anything in. Did he even look at the papers? Not really. He'd been staring at the chief in disbelief. His ears seemed to fill up with white noise, as if he were under water. His vision had blurred and he thought he would pass out.

It was embarrassing to admit to that reaction, even to himself. It was like some Kafkaesque nightmare, one that he thought he might soon wake out of, except he never did. But supposing it had been done on purpose - it would have to be someone who could meddle in the system, make it look like the records were older than they were. And that could very easily have been Notter.

'Fraser? Hey, Fraser, you still there?'

'Yes, sorry...'

'Couple of us are thinking to go for a quick jar after work. Harry suggested we could meet you. Something we wanted to talk to you about.'

'You just told me you've been barred from talking to me.'

'Yeah, but he can't stop us *accidentally* bumping into each other at the pub and, anyway, he never goes there, does he?'

'Good point. I could... what sort of time were you thinking?'

'Probably half five or six?'

'Okay. I'll be there. I assume it's the outer office as usual?'

'That's the one.'

Fraser was there before Casey arrived, and took a seat near the door, so that he'd have a good view of people coming and going. He fished out his phone, went online, and stared at the search bar. What was her name? Anna somebody... Stevens! No... nothing. He added 'Ipswich' and pressed search again. This time, a list of articles, with lurid headlines, appeared.

'Couple killed in frenzied attack', 'Bloodbath in Suburbia', 'Tragic Daughter Admitted for Treatment'.

Her name was everywhere, along with thinly veiled assumptions of her guilt, that she was mentally ill and therefore must have been involved somehow, the usual tabloid rubbish. A more sober article, from a local paper gave the important information that, at the time of the killings, Anna had been two hundred miles away, attending a concert with friends. She had travelled back the next day and blundered into the horrific crime scene. No-one knew for sure what she did next, but there was about an hour's delay between the time the taxi dropped her off at home and the time a call was received at the station.

A neighbour had called it in, after seeing the poor girl wandering along the street, covered in blood and unable to speak. It had to be assumed that Anna had been alone in the house for most of that hour, possibly trying to resuscitate her parents. By then, they had been dead for over 24 hours.

Holy shit… no wonder the lass was a little odd. Who wouldn't be? He wondered what injuries the parents had. The amount of blood described would indicate something very brutal. This would have been a scene no daughter should have had to see, especially one as young and as sensitive as Laurie.

A shout from the doorway made him look up and in came a small group of his former colleagues, including Casey and Harry. He accepted an offer of a fresh pint and scooped his jacket and newspaper off the seats next to him so they could all sit. He stowed his stuff in the window alcove behind him and listened to the chatter for a while.

Casey had been stuck for half an hour babysitting Notter's two obnoxious children while he and his wife attended a meeting upstairs. It appeared that no-one was terribly taken by the offspring. Poor little buggers. If they were selfish, or devoid of joy, then, given their parents, who could blame them? He knew that a lot of the banter wasn't real and that it might well have been there for his benefit. All those present were well aware that Fraser and Notter did not get on. This was their clumsy way of letting him know which side they were on. Fraser smiled and waited for someone to change the subject.

'Hey, Fraser, when's that review of yours happening?' asked Harry, setting a fresh pint down in front of him.

'Did you have to announce it to the entire city?'

'Oh, bugger it, Fraser. It's aw shite, anyway.'

Fraser smiled. Harry was never subtle but his heart was in the right place.

'Funny thing, though,' said Casey. 'We got a friend in forensics to run a few tests. You might be quite happy with the results.'

Fraser looked around him. They were all grinning.

'What's going on?'

'That dodgy paperwork,' said Casey. 'Turns out it was very dodgy.'

'What do you mean?' said Fraser.

'The ink was wrong. On those manual records. And strangely, on those same manual records... not one fingerprint belonging to the person who was supposed to have filled them in - you!'

'But were those things not done before?' said Fraser, feeling a strange frisson of excitement.

'Nope. No time back then, apparently,' said Harry. 'It's looking more and more like a stitch up, Fraser. You've obviously pissed off the wrong person. But then you are quite good at that!'

'I do try,' said Fraser, with a wry grin.

'Should help, anyway,' said Casey. 'Even if it just adds a little doubt.'

'But how did you get hold of the documents? How did you get them tested without anyone knowing?' Fraser asked.

'A few favours owed, here and there, and a lot of bad feeling amongst the ranks,' said Harry. 'We all thought something stunk about it, so we decided to start digging. That ink that was on the papers supposedly dating back to a couple of years ago?

Turns out the ink doesn't match the stock of pens used back then. The supplier was changed last Spring and, funnily enough, the ink from the new pens match exactly. Isn't that interesting?'

'But that doesn't prove anything. We all use our own pens sometimes,' said Fraser, feeling hope slip away again.

'Yes, but there is more,' chuckled Casey. 'The ink is a new formula, designed to work better with a particular type of pen.'

'So?' said Fraser. 'It still proves nothing.'

Harry leaned forward and fixed his hard stare on Fraser.

'Would you wait a fuckin' minute 'til we gie you the punch line? That particular pen only came out the month before you were suspended!'

Fraser felt the tension drain from him. He slumped back in his seat.

'So someone deliberately falsified those documents?' he said quietly.

'Exactly,' said Casey. 'And when we find them, we'll hang the fuckers out to dry!'

Fraser wasn't sure how to feel. This new evidence would let him off the hook for that side of things, almost certainly. That just left the wee tow rag from Peterhead... Had someone put him up to it? If so, who? Who hated him that much?

He thought about that for a minute. It would be hard to know where to start. He'd pissed off plenty of people in his time and most were not nice people. It took a bit of effort for Fraser to look happy, but he thought he managed fine. He was jostled and hugged by his triumphant friends. He had friends at least, even if he also had some enemies. The smile was making his face ache but he held it as long as possible. He suddenly wanted to be home again, wanted to hide away and mull things over. The guys weren't going to stay long in the pub anyway. There was a demo happening in the morning and most of them had been assigned to keep an eye on things along the route. He began to look forward to his bus journey home, to sitting alone and in silence, free to gaze out of the bus window and let his mind go blank.

8

Casey paced up and down outside the new shopping centre. She could see a few early arrivals heading up to Market Place for the rally, bundles of banners tucked under their arms or carried over their shoulders. Hopefully, the smiling faces would remain friendly. It would all be over in an hour or so but there was always the possibility of some psychotic numpty causing trouble and she really wasn't in the mood. The last few days had been unbearable.

Notter had been at his sneaking and pouncing worst and seemed always to notice the moment she lifted a cup of coffee to her lips or took her tired eyes off the computer screen for a second. Then it was 'oh, Casey, if you have a minute you could perhaps fetch those files', or 'Casey, if you're not busy, there is a report I want you to find for me. Could you just pop along...' et cetera et cetera et bloody cetera. She would cheerfully have decked him. She had the training. But he wasn't worth the aggro.

'All right there, darlin'?' asked a local worthy, clearly heading to the Royal for a liquid lunch. Casey managed a smile, despite feeling that 'darling' was a tad inappropriate. Still... sense of humour bypass notwithstanding, she could see the funny side of the idea that they might be on such friendly terms. The guy looked about eighty, though he was probably a couple of decades younger. Casey watched his tremulous progress over the treachery of cobblestones, hoping to God he didn't keel over and knock himself out. She really didn't want to have to get any closer to him than she'd been a minute ago. The aroma of old tobacco and stale piss had been throat-catchingly strong. He was harmless though, a local character, and always smiling. So, she smiled again as she saw him successfully negotiate the small lane and trot eagerly into the pub.

A slap on the back told her that Harry was back. He thrust a large, cardboard cup of scalding hot coffee into her hand. She was grateful for the heat. Brass monkey weather but at least it was dry.

'So, you ready for this?' said Harry.

'Absolutely.'

'I'm not. Can't stand these things.'

'Not a fan of democracy then?' said Casey.

'Not a fan of freezing ma balls off while a lot of middle class hippies chant their way down the street. Fuck's sake, could they not get a hobby?'

'I dunno. I know what you're saying, but if something's wrong, it's wrong. Peaceful protest can make the world a better place. Look at the suffragettes or the civil rights movement in the States. Big changes achieved through peaceful protest.'

'Wasn't all bloody peaceful. But yeah, good point. Doesn't mean I have to like it though, eh?'

Casey chuckled.

'What's this one about, anyway?' said Harry.

'You were at the briefing?'

'In body, yeah. Kind of switched off half way through. Christ, Notter loves the sound of his own voice...'

'Very true.'

They stood quietly for a while, sipping at their coffee and watching the road for any increase in traffic.

'Who do you think it was?' said Casey at last.

'What are you on about?'

'Fraser. Who stitched him up?'

'More than one, I reckon. They did a job on him. Makes you wonder though, eh? Was he getting too close to something they didn't want him knowing about?'

'Hadn't thought of that. Just assumed he'd annoyed the brass once too often.'

'Well, time you did think about it. Think what cases he was working on then. You were with him, so you should be able to figure something out.'

'What about Fingers?'

'Lyin' little bastard. He'd be a lot safer stayin' in Peterhead the way I'm feelin' about it. One thing's for fuckin' sure, he didn't think it all up. Some fucker was usin' him to get to Fraser. You have a wee think, Casey. If you need a hand, just tip me the nod. Okay?'

Casey thought about this for a moment. Whilst Harry carried on slurping at his coffee.

'Someone beat him up pretty bad. Fingers, I mean. Would have needed to be someone with hired muscle,' she said.

'Or someone who knows someone with hired muscle,' said Harry.

'Right. Doesn't narrow it down at all then.'

'Nope. Of course, they'd need to have some sway with said person, something to bargain with... you know, favours, debts, something...'

'You're talking either really high up or very low down then?'

'Could be just someone with a lot of money and zero scruples, like our friend Harrison. Fraser must have stepped on somebody's toes, maybe without even realising it, someone who had a bit of clout, someone who might also be able to exert some pressure within the force.'

Casey knew what Harry was getting at, but neither wanted to say it out loud. Harrison could have leaned on Notter to help get Fraser off the case. Could explain why he was so edgy around the guy.

'We need to speak with Fingers. He still at the same place?' she said.

'Expect so. Bit risky to go there though. Could look like a cover up. Better to go speak to one of his pals, if he still has any.'

'It would still be the word of one reprobate against another.'

'Two or three of them though and it'll cast doubt on the entire story.'

'I like your thinking. We should make a start on that, after this is all finished, of course.' She said, waving her hand towards the demo. 'And I know just the place.'

'Want some company?' said Harry, staring over at the gathering crowd.

'Off the record?'

'Probably best.'

Casey looked up at her burly colleague. In profile, the broken nose was more obvious, a gift from a punter in a pub brawl last year. Harry was a good guy to have on your side. He also had a fair bit on his plate recently, so might be more liable to lose it. His wife had been laid off from a high paying job and they had been struggling to make the mortgage payments. She was working again now though, albeit on a lower salary, so things must be easier than they were before.

Casey only knew all this thanks to a drunken night with the boys, when Harry got a bit maudlin. He never mentioned it again and she was certainly not going to bring it up. It was generally a good idea to avoid pissing Harry off. He had a long memory. She could hear voices raised in song. It was coming from Market Place and seemed to indicate that things were starting to happen.

'Do you think we should wander up for a wee keek?' she said.

'Why not. I could do with a laugh...'

9

Fraser watched the waves rolling in to shore, mesmerised by the strange luminous light in the water at the height of a wave and that delicate lace of foam that slid over its surface just before it crashed onto the sand. The whispered pulse of the sea was soothing and hypnotic, just what he needed to soothe the ache in his head. He hadn't slept well; kept waking with a jolt, thinking someone was creeping up behind him. The symbolism was obvious.

Someone, or several someones possibly, had stabbed him in the back. It was an unpleasant thought. He even found himself doubting some of the folk that were there last night. Surely they couldn't all be on his side? He barely knew some of them. Paranoia? Oh, yes. In spades. And no bloody wonder. It was bad enough thinking that some clerical cockup had made him look like he was on the take; the thought that someone had deliberately set him up was ten times worse. Who were they? Yes, it had to be more than one. Too neat and tidy for one guy to manage. He'd have to have help. High up help for some of it. That was an even worse thought. You didn't want to mess with some people in this city. If they could destroy his career, what was to stop them from destroying him?

Fraser shivered, and not just from the cold. Still, his feet were turning numb. Probably not a good idea to add hypothermia to his list of problems. He walked back over the dunes to the safety of his wee house.

The stove was belting out heat and Fraser stripped off his jacket quickly and hung it on one of the hooks behind the door. He poured himself a coffee, then sprawled out on the couch and snicked on the TV.

Local news was starting. Up first, a quick round up and the briefest footage of Market Place. He thought he spotted Harry but it was too brief a glimpse to be sure. He waited until the newsreader stopped speaking and the full view of the demo filled the screen.

He knew there wouldn't be much. Demos were not too popular nowadays and Big Brother would much rather no-one knew about them at all. Fraser, though, found it reassuring. He remembered the demos he'd taken part in as a student and how passionately they had all believed in the power of protest. He wished he still felt as optimistic now as he had back then. Still, despite years as a policeman, he felt more in common with demonstrators than he ever had with any of the politicians he had been expected to watch over on their pre-election visits to the city.

There she was. Casey was standing speaking to a couple of demonstrators. They were all smiling. Seemed to be going okay then. Harry would be pleased. Fraser smiled to himself, remembering numerous friendly arguments with Harry on the subject of demos. Harry just hated them. Not from any ideological perspective; it was just that they took him away from what he saw as his proper job, catching bad guys.

Harry enjoyed nabbing crooks and seeing them locked up. It was all he cared about. Or so he would have you believe. Fraser knew different though. He had discovered long ago that Harry volunteered in a sports project with young offenders, that he took his elderly neighbours in his own car, and at his own expense, to do their weekly shop, that he was the one who had nursed his little daughter through endless nights of sickness after brutal cancer treatments, because his distraught wife was struggling to cope. Harry was a softie. Everyone on the force knew it and nobody would ever have dared to point it out.

Fraser switched off the TV and stretched out on the couch. The fresh air had done for him. He decided a quick snooze was called for, and then he might call along Laurie's and make sure she was okay. She hadn't phoned for a couple of days and, whilst he was relieved, he did not want anything else on his conscience just now. He made himself think of happier times, lay back, and closed his eyes.

It was late afternoon when Fraser arrived at Laurie's cottage. She was standing in her doorway as he stopped the car. Must have seen him coming. She was smiling and seemed happier than he'd seen her lately.

'Hi there,' said Fraser, striding over.

'Nice of you to drop by to check on me,' she said. An amused smile twitching at the corners of her mouth.

'Yeah, well. I hadn't heard from you so I thought I'd make sure you were okay now after... after what happened.'

'Tea is just made and there's also some ginger cake.'

'Ooh. My favourite. Careful. You might not get rid of me!'

'I kind of doubt that. Isn't that nice young policewoman more your type?'

She smiled at him.

Fraser felt himself colour. It made him feel faintly ridiculous. He wasn't a schoolboy any more but thinking about Casey returned him swiftly to those days of clumsy feet and tongue-tied helplessness. Fortunately, he managed to disguise that when she was around, covering his feelings in a rich lather of sarcasm and cynicism.

They went through to the sitting room. Laurie had obviously been working. A jam jar with paint-coloured water in it, sat to one side on the table, two sable brushes lying across the open top. A pile of papers and scribbled notes lay next to it and, in the window, a drawing board with a half-finished watercolour taped in place, lay drying in the breeze from the half-open window.

'I've never been any good with watercolour,' said Fraser.

'Practise. That's all it is. But you know that anyway.'

'I'm not so sure. I think I'm an oil painter through and through. I'm not much of a planner. I like to feel my way with a painting, so, naturally, I make a mess of things fairly regularly. But oils are quite forgiving. You can scrape off your disasters and paint over them. Can't do that with watercolour.'

'No, indeed. That is true…'

'I sometimes wish life were more like painting in oils. Sadly, it seems to be more like watercolour, which explains why I make such a mess of it.'

Laurie smiled. Fraser suddenly felt embarrassed. And more than a little confused. What on earth was he doing talking to her like this? As if they were old friends. It was odd. He must be losing his mind.

'It will work out for you, you know. You have more good friends than you know.'

'Forgive me. I shouldn't be yapping away like this…'

Laurie ignored him, instead proffering a plate of sliced, home-made ginger cake, in order to shut him up. Then she settled down at the table with him and started pouring tea. They talked for a while, exchanging stories about their student days at their respective art schools. They chatted about the beauty of the coastline and how sad it would be if developers were allowed to ruin it. They chose to avoid mentioning the body that had washed up there, or how that small death had changed their feelings about the place, perhaps forever. There was no need. It was obvious.

As Fraser stood to leave, Laurie touched his arm. Her face was suddenly serious.

'Take care of your friend. She is in danger. I can feel it.'

Fraser stared at her.

'What are you talking about?'

'I... I can't be sure of the name, but there's –'

'Stop! Just stop this! This... I don't even know what this is but it's not helpful!'

He broke free and made for the door. He was angry but worried too and already he felt the weight of guilt at his own impatience and rudeness. She couldn't help it after all.

'She paints too,' Laurie added, raising her voice to be heard as Fraser walked away. 'You know who I am talking about now, don't you? She is surrounded by danger. She has something they want, knows something they don't want her to know. You must warn her!'

Fraser turned back and stared at Laurie. Her eyes glittered but her chin was raised defiantly. He realised what courage it took for her to talk to him like this. Maybe she *was* mad, but, even so, he knew he would have to check in on Jamie. And soon. He nodded solemnly to Laurie and fled to his car, feeling that same creeping fear that had haunted his dreams.

10

The bar was almost empty. Casey nodded at the barman, who winked back and nodded to the far corner, behind the fruit machines. Harry scanned around them but saw no-one to worry about. Their quarry was half-slumped over a table. A young girl was sitting next to him, smiling and whispering in his ear. Casey and Harry watched as she dropped her scarf over his phone. She stood up and reached for the scarf and its contents.

'Oh, I wouldn't do that, Karen,' said Harry.

'Oh, shit! What do you want?' said the girl, losing the smile immediately.

'Take the scarf, leave the phone, and, make yourself scarce, there's a good girl.'

'Fuck you!'

The girl whisked her scarf off the table and flounced off. As she left, her companion looked up. His face crumpled with disgust.

'Awww, bloody hell!'

'Hello, Toomey,' said Casey. 'Who's your young friend?'

'Fuck you, Sergeant!'

'Well, now, that's not very nice,' said Harry. 'No way to talk to a lady.'

'She's no fuckin' lady.'

Harry launched himself into the seat next to Toomey, and leaned on him so that he was forced into the corner.

'Now, now, Toomey. Play nice,' said Harry, as he watched Casey take the chair opposite them. 'Sergeant Drummond is going to ask you a few questions, which you are going to answer.'

'Am I fuck!'

'Well, you see, if you don't answer her questions, then she and I might have to accompany you down to the station instead.'

'Oh, yeah. On what fuckin' charge, ya big eejit?'

'Well, we could start with possession and work our way up from there.'

'Fuck off.'

Harry shoved his hand in Toomey's jacket pocket and drew out a small foil-wrapped square.

'Well, what have we here?' said Harry. He sniffed at it and then lifted one corner and looked inside before sealing it up again. 'Leb Gold, I'm guessing. Very nice.'

'Okay, okay...What do you want?' Toomey snatched the package out of Harry's hand and shoved it back in his pocket.

'Just some information about your friend, Fingers,' said Casey.

'Him! No fuckin' friend of mine... bastard!'

'Oh? Since when? You two used to be as thick as... well...'

'Ha-bloody-ha! Fucker stole from me.'

'He's a thief. What he does, surely?' said Casey, with a smirk.

'Ya don't fuckin' rob yer mates. Only a right arse-hole does that. Bastard.'

'So how long ago are we talking?' said Casey.

'Couple o' weeks. Just after he came out o' the jail. Stayed on ma couch a couple o' nights. We were havin' a wee bevvy an' 'at, ken... then the wee shite nicked off wi' ma money. Left me wi' nothin'. I mean, if he'd asked, I might 'a lent him a few quid, but naw... selfish bastard... So, what's he done now?'

'More a case of what someone else did to him,' said Casey.

'Ahhh, I get you. That copper got stitched up like a kipper, eh? Hahaha... makes a bloody change. Yer aw bastards.'

'Got your cuffs on you, Sarge?' said Harry. 'I think our friend here's wanting a wee dander down to the cells.'

'Oh, all right, all right... yeah, he t[lt me aboot it. Some bad bastards jumped him one night. Beat seven bells oot o' him. Told him what to say. Said if he didn't, they'd come back to see him again. He didn't need tellin' twice.'

'Did he say if he knew them?'

'Aye. He knew them. We aw do. It's they three numpties Harrison sends roond tae pick up rents or whatever else he's after. Harrison's who you should be lockin' up, He's one dirty bastard. The girls have told me some stories...'

'That'll be the girls that sell you your dope?' said Casey. 'It's okay. Couldn't care less about that right now, by the way. We might need a statement from you.'

'What? You out o' your mind? They'd fuckin' kill me. Kill Fingers too.'

'Oh, I don't think so. We're going to be speaking to a couple of other people as well, and they're not likely to know who's told us, are they? All I need from you is some information about exactly when this happened to your friend. Do you remember when he got hurt? Was it before or after the week-end? For example?'

Toomey grinned and relaxed.

'Well, that's all right then. I can help you there, as it happens. See, I'd been down to Glasgow to see ma wee sister. Came back up on the Friday. We'd arranged to meet up here that night, but he never showed, so I went round to his place, What a fuckin' state he was in. They'd broken in early hours of Friday morning. They'd hauled him out of bed, poor bugger. No chance to get away or defend himself. Three of them for that one skinny wee middle-aged drunk. Not fuckin' super-heroes, eh?'

'Would you be prepared to sign a statement to that effect, just the time it happened?' said Casey.

'If that's what it takes to keep you fuckers off my back then yeah. Are we finished here, 'cause I really need to get away,' said Toomey, rising unsteadily to his feet.

'What time suits you to come to the station?'

Toomey stared down at Casey.

'Really? Fuck's sake... tomorrow? Usually down the centre about eleven. Could come along after that, I suppose. Pain in the ...'

'That's great," said Casey. 'We won't keep you long.'

'Aye, right.' snorted Toomey and started rolling and staggering towards the door.

'Is he gonna be all right, do you think?' said Casey.

'Toomey? Been the same for years. The man's bomb-proof,' said Harry.

'It's not bombs I'm concerned about; it's pavements and traffic.'

'Pfft... I'd be more worried about the pavement!'

11

Casey scrolled through her mobile, searching for that e-mail Fraser had sent her all those months ago. She needed a date. Some sort of clue to start her off. Eventually she found it:

> *Hi Case.*
> *I won't be around for a while. Been suspended. Cock-up somewhere, I assume. Didn't want to go without saying good-bye.*
> *Thanks for everything,*
> *Fraser x*

The message was dated 17th July. Four months ago. What was he working on back then? She rummaged around her desk drawer and found an old notebook. She rifled back through the pages to the beginning of June and started to read.

There were a couple of fatal muggings, a handful of burglaries where extreme violence had been used but no-one had died thankfully, and a couple of attacks on young prostitutes, one of whom had died. She read those carefully. The first, a girl who called herself Rosie, had been left in a coma for three days. Severe head injuries and her money had been taken. Sad, but not out of the ordinary. The second was different. An unidentified young girl. Mid to late teens. Severely beaten and possibly tortured. Cause of death, ligature strangulation. The two events were so similar. Could there be a connection? But why would that have anything to do with Fraser's problems? Seemed very unlikely.

There were those at the station who showed a total lack of interest in assaults on prostitutes but that was usually indicative of professional frustration rather than callous disregard. It was so difficult to solve those cases. The girls were reluctant to speak out and there were few, if any, witnesses to the attacks. DNA evidence was next to useless as well, since some of these girls had been with at least half a dozen different and unidentified males immediately prior to the attacks. It was an investigator's nightmare.

Only rarely did they have any success, and that was usually down to the courage of someone daring to speak out. Like Maggie, for instance. Maggie Clark. Christ, Casey had almost forgotten about her! She'd been off the streets for a while now. In her mid to late forties. Rented out a couple of rooms in her flat, now her kids had left home. The girls who stayed there both worked the streets but the police left Maggie alone. She might be living off immoral earnings, but she wouldn't be abusing the girls, and she would argue she only charged them a fair rent. And a fair rent, in Aberdeen, was worth having.

Casey switched on the computer. Maggie was still a valued contact. Had Fraser been to see her back then and would he have logged it? She found Maggie's file. The last contact had been in May. Fraser had been to see her, probably to do with the other girl. Still, it was worth paying her a visit. It would have to be on her own time, though, reasoned Casey, so that Notter wouldn't ask her what she was up to. She closed down the file and checked her e-mails. Time to clock off. Time to go speak to Maggie.

Maggie lived in one of the anonymous tower blocks near the links. Casey had always hated these flats, hated how the walls moved in a strong wind, hated how thin the walls seemed to be, how the windows looked like they might just pop out, allowing the wind to suck you out to fall fourteen stories to oblivion. She couldn't stand close to the windows, would agree that the views were great but keep her distance. She remembered the amusement on Harry's face when he twigged. God bless him though, he never mentioned it again. And Fraser wouldn't because he suffered from exactly the same problem.

Casey rang the bell to the flat. A few moments later, the door opened a crack and a wary blue eye appeared. Casey had her ID out, and pointed at the door. There was a husky cry of recognition, the door closed briefly, a chain rattled and then the door opened wide, showing Maggie, perfectly dressed as usual, puffing on a cigarette, and reeking of expensive perfume.

'Casey, my darling. Not seen you for months. Come in, dearie,' said Maggie, waving her free hand towards the sitting room.

Casey stepped inside. The place was spotless, with a heavy smell of air freshener that struggled to compete with cigarette smoke as the dominant perfume. Casey sat down in a soft and very comfortable leather armchair and waited whilst Maggie, having offered coffee and almost every other drink known to man, eventually gave in and sank into, and then sprawled across the couch, puffing on a cigarette.

'So, you're on your own today? I'm guessing your new boss doesn't know about this? Or maybe you're here to ask about some work. I could fix you up with one of the girls you know. You could make a fortune, pretty little thing like you!'

Casey laughed. It was a familiar conversation and oddly flattering, provided you didn't think too deeply about it.

'No, my boss doesn't know. It's about Fraser.'

'Oh, yes, I heard about that, poor boy. He's one of the good ones. No way he did any of that. Fix-up, that's what it is,' said Maggie and there was genuine outrage in her voice. Casey warmed to her even more.

'I was just wondering if he was looking into something he shouldn't. Or if he might have stumbled onto something without realising... had you seen him around that time? Before it all happened?'

'Matter of fact, I saw him just a few days before. He'd been asking about two girls that were attacked. Said he'd heard they knew each other and wondered if there was any connection. I told him. Lots of these girls know each other. It's like a family, even if it's a pretty fucked up one. You know... don't necessarily get on. But, yeah, they could well have met, especially if they worked the same patch. Think they worked just along the harbour there.' She gestured vaguely out of the window.

Casey couldn't help thinking that this was not much of a clue. 'The harbour' covered a wide area.

'So, was there anything in particular that made you remember that conversation? Seems odd that you remember the timing so well,' said Casey.

'Not so odd really, dear. I've known Fraser a long time, ever since he first joined the force, all fresh-faced and innocent. I worked the streets myself then, and he arrested me a couple of times. Always polite though. As I say, he's one of the good ones. It wasn't long after we spoke that I heard about his troubles. That's why I remember. Spent days thinking about it, questions he asked and all that stuff. I do remember warning him off asking too many questions. If there was something he wanted to know, it was safer to come to me and I'd try to find out for him. There's some bad buggers out there, you know. Knife you as soon as look at you. He knew all that though. Course he did. No fool, Fraser... a little too trusting sometimes but that's not necessarily a bad thing. Unless you go asking questions round the harbour. But, yeah, nothing strange about me remembering. We're kind of like old friends.'

Casey absorbed this information. She could believe this of Fraser. There was an old-fashioned courtesy to his manner, probably from his very middle-class upbringing. It sometimes seemed comical, but it was always charming. She felt herself smiling.

'You two still not hooked up then?' asked Maggie.

Casey looked up, startled, and saw Maggie grinning, her eyes sparkling with mischief.

'I'm... er... no.'

'Och, you're all right. Don't mind me. You just always seemed so comfortable together, as if you belonged... I'm allowed these little romantic fantasies about other people. Never going to land anyone myself, at my age.' She said and started to laugh. The laugh developed into a cough. She struggled up into a sitting position and coughed until her face turned scarlet. Casey crossed over quickly and patted her back.

'Do you need anything? Glass of water?' Casey asked once the coughing subsided.

'Och, I'll be fine in a minute or two. Glass of water might be good though. Right hand cupboard above the kettle.'

When Casey returned with the water, Maggie was dabbing at her nose with a tissue. Her colour had almost returned to normal. Maggie drank the water in great, hungry swallows. Casey sat back down in the armchair.

'So, there was nothing unusual in what he said?'

'No... at least... there was one thing. He asked about the girls' families. They'd both been in the care system. Mind you, that's quite common really. Doesn't necessarily mean much. Far as I knew, neither of them had any contact with their natural families. Damned shame for them. Might have had a chance if they'd just got a better start in life. I sent two kids to university, you know. I might have been an old tart but I brought those babies up right. James is an accountant down in Edinburgh now, and Jessica is nursing in Canada. So proud of them both. Just a shame I never see them nowadays. Probably don't want their friends to know how their studies were paid for, eh? Didn't stop them taking the bloody money though, did it? Ah, well, I did my best. Maybe they'll understand some day.'

Casey felt sad for Maggie and hoped that her two children would reach out to her again before it was too late.

'Sorry for going on,' said Maggie. 'You were asking if there was anything strange. He did ask if they had the same pimp, or if there was someone in their lives with military training. That made me laugh. As if I'd know! All they had in common, far as I knew, was they both lived at one point at Oakland House, you know, that kid's home. Used to have huge grounds but they sold off the land. Got all those greedy developers sniffing around. It's what those guys are all protesting about. Not that I pay any attention to that. No time and no energy at my age... Can't see what relevance that has to anything, though. He made a note about it all in his little book.'

Casey wrote this down. She'd have to find out about Oakland House. Might be something there. Casey thanked Maggie for all her help and saw herself out. A minute later, she was stepping into the stinking lift and wondering once again why some folk seemed to use them as travelling urinals. The graffiti on the walls was unimaginative and crude. Apparently, Sadie gave a good blow job and Martin had a massive dick. Genius.

The cold air outside was a welcome relief, smelling as it did of salt water and distant ice. She decided to take a walk along the beach, while it was still light. Then, she might have to give Fraser a ring and invite him for a coffee. Notter wouldn't be happy about it but this was her own time now, so he could just go and do one, as far as she was concerned. She'd had just about as much of his bullshit as she could stand this last few days.

There weren't many people at the beach, just a couple of hardy joggers, some teenagers on bikes and an elderly couple walking an overweight Labrador. Casey allowed her mind to go blank, walking along the pavement in a half-dream and drinking in the soft whisper of the sea and the crunching of windblown sand under her shoes. It was bitterly cold, so she dug in her pockets for her gloves. Must have left them in the car, damn it... She stood, for a moment gazing out to sea and blowing into her cupped hands. Bugger it, she would just phone him now. She walked over to a bench and sat down, feeling the icy cold of the seat biting into her bum, through the thin cotton trousers she'd unwisely donned this morning.

'Hello?'

Fraser's soft tones caused a quiver in her belly again.

'Hi, it's Casey.'

'Hallo, "It's Casey", what can I do for you?'

'Just been to see Maggie. I need to speak to you.'

'Casey, you were warned off. Remember?'

'It's my own free time. I can do what I want.'

'Okay. I just don't want you ending up in my position, that's all. Could do without that on my conscience.'

'It's okay. Just wanted to check over a few things. Can you meet me?'

'Sure. You mean now?'

'Yes. That being cheeky?'

'Of course it is,' chuckled Fraser. 'Where?'

'You know that place on the corner of Commercial Lane? I'll be there in about twenty minutes but I can wait for you. Take your time. It's frosty out.'

'Okay, mummy. See you soon.'

Casey smiled to herself, as she turned and wandered back to where she'd left her car. She really shouldn't feel this happy, but having Fraser all to herself was probably just what a doctor would order, even if it turned out to be professional suicide.

Half an hour later, they were sitting together, drinking good coffee and talking about old times. Eventually, Fraser gave Casey that "get on with it" look.

'So, you were looking into a possible series before you went off?'

'You make it sound like I booked onto a round-the-world cruise or something... but, yes. Thought I told you?'

Casey shook her head.

'So, how do you know then? Been rooting around in my notebooks?'

'How the hell would I do that? No, I went along to see Maggie. She remembers your last conversation. You were asking about their families, the children's home... did you ever go there?'

'Casey, where are you going with this? Notter dismissed it. Case closed.'

'I know but... well, if you don't mind, I'd like to pick things up where you left off. Just until you get back.'

Fraser leaned back in his chair and stared at Casey. he looked anxious or, possibly, annoyed. What was bugging him?

'I don't want you doing this, Casey. It's too big a risk. Be viewed as insubordination by certain people. Don't want you joining me on the benches.'

'That's your only objection?'

'Well, yes, but it's a big one, Casey. You know as well as I do that there's every possibility that my investigation landed me where I am. Somebody wanted me to stop digging. Easiest way to do that is to get me off the force.'

'Did you go to Oaklands?'

Fraser sighed theatrically and rolled his eyes in frustration.

'No,' he said. 'And neither will you if you know what's good for you.'

'Were you planning to go?'

Fraser nodded.

'If we can find enough evidence, Notter will have to listen.'

'I'm not so sure.'

'Then we'll go above him.'

'Casey, please! Think about –'

'I have. I saw that girl on the slab. A teenager. It has to stop!'

Fraser frowned and peered into Casey's face.

'What's this really about, Case? Why does it matter so much to you?'

'I... it just does... I have to do this. I can't...'

To her horror, tears began to spill from her eyes. It had been so long since she thought about all this. She brushed the tears away and reached in her pocket for a tissue.

'Sorry.'

'Don't apologise. Want to talk about it?'

Casey shook her head.

Fraser reached across and placed his hand lightly over her forearm.

'Whenever you're ready, Case. Meanwhile, just be careful. Please?'

Casey nodded and stared at his hand on her arm. He moved it away again. She wanted to tell him everything, but not yet, not now, and certainly not here.

12

Fraser had been dozing off and on for the last couple of hours, the result of two almost entirely sleepless nights, the soporific effects of some rather nice malt whisky and the sultry heat of the log burner. Maybe he should just take an early night, he thought. It had been great catching up with Casey, though he was worried that she might be getting recklessly rebellious. It would not be a good idea for her to piss Notter off too much. The sneaky bastard would find a way to make her life hell. It was good to hear that Maggie was getting on okay. Fraser had always had a soft spot for Maggie. She had guts and she took no shit from anyone. She also hated Notter on sight, something which further warmed Fraser to her.

It had happened years ago. Someone had been going round beating up the working girls and taking their money. It was an especially cowardly crime, in Fraser's view, since it consisted of a big, strong guy attacking lone females, often quite sickly ones at that, given how many of them were serious drug users. And the bastard knew that the crimes were unlikely to be reported, or to be taken seriously even if they were. It had maddened him. He had seen a fair few of the victims lying, bruised and shaken in hospital beds, terrified to say anything in case he came back. That was exactly what he wanted of course. Unfortunately for him, he made the mistake of attacking a young girl that Maggie had taken under her wing.

Maggie did her own investigation and 'persuaded' several of the women to come and give statements. Fraser had no idea how she'd done that and he didn't ask. Notter had been on duty the night Maggie came along with the girls and he was the first to speak with her. Fraser didn't know what had been said but Maggie ended up shouting the odds at Notter and anyone else who came within earshot. Then she succeeded in pissing off both Notter and several of their superiors, by refusing to speak to anyone except Fraser. Fraser had been typing up reports at the other end of the station whilst this drama was unfolding and was a little surprised when Notter appeared, got someone else to take over, and said that there was someone in reception asking for him by name.

Fraser was remembering all this, and smiling to himself, when there was a knock on the door. He went to answer it and was surprised to see a panda car parked by his house with the engine running, and a serious looking Harry standing on the doorstep.

'Fraser. Sorry to disturb you this late at night but we've got an assault victim at the hospital who's been asking for you. Says she's a friend of yours, so I thought I'd better come myself.'

Fraser glanced over at the police car. There was no-one else in it. Harry had come alone out of loyalty. Probably get a bollocking about that too, but it would be nicer to sit up front, rather than riding in the back seat like a criminal. He was about to ask who it was when he remembered Laurie's warning. He hesitated.

'Er... who is the victim?' he asked.

'Young girl called Jamie Munro. Her boyfriend's with her if you'd rather leave it 'til tomorrow?'

'No, no.' said Fraser, suddenly aware of a cold, prickling on the back of his neck. 'Just give me two minutes.'

Harry nodded and went back to the car. Fraser closed the door and went through to the sitting room. He turned off the TV, shoved his feet into boots and grabbed his coat. There were times when he questioned his own sanity. Like now, for instance. Coincidence. It had to be. And yet... Fraser shook his head as if to shake the strange thought out of it, grabbed his wallet and keys and headed for the door.

Dod stood up as Fraser came in. They exchanged muted greetings and Fraser registered that Dod looked as if he'd been crying. Jamie was sleeping. There was a large helmet of bandaging around her head. One arm was in plaster and a cage under the blankets indicated that there was some injury to her legs or feet. Poor kid had taken a pummelling. The staff had put Jamie into a little side ward on her own, which would make any police questioning a lot easier. Fraser wondered how much she'd be able to tell anyone though. Head injuries could be bad news as far as memory was concerned. He gazed at her, noting the growing bruising around both eyes and the cuts and grazes on her face where she'd fallen onto hard ground. She looked tiny on the high metal bed, almost child-like. Fraser felt a ball of rage swelling in his chest. Why did this happen to her? She was one of the most inoffensive young women he'd ever met. Prickly on occasion, sure, but she'd have gladly helped anyone that needed it, without expecting anything in return. Fraser patted Dod on the back.

'How long have you been here?' he asked.

'Couple of hours. I think. I can't believe this has happened...' Dod was trembling and pale. He looked so lost that Fraser had to resist the temptation of giving him a hug.

'Why don't you let me take over for a while,' said Fraser. 'She's sleeping anyway. Go and grab a coffee. Have a walk outside. She might be awake by the time you get back.'

Dod mumbled something incoherent, grabbed his coat and went out. Fraser sat down in the chair Dod had just vacated. Dod's body heat was still on it. Fraser let his mind wander. He knew they had both been on the demo this morning, but it was unlikely to be connected to this. The attack had taken place just outside her studio, a cold, draughty little workshop Jamie had inherited from her father. She virtually lived there and was used to the area, a warren of narrow streets down by the harbour. Fraser had visited her there once, when he came to buy a painting he didn't want or need, a painting he knew she needed to sell in order to make ends meet. It wasn't exactly a salubrious area but there were worse places in the city, and at that time on a Sunday evening, she should have been safe.

For a moment, he wondered why Dod had not gone with her but shrugged that off. He knew her well enough to know that she had probably told him quite forcibly that she wanted to go on her own. Dod was a softie, especially where Jamie was concerned. Whatever his thoughts had been, he'd have gone along with anything she said. Besides, if Dod had been there, given the level of violence Jamie had been exposed to, he would most likely have been in hospital too. He might even have ended up on a slab under Tony Fields' cold gaze.

A small, low moan told Fraser that Jamie was surfacing from the morphine. He watched her, saw her eyes twitch and flicker, then slowly open.

'Hello, Jamie,' said Fraser softly.

Jamie turned her head slightly towards him, wincing with either effort or pain, Fraser couldn't tell.

'Hi,' she croaked and managed a faint smile.

'Are you able to remember anything?'

'Every...thing. Don't... understand though...'

Her voice was very faint and rasping. Each word seemed to cause pain. She held a hand over her throat as she spoke, as if trying to stop the vibrations.

'Who was it? Did you know them?'

'I... ah...didn't know him... never... saw him... before.'

'Could you describe him? There is a sketch artist they might ask you to talk to?'

'Yeah... H...he was big... snake tattoo. J... Jade... was there. H...he hurt her too.'

Jamie coughed and gestured to the glass of water by her bed. Fraser gave it to her and watched as she downed it and then lay back on her pillows.

'Jade?'

'Ask... ask... at the project. Th... they know her. She ran away... Y...you have to find her... help her...'

Jamie's eyes pleaded with him. Fraser patted her on the arm and whispered some reassurance.

'Was she with you at the studio?' he asked, desperate to understand what had happened.

'No. They were... waiting for me... outside. I...I... think Jade... led him to me. She... she was hurt bad... He must have... f... forced her... to take him there.'

'But why?'

'I don't know...' Jamie wailed and began to cry. Great, racking sobs tore from her throat. She moaned in pain. Fraser watched, helplessly. He reached over and held her hand in a gentle grip until the sobs subsided.

'Do you want me to fetch someone?'

'No... I'm... okay. Dod's called Suzy. She's coming in... Bringing me in some pyjamas an' stuff.'

'Is there anything else you want to tell me?'

'Just that... he wanted something... H...he said I had it. But... I don't have anything he could want.

All that was... in my bag... clothes and toiletries....
All I had... And now... lying all across the lane...'
Fresh tears trickled from her eyes but she managed
to control it this time.

Fraser stood and poured some water into a
glass. He supported Jamie's head while she drank.
Then he fetched a tissue and dabbed at her eyes.
Jamie snatched it from him and blew into it loudly,
just as Dod walked back in. Fraser saw her eyes
light up at the sight of Dod and wisely moved out of
the way, so Dod could resume his vigil. Then he
wandered out into the corridor and went in search
of Harry. He found him chatting up the nurses at
the reception desk. When Harry saw him he
straightened up, threw a wink at the nurses and
then walked out of the ward with Fraser.

'Needin' a run home?' said Harry.

'Not much I can do here,' said Fraser. 'By the
way, aren't you supposed to be off duty now? You
were on demo duty this morning. That's a long day!'

'I came back in to pick up some stuff I'd left.
Was all a bit of a shambles earlier. You know how it
is. Anyway, I was just about to go when the call
came in. Casey was there and mentioned that Jamie
was a friend of yours. Bit young for you, isn't she?'

Fraser laughed.

'You're incorrigible. I know her through the
blues nights. She and her boyfriend often sit with us
old crusties. They appreciate all the witty banter.'

'Hah! Witty, my arse...'

'So, Casey was here too?'

'Yeah. She'll be back here shortly if you wanted to see her? She went to pick up Jamie's pal, Suzy, from the centre.'

'No, it's fine. I take it there's someone here to keep an eye on things?'

Harry pointed to something behind Fraser. He turned and saw two young uniformed officers approaching, carrying polystyrene cups, presumably filled with coffee, and what looked like sandwiches.

'Thought it only fair to let them go and grab a bite while I was here.'

Fraser nodded.

'Fair enough. Shall we go then?'

'Your wish is my command, O Master!'

Fraser grinned. Harry always made him feel better. Even on nights like this, when the world seemed like one enormous shit-hole.

13

The following morning, Fraser woke early, after a restless night. It was as if his brain were driven by some relentless motor, one that couldn't be switched off. The thoughts kept churning around, over and over again. Shit thoughts. First the fire, always that... if he could just get a handle on what happened there, who was responsible... but it might have been any one of the hundreds of people he'd helped put away over the years. But why then? Unless it was someone who'd just got out of jail... He'd have to look into that. But, of course, he couldn't. He was suspended.

There was that too, of course. Some wee shite-bag accuses him of beating him up. As if... But it had to be looked into. He accepted that, well almost anyway. Not really though. Did anyone actually believe it? Of course... some were bound to. No smoke without fire as they say. Bad analogy given the other thing. And now this body washes up just down the coast. Another lass killed and no-one paying any attention. It was a series. No doubt about it. Notter would never listen of course. Had to be his idea or it was shite. Every time. Wanker.

Poor Casey, having to deal with him every day. Why had he suggested she come to the blues night? Stupid move. She was obviously uncomfortable about it. Not easy for her to deal with it all, his suspension and the rumours, plenty of them. Why were people such arse-holes? They worked together. End of. Never been anything else. Never would be either. No lass in her right mind would take him on. Depressing thought but true.

Strange to think that he had once had it all – beautiful wife, a son he adored, a career... all gone now. Bloody mirage really. None of it had been real. Except his boy... Fraser felt a lump in his throat and shook off those thoughts. One more mug of tea and then he'd get out for a walk, blow the cobwebs away.

He'd only just switched the kettle on when the phone started ringing. It was Tony.

'Hi Fraser. Courtesy call. Thought you'd want to know about your mermaid from yesterday.'

'Oh, right. That's good of you but won't it upset the powers that be? Like Notter.'

'What he doesn't know...'

'Okay. So, what have you found? You never called me at home before.'

'That's because I could always call you at work before, but anyway... Astonishingly, we have an identity. I can't tell you what a relief that is. I hate it when we have to start putting out feelers just to find out who it is we just carved up.'

'And?'

'Oh, yes. Sorry, Her name is Stephanie Arnott. Twenty-two years old, though she looks much older, poor thing. Severely under-nourished. History of drug and alcohol misuse. Been arrested several times for soliciting and once for possession. Anyway, she'd been badly beaten but you saw that yourself. And although I can't be certain, I would guess she suffered more than one such attack before she was killed. Ligature mark around her neck. Our young lady was strangled and then dumped at sea.'

'Thanks, Tony.'

'Yes, well. There's more. It would appear that our young lady had a run-in with someone who was quite practised. I would guess that she was unconscious fairly quickly.'

'What do you mean?'

'Bruises on her neck, under the ligature marks. I can't be certain, but, remembering the cases you were looking into before, I paid special attention to the marks on her neck. Found some faint signs of bruising that could indicate an arm lock was used on the poor girl. I think she was overpowered first and then strangled. Extreme pressure on the carotid artery cut off the oxygen supply to the brain. He, (and I'm assuming it's a *he* since they would need a reasonable amount of strength), probably came up behind her, forearm across her throat and squeezed. It's not difficult if you know how, and I get the feeling this guy has had practice. Why he did that I'm not sure, since he was going to kill her anyway, but I'm thinking he maybe used it to stop the victim from crying out. Important when you're operating in a busy city. And it is a pattern. One we have seen before.'

'I thought so. It's worrying. He's not going to stop... Any clue where she went in the water?'

'Nope. That's your job, not mine. And please do not ask me the time of death! All I will say is that if she'd been in the water long, I would have expected more nibbling – crabs and suchlike, as well as damage from being dragged along the sea floor or generally tossed about. Couldn't have been in the water more than a couple of hours or so. Any longer and there might have been less of her for me to examine, if you understand me... erm... anyway, that's all I have right now. Of course, there will be stuff coming back from the labs but that'll take time. Do you want me to keep you posted if there's anything else?'

'If you're really determined to piss off Notter.'

'Wouldn't dream of it,' said Tony. 'Anyway, must go. Don't be a stranger.'

Before Fraser could reply, Tony rang off.

Stephanie Arnott - where had he heard that name before? Maybe he hadn't. It wasn't that unusual a name, anyway. Or maybe he'd arrested her. Didn't think so though. He was good with faces. Jamie would know her. She knew a lot of the working girls. Might even know who her friends were. Not that it was any of his business really. He should keep his nose out of it. Still, it wouldn't do any harm to put some feelers out. He could pass on the info to Casey after all. Let her take the credit, if there was any to be had. He'd ask Jamie about it tonight. A sudden weariness washed over him and he knew he could sleep now. Typical. He abandoned his tea and trotted back through to his bed.

Fraser was on his second mug of coffee. The fire was lit and soup was bubbling away on the stove, ready for later. He had already checked up on Jamie and found out that she was much better, had slept well and might even be able to go home if someone could be around to look after her. Dod would do that. Fraser tried not to think about what might happen if that guy decided to come back looking for her and he struggled with an irrational guilt. Laurie had told him to check on Jamie. Perhaps if he'd not gone to meet Casey... no, there was no point thinking that way. Concentrate on now... Jamie had asked him to look out for someone she called Jade, though God knows why. She was the one who'd led that animal right to her. But, he had the number for the project, and he would phone them later. After this coffee, maybe, he thought. Then Fraser heard the sound of a car pulling up outside and went to his kitchen window to see who it was. Before he got there, he heard a tremendous hammering on his door, so he turned and went to answer it.

'Fraser,' said Notter. He didn't look happy, although that was not unusual, in Fraser's experience.

'Correct. What brings you out here?'

'Just need a word.'

Fraser noticed movement and saw Harry standing behind Notter, making certain disrespectful gestures at his new boss. Fraser pressed his mouth together in an effort to avoid laughing in Notter's face. Notter noticed this and, without turning round, he snapped at Harry.

'You can wait in the car!'

105

Harry pulled a face and marched back towards the vehicle.

'What do you want?'

'Aren't you going to invite me in?'

Fraser would rather have admitted a nest of tarantulas but he stepped aside, cursing his mother for teaching him manners. Notter walked into the sitting room and stood in front of the stove, looking around the small room.

'Very cosy here, Fraser,' he said.

'Listen, I'm pretty sure you didn't come all this way to offer me tips on interior design...'

Notter turned and glared at him.

'No, indeed I did not. I came to warn you off.'

'Warn me off? What are you on about?'

'You have been tramping through the middle of an ongoing investigation.'

'What investigation?'

'You were at the hospital, asking questions.'

'I was visiting a friend who'd just been mugged.'

'And who told you about it?'

'Her boyfriend called me.'

Fraser felt his colour rise at the lie he was telling but the alternative was to drop Harry right in it. And that wasn't happening.

Notter stared at him. He looked sceptical but didn't pursue it.

'You will stay away from the investigation, and that includes the current patient at ARI.'

'Now, you just wait a minute. I am not answerable to you. That girl is a friend.'

Notter sneered at him.

'Oh yeah? What do you two have in common?'

Fraser felt his rage building. He could feel a dangerous trembling in his fingers.

'It's called a social life,' he spat. 'You should try it some time. It enables you to meet a range of people of all ages and social backgrounds. Unlike the brown-nosing and social climbing you go in for, where everyone is in everyone else's pockets, they all join the Rotary club and no-one ever owns up to anything!'

Notter's face turned pale with fury.

'You will stay out of this investigation,' he said. 'Don't want any more innocent people getting killed because of you.'

Fraser felt his heart thumping in his chest.

'What did you just say?' said Fraser. Then he stepped over and stared right into Notter's face. 'Right now, I have absolutely fuck all left to lose! Remember that'

Notter flushed but said nothing.

Fraser stared at him for a moment. He turned on the spot, agitated and upset. Then he stopped, was dead still. He slowly turned again to face Notter.

'Do you know who set that fire, who killed my family? Do you?'

'No, no, no... of course I don't! But... well, it had to be someone you were investigating, and now you're meddling in this stuff... and without any back-up.'

Fraser stared at Notter.

'I think you should go,' said Fraser quietly.

'Just stay away from the investigation. Understood?'

Notter went to walk past Fraser to the door. Fraser grabbed his arm and leaned close in to his face.

'I will not interfere with your investigation but I *will* be looking in on my friends. And *you* had better think about your involvement in all of this. Because if I ever find out that you knew something and didn't tell me, I will *fucking* disembowel you. Understood?'

Notter swallowed hard and a splinter of panic flashed in his eyes. He wrenched his arm away and stormed out of the cottage, slamming the door behind him.

Fraser stood for a while, his back against the wall, thinking about what had just happened. What did Notter know about the arson attack? Probably nothing. Just verbal diarrhoea, as usual. Imagine threatening him like that; how did he think Fraser would react? The man was an idiot. He looked over to the photograph on the shelf by the fireplace. A picture of Fraser's mother, Isla, and his own beautiful boy, Finlay. A day at the beach less than two years ago, although it might as well have been two lifetimes. They were laughing, blissfully unaware that they only had a few short months left to live.

14

Fraser was about to go to bed, when his phone rang. He thought about not answering it, in case it was Notter again. But it might be Casey, or news from the hospital. He snatched it up.

'Hi, Fraser, it's Eddie.'

'Hi.'

Weird... Eddie never phoned.

'Is it true?'

'What?'

'Is young Stephanie dead? Come on, man. Jamie said you found the body on a beach.'

'What do you want, Eddie, only I've been getting shouted at a lot lately and I'm getting a bit pissed off with it!'

'She was Sarah's daughter, Sarah that I was at uni with, Sarah...'

Fraser let that sink in. Sarah Arnott, That's why the name sounded vaguely familiar. He hadn't thought about her in years. He remembered the two of them were close back then. Just pals, only ever pals, but very close nonetheless.

'I never knew she had a daughter! Christ, almighty, I'm sorry, Eddie. How is she?'

'She's dead.'

'What? When did that happen?'

'About a year ago. Car went off the road. Accident they said.'

'Fuck! I never heard about that.'

'Well, you wouldn't. I was told there was nothing to investigate, and, anyway, I think you had other things on your mind. It was just after the fire.'

'Yeah. I wasn't really listening to anything back then. I'm sorry. Should have been there for you. Strange for them both to be gone, and in such a short space of time too. Weird coincidence.'

'I don't think it was. A coincidence, I mean. Sarah was working on something. She wouldn't tell me what it was, some sort of conspiracy, high up.'

'I thought she'd have been glad of help with something like that.'

'Me too. It wasn't like her. We often worked together. But she said she'd been hired by someone. They were paying good money but it had to be confidential. She wouldn't say who.'

'Sounds a bit dodgy to me. Why take such risks?'

'That's the thing. Her daughter had got mixed up with some bad stuff. Sarah was trying to get enough money together so they could move away. It was putting a huge strain on her finances. Stephanie was always mooching off her and what Sarah wouldn't give her, she just took. There was a lot of stuff went missing from the flat. Sarah almost threw her out a couple of times.'

'What about the father?'

'What about him? Oh, he sent them money when Stephanie was at school. Once that stopped he must have figured out that his job was done. Met him once. Bit of a wanker. They met at uni., like countless others, and married just after graduation.

She got a job at the local paper. He was a junior doctor so was moving around a lot. When Sarah fell pregnant, things just started to go downhill. He was still studying and working crazy hours. The strain got too much for them, so they were hardly speaking. Then, while he was on placement in Edinburgh, he fell in with a young medical student. You can guess the rest. Anyway. That was Sarah's story. Pretty crap life she had, really, poor cow.'

'I'm sorry,' said Fraser.

'Yeah, well... So, what happened to Stephanie?'

'She was washed up on the beach, just along the coast from my place, right by a neighbour, Laurie's house. Laurie called me to come over, which I did, of course and then I phoned the station.'

'Why did she not do that herself?'

'Long story, I think. She's a wee bit... what would you say? ... lives on her nerves sometimes. Anyway, she was freaked out and couldn't go to check.'

'Fair enough.'

'So, what had happened to her?'

'Someone knocked her about quite badly. She was... listen, you don't really want-'

'Fraser, don't. I have to know.'

'Okay. Well, it looks like she was strangled and then dumped in the sea... but I don't know any of this, and neither do you... understood?'

Fraser heard a slight choking sound at the other end of the phone and realised that Eddie was crying.

'Eddie? You okay?'

'Not really. Probably hard for you to understand, but I knew Sarah's daughter as a little kid. Later on, she started that teenage thing of hiding in her room with her pals and being embarrassed or irritated by anyone over twenty-five. I kind of drifted away from both of them, although Sarah would phone for a yap now and then. Anyway, couple of years later, Stephanie started to go off the rails. Her dad blamed Sarah, of course. Said she should have sent the kid to boarding school, like he'd wanted her to do. Sarah couldn't bear the idea of sending her away and, anyway, Stephanie just wanted to stay with her friends. They were good, decent kids too. Unfortunately, she got in with a different crowd later, made new friends, ones that weren't quite so positive.'

'A familiar story, sadly... By the way, the body will probably be released for burial shortly. I suppose her dad will be making all the arrangements but if you wanted to see her first, I could give the pathologist a call...?'

'No... no, I don't think so. If what you say is true, then I'd rather remember her as she was.'

'I think that's probably wise. I'm so sorry, Eddie I never made the connection.'

'It's okay. Not your fault. Anyway, see you on Wednesday?'

'You bet!'

Fraser stood for a moment, looking through the window into the velvet darkness of the night. He knew what was out there, even if he couldn't see it now - the wind playing through the long grass that led to the dunes, fields of it undulating, and rippling with waves, like a yellow-green sea.

He wondered about Sarah's parents. How could they have survived this double blow? Of course, he was making assumptions here. First, he was assuming that her parents were still alive. Second, that they were still involved in their daughter's life and actually gave a damn. It wasn't inevitable after all. Twenty years of dealing with society's darker recesses had shown him that not all families were happy ones, and that even those that seemed happy often had some very dark secrets.

He thought again about Sarah. Car accident. Sometimes it was just bad luck. Bit of black ice on the road, or some sort of engine failure, dodgy brakes... or maybe just wrong place, wrong time. So sad that her daughter died so soon after her, and in such a terrible way. He would have liked to get a look at Sarah's accident report, but he would have to ask Casey to look into it instead. See if there were any other cars involved, any witnesses. More than likely Eddie was making connections where none existed. He was an investigative reporter after all, liked his conspiracy theories. Fraser turned away from the window and headed for bed, knowing he wouldn't get much sleep, his mind buzzing with possibilities.

Next day, Fraser scrolled through his phone. He found what he was looking for. Jamie's work number. Hopefully, there would be someone there who could help him out. He dialled and waited. It rang several times and then went to an answering machine. Fraser sighed, and prepared to speak.

'Hi. Suzy? My name's Fraser Gilchrist. I'm a friend of Jamie Munro's. I need to speak with you urgently. If you could call me back on this number, as soon as you get this message. Okay...er... Thanks.'

Fraser thought about how deeply he hated answerphones. He hated the waiting as well. Would she get the message? How long should he wait before he tried again? He wondered where this young friend of Jamie's might be hiding. He hoped she was safe. He paced the floor for a while, then sat and stared out the window. Then he started pacing again. Oh, bugger this. Fraser stamped through to the kitchen and started to make more coffee. He'd have another cup and phone again. Surely it couldn't be so busy in that place that they couldn't answer the bloody phone?

He was just pouring the milk in, when the phone rang. He jumped at the sudden noise, sloshing milk all over the work surface. He slammed the bottle down, tossed a tea towel over the mess and grabbed the phone.

'Hello?'

'Hello, is that Fraser?'

Fraser didn't recognise the voice. Female. English accent.

'Yes. Yes, who's calling?'

'It's Suzy from the project. You left me a message?'

'Oh, right. Yes. Thanks for calling me back so soon. I was wondering if I could possibly call along for a chat? It's to do with the attack on Jamie.'

There was a muffled sound at the other end of the phone. She must have had someone with her.

'Suzy? I'm sorry, is this a bad time? I can always call back later.'

'Erm.... Hah... no, I'm fine...bit busy here. Just me working now Jamie's out of commission. Was it something in particular you wanted to know?'

'I'm not sure yet. Be easier just to come down there and have a chat about things generally if that's all right? I'm trying to trace someone that Jamie's worried about, someone from the centre. Would there be a good time to call?'

'She'll be all right though?'

'She'll be fine I'm sure. So, do you think I could come by and see you? I could probably help out a bit if you like?'

Suzy laughed at this.

'I'm sure you'd be a great help but the management committee decided a while ago that this should be a "women-only" service. You understand?'

'Yeah, sure. Erm... so...?'

'Oh, sorry, yes. We'll be closing for a few hours this afternoon, so that might be the best time to come. Maybe some time between three and four? If you walk down the alley at the side, there's a door at the back. You'll have to knock.'

Fraser glanced at the clock. It was just gone half two.

'That's great. I'll be there just after three.'

'See you then,' said Suzy.

'Bye.'

Fraser put the phone back on the charger. She sounded nervous. But then she might be thinking it's connected to the work at the centre. Unlikely though. Probably has a thing about the police... or ex-police in his case. Maybe had some secrets of her own. Well, there was only one way to find out. Fraser switched off everything, grabbed his jacket and headed outside.

15

Casey and Harry stood, waiting for Notter to finish his phone call. It was a schmoozy session with his immediate boss, nauseating in its creepiness.

'Yes, yes. Of course, sir. I will inform you straight away. Thank you, sir.'

He put the phone down, cleared his throat, and then looked vaguely over at them, with a slightly puzzled expression.

'You wanted to see us, sir,' said Casey.

'Yes. Any progress on the I.D. of the attacker?'

'Nothing definite yet, sir,' said Casey. 'No-one local on the system that has a snake tattoo on his neck, so we did a UK-wide search. Got a list of fourteen. Eight were inside or verifiably elsewhere at the time of the attack, which left six. We showed their pictures to the victim, who was unable to identify him with any degree of certainty.'

'I see... okay. Right. I need you to go and speak to whoever it is that runs that project, you know, with the street girls. Put some pressure on. See what they know about this murder.'

'They might not know anything, sir. They're often the victims after all,' Casey said.

He stared at her as if she were a microbe.

'You do understand what I just said, Sergeant? I am ordering you to go down there and get some information for us. They must know something!'

Harry touched Casey lightly on the back, encouraging her to move.

'Right away, sir,' he said, and held the door open for Casey.

She coloured and did as she was bidden.

They walked down the corridor together, without speaking. Once they were in the lift, Casey exploded with rage.

'Why did you do that? Made me look like a right prat! I'm the sergeant, remember?' she said, knowing how pathetic she sounded and how unfair she was being on Harry, who had only recently failed his sergeant's exam.

'I think you were managing that fine all by yourself. *Ma'am.*' As he said this, Harry stared straight ahead.

They stood frozen in silence. Casey broke first.

'Shit, Harry, I'm sorry. What's the matter with me?'

'He's an arse, Casey. But he could really fuck with you if you give him the slightest reason. Don't do it.'

The lift doors opened. Casey smiled over at Harry. He threw her a wink and then stepped out and led the way.

'I don't get it. A few days ago, he could not have been less interested in the deaths of these girls.'

'Maybe he still isn't. Maybe something about this one in particular. Can't think why though. Anyway, ours is not to reason why and all that.'

Casey thought about that. Why was he interested? Was he under pressure from above, to get a result or was it something else? Wasn't that unusual for the top brass to bleat on about clear-up rates. Suppose they have bosses to answer to as well... But what if it was the opposite? Could they be involved in some way? No reason why the killer couldn't be a boss man or a toff. Some theories about Jack the Ripper implicated people in positions of power, some even hinted at royalty. But... yeah, it didn't matter why anyway. He said jump, so they would jump. Superior officer and all that.

So, where to first? Should we phone the centre and ask to speak to someone?' said Harry.

'Let's just wander down. Take our time. Do *exactly* what we were told to do. That okay with you?'

'Perfect. We could have a dander through the square. Grab a half-decent coffee to drink on the way?'

Casey grinned at him.

'I knew there was a reason I liked you.'

Casey and Harry sipped at their coffees and chatted, as they sauntered towards the support project. They paused at the corner, to finish their drinks and then tossed the empties into a waste bin.

'Right,' said Harry. 'What's the best way to go about this? I don't believe that police are too popular at these places,'

'True. Still, we have to follow orders. And if they won't talk to us, we can tell shit-face that we tried and suggest a different approach maybe? Like phoning first?'

'We should have done that...' said Harry.

'It wasn't what we were told to do,' snapped Casey. 'He insisted that we march down here and force them to speak to us. So, we will do *exactly* as he told us. Can't see what he expects to get out of it, anyway.'

'Jamie was attacked. She works there. Maybe there's a connection.'

'Yes, she does work there, but the attacks are very different. Stephanie Arnott was beaten and strangled, dumped at sea. Whoever attacked Jamie was after something in particular, something he thought she had. Could have been money or drugs. Mistaken identity. Could have been a simple mugging. More than likely it was.'

They walked along the lane to the door of the project. It was firmly locked. A notice in the window gave the opening times. Casey checked her watch.

'Not open again for a couple of hours... typical...' she muttered.

'I think there's a light on at the back, though?' said Harry, peering in through the small window at the side of the door.

'Someone's in there then,' said Casey. 'Let's check round the back.'

She looked around.

'Maybe get to it down the next alley,' said Harry pointing along the street.

They wandered along, down the alley and into a small courtyard. Casey spotted the centre's logo on one of the doors. She marched up to it and knocked. There was a murmur of voices inside. Then, they heard the rattle of a key in the lock. The door swung open.

'Well, fancy that!' said Fraser.

Casey and Harry just gawped at him. Fraser burst out laughing. Then he stood aside and ushered them in.

'So,' said Fraser, 'I'm assuming you were sent here without warning?'

Suzy was making two more cups of coffee, but casting fairly hostile glances in their direction. Casey nodded, feeling like a kid who's been caught with their hands in the sweetie jar.

'You know, you could have phoned. Even if your lord and master didn't think of it, that's no excuse to behave like an idiot,' murmured Fraser, quietly.

Suzy appeared with the coffee and set it down on the table in front of them. Casey and Harry muttered their thanks, looking suitably chastened.

'Hey,' said Suzy. 'We got off on the wrong foot. Doesn't mean we can't get on. Just, please, if you're wanting some help from a project like ours, phone first! Some of our customers'll stop coming altogether if they see police here. You can understand that, right?'

'Yes, of course,' said Casey.

'Sorry,' muttered Harry.

'Okay then,' said Suzy. 'What was it you wanted to know?'

121

'Our boss thought you might be able to give us some information. About who might have attacked Jamie and also if there's anything you could tell us about Stephanie Arnott, the girl whose body was found recently?' said Casey.

'I'm sorry but I don't really think I can help you,' said Suzy.

'Can't or won't?' said Harry.

Casey shushed him.

'I'm not sure you understand what we are trying to do here,' snapped Suzy. 'These girls have no-one to look out for them, no-one they feel they can trust. We do whatever we can to keep them safe. A GP volunteers once a week here. We have a needle exchange programme. There's counselling services, free condoms, rape alarms sometimes... It's not much, I know, and it's not going to stop any of these attacks... but it is something. We start breaking confidentiality, they stop coming... are even more at risk.'

Harry coloured.

'Sorry,' he said. 'Makes sense.'

'However,' said Suzy. 'If you leave me your card, I could let you know if I hear anything that I think you might find helpful. No promises though.'

Harry handed her a few cards.

'Maybe you could give them to the girls. If they hear something or if they're scared?' he said quietly.

'Maybe,' said Suzy, taking the cards from him and placing them on the table in front of her.

'Please don't put yourself at risk by asking questions,' said Casey. 'Whoever is responsible might come after you next.'

Suzy just smiled in response. It was an odd smile, a little patronising and almost cat-like. Then Casey and Harry got to their feet. Casey looked at Fraser.

'Are you needing a lift anywhere?' she asked.

'I've got my car,' said Fraser.

'So... do you need a lift anywhere?' she said with a grin.

'Cheeky mare,' said Fraser. 'Nothing wrong with my car.'

Laughter peppered the air as Casey and Harry let themselves out.

16

Suzy had been a little more forthcoming with Fraser. It turned out that the only address the centre had for Jade, was a 'care of' one. She had her mail delivered to her friend, Tara. Fraser had recognised the address straight away. Maggie's place. Well, well, it had been a while. He'd heard she was a landlady now. Or was she a madam? And did Fraser even care? He smiled to himself. It would be nice to see Maggie. A hard woman but not a bad old sod, really. He headed straight there. On the way, he sent a quick text to Casey, telling her that information. She might need it. About ten minutes later, Maggie opened the door cautiously and then, seeing who it was, flung the door wide open. Her shrieks of delight were probably heard half a mile away.

'Fraser! Darling!' she cried and flung her arms around him. He staggered backwards, laughing. She let him go and then grabbed his arm and dragged him inside.

'Let me introduce you to my lodgers,' she trilled.

Fraser trotted through to the sitting room with her and sank into a big, soft armchair by the fireplace.

'This is Ivy,' she said, gesturing towards a tiny, dark-haired girl, with warm, tea-coloured skin and almond eyes, who smiled and said hello. The ease with which she spoke to him and something in her body language told him she was probably a lot older than she looked but she looked like a teenager.

'And this is Tara.'

Fraser smiled and said hello to a young woman with shoulder-length red curls, creamy-white skin and a smattering of freckles over her nose, which even the thick make-up she had on could not disguise. The girl seemed much less self-assured than Ivy. Her blue eyes were wary, with the quick, unsteady focus of a trapped animal. She whispered hello back, fidgeting uncontrollably. Fraser felt a pang of pity for her and wished there were something he could do to make her less anxious. Maggie noticed this exchange and made a poo-pooing snort.

'For goodness sake, Tara. This is Fraser. He's a friend of mine. He won't eat you!'

Fraser smiled from one to the other and Tara seemed to process this, relaxing slightly.

In five minutes, all small talk had been exhausted and strong, fresh coffee had been pressed on Fraser, yet again. At this rate he would get no sleep tonight at all.

'So, I'm assuming you haven't come here to do business, so what are you here for?' said Maggie at last.

'Well, actually, I was wondering if I might have a word with young Tara here? Trying to track down Jade, just to make sure she's all right. Jamie asked me to.'

At the mention of Jamie's name, a light seemed to come on in Tara's eyes.

'Is... is she all right? Jamie, I mean,' she said.

'She's going to be okay,' said Fraser.

'That's good. She's really nice.'

'I know... so... have you heard from Jade at all?'

'No. I mean, I usually only see her on Mondays, when she comes to check her mail, or if we happen to be at the centre at the same time.'

'I thought you two were pals?'

Tara looked a little uncomfortable for a moment.

'We were.' She said, eventually. 'But, she got too into the drug scene. I don't do drugs.'

'So, why...?' Fraser stopped himself, just in time, before he made a total prat of himself. Now, it was his turn to look uncomfortable.'

'Why am I doing this?' said Tara. 'It's okay. Well, I was on the stuff, same as Jade, but I got really ill. Infection. All cleared up now. Maggie helped me get clean. I can never repay her.' Tara's eyes started to fill. Maggie ruffled her hair affectionately.

'Now, don't you go turning all soft on me, Tara!' she chuckled.

'I'm saving up,' said Tara. 'I missed a lot of school. I can't get a good job without qualifications, so I've been going to classes. I want to be a nurse.'

Fraser looked suitably impressed. It was working with people, he realised. Not dissimilar, in that sense, from what she did now.

'So, can you tell me where Jade's been staying then? Any ideas where I might find her?'

'She spoke about some guy a few times. I doubt she'd be staying with him but he might know where she is. He's a bad sort though, so be careful.'

'What's his name?'

'Danny. Danny Wilson. They call him "Rat".'

'Oh... yeah...' said Fraser, almost to himself.

'You know him?' asked Tara.

'Run into him from time to time. Nasty little sod. What's she doing hanging round with him?'

'I... I'm not certain... but I think he gets her... her stuff, ken?'

'I see,' said Fraser. 'And do you know where I might find him?'

'He hangs about near the bus station most days, in the early evenings. Think he does some trade there. On the quiet, like. If the guys at the station knew, they'd chase him off. But he's pretty sneaky about it I think.'

Fraser fished in his pocket for a card. He gave it to Tara.

'That's got my mobile on it. If you hear from Jade, give me a ring, okay? Been really nice meeting you. You've been a good help.'

'Have I?' said Tara, sounding far from convinced. Fraser wasn't too convinced either, but at least she'd spoken to him.

On the way down to the bus station, Fraser pondered over what he'd heard. So, it sounded like young Jade was on a determined downward spiral. Hanging around with a scumbag like Rat was likely to prove unhealthy for most people. The wee shit had a notoriously violent temper and always carried a knife. Fraser had seen the mess he'd made of various people over the years, none of whom would ever put in a complaint or give evidence. As a result, apart from a few short sentences, for relatively minor offences, he had not yet got what he deserved. Half the police at the local station longed to get the little prick put away for good. Fraser, on the other hand, had often wished for a more permanent solution.

Fraser wandered into the bus station and out again, several times. He kept his eyes flickering over the faces of young men as they came and went. A couple of times, he thought he spotted Rat but, when he got closer, realised it was just another young man of similar height and build. Frustrated, he sank down onto a damp bench outside the station, leaned back and stretched out his legs.

He felt weary and chilled to the marrow. The temperature had been dropping rapidly since about five. He was hungry too. He would just have to give up for tonight and hope that Jade was somewhere safe and warm. He stood up and headed for the pedestrian crossing. He had parked his car on a side street, in the hope it might be safer there. There was no irony in his thinking. Fraser was genuinely fond of his car and failed to recognise that, faced with a choice between his car and a pile of junk, most joy riders would go for the pile of junk.

He pressed the button and waited for the green man. Another legacy from his mother, he often erred on the side of safety, rather than speed. Still scanning the faces around him, he glanced at his watch. Almost seven. Definitely time to go home. Jamie would be safely tucked up at Dod's place, Casey and Harry would no doubt be propping up a bar together somewhere, and Laurie would, hopefully, be back to painting watercolours and living a quiet life. He was almost at the car when his phone rang. He fished it out of his pocket and answered it.

'Fraser?'

'Who is this?'

'Dod.;

'Oh, sorry Dod. You don't usually phone me. Everything okay? Is Jamie all right?'

'Oh, yeah, yeah, Jamie's fine. It's just... it's kind of difficult to explain on the phone. Do you think you could come round? Jamie says you're the best person to call.'

'Well, I was just about to drive home. I don't suppose this can wait 'til tomorrow?'

'Not really. I'm sorry but this is really... I don't think...'

'Are you sure this wouldn't be better dealt with by the police?'

'No. No, definitely not. It's hard to-'

'Yeah, yeah... hard to explain... what's your address?'

17

Fraser sighed and rubbed his head, wearily. He had been scrolling through some computer files on a pen drive Jamie had found amongst her things. She had no idea whose it was or how it had got there. It was not a fun experience. There were documents related to the Oaklands development and photos of a disturbing nature, involving what seemed to be very young girls. Fraser's appetite had vanished. He wanted to claw his eyes out of his head.

'Shit,' he muttered. 'Shit.'

'So, what do we do?' asked Jamie.

'You've no idea where this came from?' asked Fraser. 'There's a lot of stuff on the Oaklands development. It has to be someone connected to that demo you were on. Think!'

'I... I don't know. Didn't know I had it. Must have been in my bag but don't know how it got there.'

'Don't you get it, guys? This is what that bastard was after, Jamie. Someone must have put it in your bag. Try to remember. It's important. And shut that thing down now. I've seen more than enough.'

Jamie quickly closed it down.

'I'm telling you I don't know!' cried Jamie, close to tears.

'You must know. It's important. Think!'

'Jamie,' said Dod. 'That girl. In the Royal. It's the only thing that makes sense.'

'What girl?' snapped Fraser. Tiredness and low blood sugar, combined with the burst of adrenaline he'd got from watching the stuff on that pen drive were turning him into a snapping turtle with an attitude problem.

'Jade,' said Jamie. 'Of course. She was in the pub. Bumped into my chair, knocked my bag over the floor. She started to pick stuff up for me but I was scared she'd steal something so I told her to stop. It must have been her. But why?'

'Either she was trying to get rid of it, or she was making sure someone else didn't get hold of it. Explains why that guy came after her first, why she led him to you. Do you think she's involved in any of this?' said Fraser.

'I don't know. Seems unlikely. Where would she have got it from though? It can't be hers. She wouldn't have a clue about that stuff, wasn't interested in politics or corruption. Only cared about the next fix, truth be told.'

'We have to find her,' said Fraser. 'Be easier if I had a recent photo to show people.'

'I did a drawing of her,' said Jamie. She gestured to Dod to hand her a small sketch pad that was sitting by the television. She leafed through it and handed the sketch to Fraser.

'That's great. Brilliant drawing. Should help. Thanks. Important we find her soon as possible. People like this, they don't like loose ends.'

Jamie turned pale.

'Will you find her in time?' she whispered.

'Well, she's not an easy lass to find, which has to be good news, I'd have thought. Hopefully, we'll hear something tomorrow.'

'What about the guy that attacked Jamie? The police must know who he is. Can't be that many with a snake tattoo on his neck.' Dod's voice was as close to angry as Fraser had ever heard it.

'You'd be surprised,' said Fraser.

'Would help if I wasn't such a lousy witness,' murmured Jamie. She looked at Fraser, her face a study in misery.

'Who says you're a lousy witness?' said Fraser. 'I don't suppose memorising every tiny bit of your attacker's appearance was uppermost in your mind at the time. It's just what happens. Stress fucks with your memory. That's the technical term you understand?'

His last statement brought a smile to Jamie's face.

Fraser picked up the flash drive.

'Do you mind if I take this? Might have to run it past a friend of mine.'

'Please do. I don't want it anywhere near me,' said Jamie, disgust sharpening her soft features.

'I'm gonna go now. Starving. Need to get home. You two gonna be all right?'

'Yeah, we're fine,' said Dod. 'They won't know where Jamie is. She'll be safe here with me. Sorry 'bout keeping you.'

'No, that's fine. You were quite right. This needs to be looked into. Pronto. I'm just a cranky old bugger when I'm hungry.'

'So, next time we keep you out, we should lay on curry?' said Jamie.

'That would be preferable, but I'm kinda hoping that this is a one-off, to be honest.'

Fraser didn't say it but he was also hoping that no-one had followed any of them here, that whoever had attacked Jamie would not be able to get to her again. Always delusional on the subject of his old car, he was also hoping that no-one had stolen it. On that subject, at least, he was soon satisfied.

18

It only took five minutes to get to Eddie's. It took a lot longer to explain why he was there. Fraser took a seat whilst Eddie explored the files.

'Where did this come from?' he said.

'Someone planted it in Jamie's bag. She didn't know it was there.'

'So, that's why Jamie was attacked. This was what that bastard was after.'

Fraser said silently for a few minutes, listening to a stream of expletives from Eddie as he opened each file on the pen drive.

'What do you want done with this?' said Eddie.

'I need you to get it to Casey, but you need to warn her. There are some powerful people involved. It's high risk. What happened to Jamie may be just the start. And make sure to save copies or hide stuff somehow. You know more about all that crap than I do.'

'The average five-year-old knows more about computers than you do.'

'Yeah, okay... anyway, do what you do... and then phone Casey. Ask her to come over. She'll ask where you got it. Tell her the truth. She'll know what to say or not say at work, at least I hope so.'

'So you expect her to lie for you? Not cool, Fraser.'

'I know. Up to her though. Tell her she can tell the truth. I was getting past the point of caring about it all to be honest, and after seeing the sick stuff on that thing, I care even less. So yeah. Up to Casey. Anyway, I'll be off. My stomach thinks my throat's been cut.'

'Okay. I'll call you once I've made some sense of this stuff. And I'll fire off a text to Casey just now.'

Fraser had spotted a chip shop on his way there and wandered towards it, salivating. He bought a fish supper and a carton of milk and took them to his car. He decided he had to eat then and there and began to tuck in. Under most circumstances, the sights he had seen on that computer might have ruined his appetite but, despite a residual nausea when he thought about it, the fact that he'd had no solids for over twelve hours meant that his desire for food assumed a greater urgency than usual.

He groaned with pleasure at the first, vinegar-sharp mouthful. Barely chewing it, he wolfed the lot. Then, he opened his carton of milk and drank it slowly, in the possibly vain hope that it might counteract the acid-inducing effects of a deep-fried supper. He'd worry about his arteries later.

He was just finishing the milk, when he spotted a familiar figure across the road. Rat. Fraser was out of the car and on the trail before the carton hit the floor.

Fraser had to walk faster than he was accustomed to, in order to keep Rat in sight. For a wee runt he could get up quite a head of steam.

135

Clearly very fit. Gasping along in his wake, Fraser told himself that he needed to start living healthily, staying off the coffee maybe, or at least steering clear of fried food.

His guts were not happy with him right now. Probably isn't wise to stuff your face with instant heart attack and then attempt the four-minute sodding mile. Still, he had to keep him within sight, see if he would lead him to Jade.

Christ, he hoped she was okay. How would he tell Jamie, if anything happened to her? Rat rattled along like the hounds of hell were after him. Could the wee shite not slow down just a bit? As if he had heard him, Rat's pace diminished suddenly. They were at a small park. Its black metal gates were wide open but a uniformed policeman barred the gateway. Rat seemed to be remonstrating with him. Fraser moved a little closer so he could hear.

'You've fuckin' got to let me in. I've got to see her!'

'Sorry, son. Crime scene. You'll have to wait and speak to the guys in charge. They'll be out shortly, if you want to wait.'

'But it could be my fuckin' girlfriend in there. Don't you understand, ya fat fucker?'

Fraser sighed and crossed over to intervene.

'Rat?'

The boy turned round.

'Awww, fuck me!'

'Thanks for the offer but no,' said Fraser. 'Come on. I'll buy you a coffee?'

'Don't want no fuckin' coffee. Want to see Jade, see if it's Jade in there.'

Fraser stiffened. His mood plummeted.

'Jade? Your girlfriend Jade?'

'Yeah. What the fuck other Jade would I fuckin' mean, ya daft cunt!'

Fraser looked at the constable guarding the scene. Behind him, Fraser could make out the yellow flicker of crime scene tape. This did not look good.

'Who's in charge here, constable?'

'Inspector Diamond. But he's been called away. Sir. And who might you be?'

'Up until recently, I was an Inspector. Fraser Gilchrist.' Fraser held his hand out and the constable shook it.

'I heard about that. Sorry, sir. Sergeant Drummond's here. Do you want me to...?'

'If you would, constable.'

Fraser took Rat's arm and led him over to a low stone wall.

'Sit,' he said. 'Once the sergeant's here, we should find out what's happening.'

'Yeah, right.'

'What makes you think it's Jade?'

'Didn't come back last night, did she, stupid cow. Supposed to be seeing some people, ken. But she was a no-show. If I'd got hold of her...'

'Well, let's hope, for your sake, that you didn't.'

Rat shot him a look of undiluted poison.

'Fuck you. Fuckin' pig.'

'Not very original,' said Fraser, with a theatrical sigh.

'Fuck off.'

'Repetitive too.'

Then Fraser heard his name being called. He turned to see Casey coming through the gate towards him. He moved over next to Rat so that they were both facing her.

'What brings you here, Fraser?'

'I saw our friend here and thought I'd tag along. He seems to think his girlfriend might be in there. Could you tell us what's going on?'

'An incident. Young woman been attacked. Could have been a mugging. Although there's no way of knowing at the moment'

'Any idea when this might have happened?' said Fraser.

'You know better than that, Fraser!'

Fraser shrugged, a smirk pulling at the side of his mouth.

'What can I say? I live in hope,' he said.

Casey sighed.

'If we knew who she was, when she was last seen... she wasn't that well hidden and the park's a useful short cut for a lot of people, so she can't have been here more than a few hours, I wouldn't think,' said Casey, almost to herself.

'So it could be Jade! When can I see her?' shouted Rat, and he leaned forward as if to stand. Fraser pulled him back. Rat settled down again, muttering curses.

'Young? Drug user? Previous trauma?' asked Fraser,

Casey nodded.

Fraser reached into his pocket and pulled out Jamie's sketch.

'This her?'

Casey stared at Fraser and nodded.

'I thought so... This young man is out looking for his girlfriend, who appears to have gone missing late Sunday, early Monday. You can see why he might be interested.'

Rat suddenly stood up and snatched the drawing out of Casey's hand.

'That's her! That's ma bird" She deed? That what you're sayin'?'

'Look, if your young friend here would come down to the station we might be able to arrange a formal I.D. of the body.'

He was too late, after promising Jamie... It felt like a punch to the guts. Rat shoved the sketch back into Fraser's hands and went back to his seat on the wall. When Fraser turned to check on him, he was surprised to see that the boy had his head in his hands. Maybe he did care after all. He was actually crying, but whether from rage, grief or fear, it was impossible to say.

Fraser found himself wondering whether Rat knew about the pen drive, and if so, how many others also knew. Were these young kids dying simply to protect the interests of a small group of twisted but powerful people? Were the girls viewed as disposable? And was Rat upset about his girlfriend, angry at losing potential blackmail material, or terrified of someone else who was after it?

Casey gave Rat a lift to the station. Fraser walked, at a sensible pace, back to his car. Before he got in it, he glanced up at Dod's flat. The flickering light told him they were watching a movie. If he had found Jade alive and well, he would have interrupted them to give them the good news. But this could wait. Bad news could always wait.

As he left the city, heading north, and home, a light rain began to fall. It seemed to reflect his sombre mood, so he almost welcomed it. He switched on the radio and allowed someone else to take control of the music; it was hard to care what he listened to, considering the circumstances. He hardly knew how he felt. The music neither delighted nor disgusted him; it was grey music, suitable for a grey evening, on the outskirts of a grey city.

For some reason, as he approached the turn off to Laurie's house, he slowed down. He found himself driving down her road, with no particular purpose in mind. He just felt that he had to go there. As he crested the brow of the hill, he spotted Laurie watching through the window. As he pulled up outside, her door opened and she beckoned him inside. The table was set for two.

'Are you expecting someone? I could just go. Don't know why I-'

'Shhhh,' said Laurie, patting his arm and pointing towards the table. 'I've been expecting you.'

19

Casey was shattered. It had been a stressful shift. Notter had seemed even more uptight than usual. She got the feeling that it had very little to do with work. What was bothering him? Must be trouble at home, she was guessing. She'd heard the rumours about his wife. Some of the guys had seen her at various venues, draping herself over a succession of younger men. Notter had to know what was going on but appeared not to care. Or that's what she used to think. Maybe it bothered him more than he let on. He was only human after all. It was humiliating for him.

She found herself feeling vaguely sorry for the guy, even if she had no respect for his abilities as a police officer. It was well known around the station that no-one below him in rank would ever be given credit for any successes they might have had. He always claimed the ownership of any new insight or breakthrough. On the other hand, if he made a mistake, which happened with monotonous regularity, blame for that always seemed to trickle down to the troops. Yes, he was a joy to work for.

The young guy, Rat, had identified the body, and had appeared genuinely upset. Casey was surprised. She knew the sorts of things he was capable of and tenderness didn't rank highly in that list. Of course, his upset might not have been indicative of any particular love for the victim. The response had seemed excessive somehow. Genuine enough but just a shade too much. The poor lass had taken a heavy beating less than twelve hours before her death. Had he been responsible for that?

Rat had asked how she died, been quite insistent. He seemed desperate to know, for some reason. Casey told him that they would have to wait for the post-mortem results. When she said that, with an absolute and final tone in her voice, he had turned panicky, like she had whipped all hope away from him. It was an odd reaction. Frustration or anger she might have understood. She'd seen that many times, had even felt that way herself in some cases. But fear? What did he have to be frightened of? Casey got the impression that he might know something about it, that he had an idea who might have been responsible for it. But he wasn't sharing that information and seemed anxious to go. Casey watched him leave, saw how he hurried, constantly looking around him. He was clearly scared to death.

The end of her shift was more welcome than usual. It was always hard to deal with something like that, however often you saw it. Casey had vowed that the day it didn't affect her was the day she'd leave the force. She had met officers who appeared not to care and she had a hard time deciding if their callousness was real or a defence to stave off the horrors of what they had to deal with in the job. Either way, she wasn't sure she could cope with much more. Two bodies did not a serial killer make, but there were clear links. And that generally meant bad news. Not for the first time, she wished Fraser were there. Not that he hadn't been around a lot lately but that was different. Sometimes she felt like they were working on opposite sides. Ridiculous of course, but there it was.

Casey walked across to her car, feeling as if she'd been in a fight. Every muscle ached, every joint felt stiff. A hot bath might sort it. And possibly some muscle relaxant... there was half a bottle of white in the fridge screaming to be drunk. She got into the car and reached into her pocket for her phone. Fraser had seemed a bit shaken earlier on. Maybe a quick ring to let him know about the ID. Seemed only fair after what he'd said. She rang his number.

'Hello?'

'Hi, Fraser. It's Casey. I just-'

Casey heard the sound of a woman's voice in the background.

'Oh, I'm sorry. You have visitors?'

'I'm not at home, Casey. Can I call you back later?'

'Yes, yes of course. Sorry. Bye.'

Casey felt herself blushing. Stupid. She wondered who she was. Fraser had friends, she knew that, but she wondered if this one was special. He'd never mentioned anybody, but then he wouldn't; Fraser never spoke about his private life. Very buttoned up. Casey would have to try and practice that herself and stop behaving like a love-struck teenager.

20

Fraser put his phone away and muttered an apology to Laurie. She just smiled and shook her head.

'You should tell her,' she said.

'Tell her what?'

'Tell her how you feel about her, of course.'

'That obvious? Shit...'

Laurie laughed.

'Why not?' she said, pouring tea into his mug.

'Christ, where do I start? Professionally, it would be a no-no.'

'And unprofessionally?'

Fraser laughed.

'I think we should talk about something else,' he said. 'How's the work going?'

'Fine. It's not your fault, you know.'

'What?'

'These things that keep happening. None of it is your fault.'

'I know.'

'So, why are you blaming yourself? Your friend is all right?'

'Oh, yes, Jamie... she will be, given time. I should have been there.'

'And got yourself killed?'

'Why do you say that? I could have stopped him.'

'Maybe that time, yes. But your card would be marked, just like theirs.'

Fraser felt a shiver run down his back. He suddenly knew that Jamie was still not safe. Would never be safe, while she stayed in the city. He had to warn her. Dod, too. What an idiot he was… Laurie leaned over and squeezed his arm.

'Hey. They can come here. I have a spare room upstairs.'

Fraser stared at her.

'How did you…?'

Laurie just looked at him and raised her eyebrows.

Fraser smiled. He took her hand.

'I need to make a few calls. You sure it will be all right?'

'Absolutely. Be glad of some company.'

Fraser was exceeding the speed limit. He knew that. If he got pulled over he wouldn't have a leg to stand on. For the first time since he was about five, he wished he could fly. On the outskirts of the city, he slowed down to a speed that was slightly less than suicidal. The traffic in the centre was dreadful. Fraser swung into a side street and ditched the car. Then, he took off running. He dialled Jamie's number, as he ran.

'Hi Fraser,' said Jamie, cheerfully.

'Jamie, tell Dod to get the pair of you out of there. I'm on my way.'

'What are you on about? I'm not going anywhere.'

'Let me speak to Dod.'

'He's not here,'

'What?'

'I asked him to go fetch some of my stuff. He should be back shortly.'

'Shit! Listen, Jamie. Please listen to me.'

'Fraser, you're scaring me.'

'Good. Now, listen. I'm almost there. I'll come and get you. But for now, get yourself into the bathroom and lock the door. Wait for me. And keep your phone with you!'

'Fraser, why are you saying this?'

'Just do it!'

Fraser rang off and carried on going. As he entered the block, he heard loud thuds coming from upstairs, followed by the sound of wood splintering and the high, terrified shrieks of a young woman. Fraser flew up the stairs, adrenaline driving him faster than he'd have thought possible. He saw the door to Dod's flat lying open and ran through the opening. A young guy had Jamie pinned against the wall.

'Where is it?' he screamed.

Jamie was sobbing.

'Please, I don't have –'

'Oy!' shouted Fraser from the doorway and ran towards them. The young man pushed Jamie at Fraser, sending them both toppling to the floor. Fraser felt a sharp pain as his head crashed into a bookshelf on the way down. He looked at Jamie, trying to let her know it would be all right. Then he got up and went after the intruder. He heard the sound of glass smashing and just caught sight of his quarry leaping down through the window, onto the flat roofed extension below.

'Fuck!'

Fraser knew there was little point trying to catch him.

Seconds later, Fraser heard Dod running in through the outer door. He almost collided with Fraser, who was emerging from the kitchen, blood pouring from a deep gash just above his left eyebrow.

'Wh...what happened here?' gasped Dod, moving over to Jamie who was lying, weeping, on the floor.

'Unwelcome guest,' said Fraser. 'He had to fly.'

Dod looked over at the broken window in the kitchen. It opened onto a flat-roofed extension. Whoever had been there had obviously left that way. Whether he did so voluntarily was a question Dod chose not to ask.

'My car's outside,' said Fraser. 'Grab some things and meet me down there. Lock the door. Don't worry about that window; I'll get someone to come out and sort it. We need to go.'

With that, Fraser helped Jamie to her feet and then lifted her up in his arms. She buried her face in his neck, still weeping, as they headed out the door. Grunting with the effort, Fraser walked down the stairs carrying her, thinking how grateful he was that Dod's flat was on the first floor. He was getting too old for this. At the bottom of the stairs, Fraser set Jamie down to sit on the lower steps, while he peered outside, looking for anything out of the ordinary. His heart was hammering in his chest still, so he had to make a conscious effort with his breathing to bring it all under control again.

A few minutes later, Dod appeared and they all left the building together, Jamie leaning on Dod and Fraser carrying the small bag Dod had thrown together.

'This is heavy,' said Fraser, as he dumped it in the boot.

'Laptop,' said Dod.

Fraser almost queried that being a priority under the circumstances but then quickly realised how old he was. A few days away from his computer was no problem to him, but he knew that, for anyone under the age of thirty, it was the equivalent of losing a limb.

As they drove off, Fraser kept glancing in his rear-view mirror. Dod noticed and looked behind him. He saw nothing unusual.

'Don't do that!' hissed Fraser.

'What is it?' asked Dod.

'We're being followed but I'd rather they didn't know that we know.'

'I didn't see anything,' said Dod.

'When we were waiting for you, I clocked the cars along the street. There were two vans among them, one of which is a couple of cars back, behind us.'

'But that could be a coincidence. They might be going the same way we are.'

'What? In a circle. Look out the window, Dod, and you'll realise that we have almost driven full circle. I'm thinking...'

'How did you even remember all the cars?'

'I didn't. Couple of them had car seats, not the usual thing for hired thugs. Another couple were ones I've seen parked here before. That left five, including two vans.'

'Christ on a bike...'

'No, he wasn't there.'

'Where are we going?' asked Jamie suddenly.

'Somewhere safe,' said Fraser, sounding a lot more confident than he felt at that moment.

He racked his brains for someone nearby who might be willing to help. Then he spotted the restaurant. Of course, George! He'd be delighted to do it. A few years ago, Fraser had got rid of some problems George had been having with a property developer. He'd pledged eternal allegiance to Fraser thereafter. And he always gave him ten per cent discount too. Fraser swung the wheel and parked outside the restaurant. He pulled out his phone and dialled George's number. He asked for George.

'Hello, Fraser, my boy! What can I do for you?'

'Bit of a problem I'm hoping you can help me with?'

'Anything, Fraser. Just ask.'

'I'm outside your door with two young friends. They've been having some trouble with some local thugs and I'm trying to get them to safety. Problem is, we're being followed, so I was wondering if you could maybe help us out?'

'So, which car is this?'

'White transit van parked down the road, just outside the post office. Need the registration?'

'Wait, one moment! I get a pen.'

Fraser waited, listening to the voices that provided background noise to George's huffing and puffing. They always sounded like they were arguing but Fraser could visualise the scene and the smiling and hugging that often replaced mere words. Then George was back and Fraser gave him the registration.

'You leave this to my boys. One minute. No more problem.'

Then he hung up.

Fraser smiled, fixed his eyes on the rear-view mirror, and then sat back to watch the show. Moments later, two of George's boys came out of the front of the restaurant. At the same time, an old, mustard-coloured transit pulled into the street behind them. It drove fast, and so close in to the white van, that it tore off the wing mirror. There was a sharp squeal of brakes and then the transit turned in and stopped, right in front of the other van. It blocked Fraser's view, which was convenient; were his witness evidence to be required, (which was vanishingly unlikely given the circumstances), then Fraser would be totally unable to say what was taking place. Next a sound of glass being smashed and a roar of angry voices indicated some damage was being done to the van and/or its occupants. Within minutes, Fraser saw the white van reversing at speed and getting the hell out of there.

21

George insisted that they eat with the family, in the kitchen. It was very hot in there, but George opened the back door, which was right next to the kitchen table, so a cool, clean breeze rippled over them all. Mountains of food were placed, steaming, in front of them. Fraser watched Jamie and Dod - two stressed, frightened and unhappy people - visibly relax under the relentless cheerfulness of George's large, and fiercely warm-blooded family.

'The boys tell me who they are these people,' said George, between mouthfuls. 'They are Harrison's men, just thugs for hire. Not the best you understand. But effective. Lot of people give in to them.'

But it wasn't one of them who'd broken into the flat, thought Fraser.

'So,' said Fraser. 'You are sure it was them, that Harrison sent them?'

'No doubt in my mind. My boys know them. That man doesn't like to spend his money, just takes from other people. Idiote...malaka...My boys were younger then, still at school. That's why they manage to do what they did and almost destroy everything I work for all my life. Bastardos!'

'I remember,' said Fraser.

'Was different company then. They went bankrupt. Too many people sue them. Six months later, new name for same company. Law is crazy. Rewards people who do not pay their bills. Rewards villains. People like me, we work hard, pay taxes... where does it get me? Eh?' George's face was turning an unhealthy shade of red. Fraser decided to change the subject.

'George... you are doing okay now though? I hear you're about to become a grandfather,' he said.

'Oh, yes! My daughter, Helena, she will have our first grandchild in the Spring. Is wonderful news, eh?' The transformation in George's face was astonishing. It almost instantly relaxed, the colour fading to a warm and healthy pink. He was almost literally glowing with happiness. Fraser allowed George the leeway to talk about each of his five children in turn, how delighted he had been with his first born, Helena, and then the joy he felt at the birth of each of his four sons: Giorgos, Andreas, Alexander and Lucas. Eventually, Fraser brought the conversation back to the current problem.

'They will probably come back in a different vehicle,' said Fraser. 'I need to get these guys to safety but I daren't use my car, in case they follow me.'

'Hah! No problem. We have cars. We make a plan!'

So that's how it was that a young waitress and Lucas, being of similar heights and builds to Jamie and Dod, ended up, swathed in hooded jackets, going for a little run around town with Fraser.

Twenty minutes after they left, and with the coast clear, Georgios and Andreas helped Dod and Jamie into the back of a small hatchback, its side emblazoned with the restaurant's logo, and headed North.

After about an hour, Fraser dropped his passengers off at a city centre hotel, having called ahead to a relative of George's, who was night porter there. He assisted them to negotiate the winding corridors to the back of the hotel, where Alexander would be parked up and waiting to take them home. Fraser smiled to himself when he saw the black saloon that had been tailing them all the way. It was parked up a few cars back. Fraser picked up his phone.

'Hello? Police?' he said, in a rough imitation of an educated, Edinburgh accent. 'Ah, yes, hello. I'm just phoning in a concern. I'm a bit worried you see. Might be nothing of course, but I'm a bit worried about some men in a black saloon car, they've been hanging around here a lot. Yes... er... my name is Simon Jessop. I'm actually just a visitor here. I noticed them here last night and again tonight. Like they're casing the joint or something...hahaha...sorry to sound so dramatic... probably nothing. No, sorry, I have to rush. Have a train to catch. You understand? Yes, just outside the Benson Hotel. Yes, a black Ford, I think... registration number...'

Fraser waited until he saw the police car drawing up alongside his pursuers, then pulled out slowly, wishing he could wait around to see the chaos. Dod and Jamie should be at Laurie's by now, drinking tea no doubt. He had phoned ahead to warn her, although he was beginning to wonder how much he actually needed to tell her and how much she knew already.

About half-way home, he passed the boys heading back. They flashed their lights and beeped at him. He smiled when he saw their grinning faces. That was reassuring, he thought, as the darkness folded around him again. He wondered what was going to happen next.

They would be back, he was sure of that. They wanted that flash drive. Was it the documents they were after or was it those disturbing images? Maybe there was something else on there. Sooner he got it to Mark, the better.

He needed to speak to someone about this, someone wholly unconnected to the local courts, the council or the business community, since it was hard to know for sure who might be implicated in whatever had been going on. He needed someone who would be good at spotting evidence of fraud in account statements and correspondence, something he had little experience of. He knew he had to get child protection involved too, but who could he trust? Someone must have turned a blind eye to all of this, and that someone might even be a friend or colleague, nauseating though that was to contemplate.

At home, he parked up and, before he went in, he phoned Laurie.

'Hi, Laurie.'

'Hi, Fraser, They're fine. Just gone to bed. They're shattered.'

'That's good. I can't thank you enough for this, but if it gets too much, you must let me know. Promise?'

'I promise,' she said.

Fraser wished Casey were there. Then he suddenly realised he'd forgotten to phone her back, prize prat that he was. No wonder she hadn't been in touch. Lately, all he seemed to have done was land her in the shit with Notter. And, if he wasn't doing that, he was just fucking ignoring her. She must be totally pissed off with him. Shit! He'd call her tomorrow. It was too late tonight. He couldn't know that, a few short miles away, Casey was lying awake and willing the phone to ring.

22

Casey leaned on her desk and gazed down at the report from the geek squad, which Notter had grudgingly passed on to her. They had managed to recover tiny fragments from the flash drive the girl had been carrying. Those fragments included some vague images so damaged that no-one could be completely sure what they contained, along with random sections of business documents. However, there was nothing to suggest there was anything out of the ordinary about them. It was a dead end. Casey had been half expecting this but had hoped that there might have been less damage than there clearly was. She wondered if this was what this poor girl had died for, and whether she even knew she had it.

The phone rang. Casey snatched it up and grabbed a pen and pad of paper, as usual. On this occasion, neither were needed.

'Sergeant Drummond? There's a guy at the front desk says he needs to speak with you about the attack on Sunday night. Urgent, apparently,' drawled Jimmy Priest, clearly less than impressed by the visitor.

'I'll be right down,' said Casey, glad of an excuse to stretch her legs, rather than plough through the mountain of paperwork on her desk. As she was going out the door she saw Harry.

The man got up as she came into the room.

'Sergeant Drummond? Mark Mackenzie. Pleased to meet you,' he said. He had the sort of soft, cultured voice and apparently permanent smile that had made Hugh Grant such a big hit with the ladies. Casey could understand why Jimmy would hate him on sight; she didn't much like him either. She ushered him into the small interview room, just off reception. They each sat down, on either side of the small table that would serve as a desk.

'So, Mr Mackenzie, what can I do for you?'

'Well, it's about the girl who was attacked...'

'She a friend of yours?'

'Er, no...well, not exactly.'

'So... er... what exactly?'

'I... I organise, help organise a campaign group. We marched on Sunday. The young lady in question was part of that march. I...I just wondered...I was worried in case –'

'In case the attack was connected to the march?'

He nodded, seeming less comfortable by the second.

'There has been no indication that the march is connected in any way to what happened. Of course, we are still investigating and cannot rule out anything at the moment. Is that all you needed to know?' said Casey, wondering why he hadn't just picked up the phone.

'Erm, well, I was also wondering if I could speak to her. I might be able to help with something... I... er... did try at the hospital but they told me she'd been discharged.' As he said this, he seemed to squirm slightly. Casey paused before answering, and noticed him nibbling the inside of his lower lip nervously.

'I don't think it would be appropriate for me to give out her contact details,' said Casey, quietly. 'I'm sure you understand.'

'Yes. Oh, yes, of course,' he said and started rummaging in the pockets of his fashionably scruffy-looking jacket. Casey wondered why he was so anxious to speak to Jamie. His agitation and posh voice reminded her of an old teacher she'd known at school. Dressed similarly too. She was surprised there were no leather elbow patches on the jacket, to go with the professorial shirt and pullover, the worn but expensive-looking chinos and the badly scuffed but exquisitely made brogues. She watched as he produced a small business card. It was thick, cream card, simply embossed with what looked suspiciously like a coat of arms, together with his name and contact details. He handed it to her. His fingers trembled slightly. He seemed strangely rattled.

'Could you possibly let her know that I was in asking after her and that, if she needs anything, anything at all, to just call me? Could you do that? Please?'

'Yes, Mr Mackenzie. I can certainly do that. I can't guarantee, though, that she'll contact you any time soon. She's been through a lot.'

He nodded as she spoke and then his face, worriedly earnest, suddenly seemed to relax and broke into a smile.

'Please, just call me Mark,' he said, reaching over to shake her hand.

Casey shook hands with him but her attention was caught by an emotion she thought she saw flickering across his face. She watched him stride towards the door. Was it her imagination, or did he look a little bit relieved?

23

Casey trotted upstairs and grabbed her coat. A bit of fresh air might perk her up a bit. She almost ran down the stairs, so keen was she to get out for a while, but she made a conscious effort to slow down, look purposeful, rather than the way she was feeling – like a guilty truant. She wandered over to the front desk. Jimmy was shuffling papers, in a vain attempt to look busy.

'Quiet day then?' she said with a smile.

'Ah... aye. It is... might be that calm before the storm thing though, eh?'

'Yeah. Look, Jimmy. I'm just going to nip along the road to speak to one of our recent victims. I won't be longer than about forty minutes, an hour... getting cabin fever.'

'Okay. So, if anyone calls... you're in a meeting?'

'Mmmm... maybe not. They might ask about the meeting. I'll not be long, anyway. You can say I just nipped out. No reason to tie yourself up in knots over it.'

'Ach, well, it makes things a wee bit more interesting... don't worry, I'll think of something if I have to!'

'I always liked you. Jimmy. You know that?'

'Steady on. I'm a respectable married man. Well, married anyway.' He laughed at his own joke, as Casey walked away to fetch her jacket.

It was the sort of day Casey's father would have called 'brisk'. Perfect walking weather, anyway. Casey hurried along, thinking that she'd just deliver the message and get back to the station. Probably be less than half an hour, so there would be little need for excuses; Jimmy would have to look for his entertainment elsewhere.

Casey climbed the tenement stairs two at a time and knocked on the door. She waited. She listened. Then she tried again. She was about to knock for a third and final time, when the door to the opposite flat opened. A young woman in a fluffy dressing gown appeared. Sniffing loudly into a tissue, and looking very peaky.

'You lookin' fer Dod?' she croaked.

'Yes. He must be out. Do you know when he's likely to be back?'

'Naw. Don't think he'll be... think they had a break-in or somethin'. Lot o' noise yesterday an' then there wis a guy fixin' a board o'er the kitchen window today, so...'

'I don't suppose they told you where they were going?' said Casey, trying to sound casual. A cold knot of fear was growing, somewhere deep in her guts. What the hell was happening? How did the bastards find them?

'Naw. I saw them go though.'

'Yeah?'

'Some guy was with them. Went off in his car.'

'Do you remember what the car looked like? Might be someone I know.' Casey hated to lie but there was no point involving the lass in this mess.

'Aye, it was old... light blue. Really old. Ken? Surprised it still worked, ta be honest wi' yer.'

Casey felt her blood pressure increase. Fucking hell, Fraser. Could you not have let us know? She struggled to control her agitation at this news and just promised herself that she would kill him next time she saw him. Slowly, of course. Slowly and very painfully.

'Ah, yes,' she said, evenly. 'I think I might know who that is. Okay, well, thanks. Hope you're feeling better soon.'

'So dae I... fuckin' miserable, ken?' With that, the woman stepped back inside her flat and closed the door. Casey heard the rattle of a door chain being put into place. Sensible move.

Casey stomped down the stairs, her shoe-tacks ringing angrily on the concrete. As she opened the door, she was astonished to see Mark Mackenzie slip hastily back into a doorway opposite. He had chosen the wrong moment for his antics. Already raging, Casey flipped at the sight of him. She marched across the road and collared him before he could disappear.

'You! Are you kidding me? You followed me here?' she hissed.

'I...I'm sorry. I just wanted to sp-'

'I know! You told me, remember? About twenty minutes ago, in fact. Have you never heard of the concept of privacy, or do the normal rules not apply to posh boys like you?' As soon as she had said it, Casey knew she'd gone too far. He would be entitled to complain about that last remark. As if he had just had the same thought, Mark's expression changed. The guilty look was gone and a vaguely smug smile spread over his face. Casey decided that she hated him as much as Jimmy did and with just as little reason.

'Look, sergeant. I admit it. I followed you. I hadn't intended to but I had met someone as I came out of the station and we got chatting. I was just finishing my cigarette when I saw you hurrying out. Figured you'd be delivering my message. Thought I could just pop up there after you'd gone.'

'Not good enough, Mark. There are real risks involved in doing what you just did. Risks to the victims of crime and risks for you too, if you only realised that. Anyway, they are not there. So you might as well go home. If at all possible, I will get your message to her and she'll contact you. If and only if she wants to. Do you understand?'

'Yes, sergeant. Look. I've apologised. Why don't you let me buy you a coffee?'

Casey was struck by that upper-class confidence again. She was so shocked by the sudden offer that her mouth fell open. She closed it again, bristling with rage.

'No. Thank you. Must be getting back to the station.'

'It's okay. I won't follow you there. I already know where it is,' said Mark, with a smirk.

Casey said nothing but was glad to turn her back on the smarmy git and walk away. As she walked, her anger subsided rapidly, to be replaced by puzzlement. What had he been thinking? That was not a normal thing to do. Was he a stalker? No, it was unlikely. So why was he so desperate to find Jamie and Dod?

Casey didn't believe all that philanthropic crap he spouted before. That could have waited until later. Why the urgency? Why was he so desperate to speak to Jamie? Casey already knew that Jamie didn't know the guy. She'd said what a good speaker he was but that she'd never even heard of him before that day. That was unusual enough for Casey to have remembered it. Mark Mackenzie was a well-known figure in the town. Jamie must have been one of a very few people who didn't know about him. So why was he so desperate to talk to her? What was he after? And how was it related to the attack on Jamie?

He didn't seem like the violent type, but isn't that what they said about psychopathic killers, that they were often very charming, or just really ordinary? Suppose he was like that; suppose he had attacked Jamie and had been planning to finish the job? It was certainly possible, if rather unlikely.

Casey was puzzling over all this when she walked into the station. Jimmy looked up and grinned.

'Message for you.' He said, handing her a scrap of paper. She read it.

FROM: *Fraser Gilchrist*

DETAILS: *Please call above-named. Information re: Jamie Munro case.*

'Thanks, Jimmy,' she said. 'Best not to mention this to you-know-who, okay?'

'My lips are sealed. Be careful though, eh?'

Casey smiled and nodded before heading for the stairs. Fraser would be the death of her. She wondered where she could make the call without attracting too much interest from other people. She decided a text might be safer.

On the half-landing, she stopped, fished her phone out of her pocket and swiftly sent a text. By the time she reached the next floor, she had a new message. It contained the initials of Jamie and Dod, followed by Laurie's address and phone number, a smiley emoticon and five 'kisses'. That didn't come close to making it better, she thought, but found she was smiling anyway.

A proper apology would require at least two bottles of decent fizz and preferably some chocolate cake. Maybe she'd suggest it some time. But at least she knew they were safe and where she could find them. Right now, she needed to update some records and do some background digging on Mr Smarmy Mackenzie. There had to be a reason he was doing that stalker thing, and Casey intended to find out what that was.

24

Casey began to calm down after ploughing through some routine paperwork. Why had Mackenzie got to her like that? She realised it was nothing to do with Mackenzie. It was all about Fraser. It always was. As if on cue, her mobile began to ring. She looked at the screen. It was Fraser. She left her desk and trotted downstairs before she answered it.

'I'm at work, Fraser,' she snapped.

'Yes, I'm sorry about that. It was too late to phone you last night. But thought you'd need to know, there was an incident at Dod's place.'

'I know. I spoke to his neighbour.'

'Oh, right. That's why you're pissed off with me. Sorry.'

Casey sighed.

'It's okay. Yesterday was just a really bad day. So, how are they?'

'They're fine. I think so, anyway. But you may be looking for more than one person, I'm afraid.'

'How do you figure that out?'

'The man who broke into Dod's place was someone I'd never seen before. Young, athletic, very fit, unfortunately. He got away fast. I could give you a description but I'm not sure it would do any good.'

'Why's that? We'll still need that description, Fraser.'

'I know, but I get the feeling he's not going to be on file anywhere. Just a hunch though. Anyway, as we were driving away, I spotted a van tailing us. It was Harrison's lot. No idea what they were planning to do, but it might be an idea to look at them. They're on file but nothing ever sticks. Worth a try though.'

'Gives me a chance to ruffle Harrison's feathers too. Thanks, Fraser. Was hoping for an excuse.'

'Okay, so are we all right? Am I forgiven?'

'Almost.'

Fraser chuckled.

'Speak again soon. Take care.'

Casey was smiling as she climbed the stairs back to the office.

She gazed at the stack of papers she still had to wade through and decided it was time to go and ruin someone else's day. She found Harry in the canteen, laughing with a couple of young constables. She walked straight over to him.

'You just about finished there?' she said.

'Only just got here, ma'am.' Harry popped the last morsel of his bacon roll in his mouth and reached for his coffee. The young constables looked suitably impressed by his chutzpah. Casey decided to ignore it. She wanted to stay on his good side right now. But it still rankled, nevertheless, to have him dismiss her like that in front of two, much more junior colleagues, especially since both were male, and both had smirked in that irritatingly juvenile way.

'Okay. Well, when you're ready then?'

'Absolutely, ma'am.'

She walked away and headed back to her desk. Was there time for another coffee? Probably best not. Her bladder would never forgive her.

A few minutes later, Harry appeared.

'You needed me, Sarge?'

Casey pretended to be busy with paperwork.

'Yes,' she said. 'Need to go and have a word with Harrison. See if he knows anything about the attack on young Jamie Munro.'

Harry frowned.

'Oh, I thought she said there was only one man. Only Harrison's men travel in threes, don't they? Er, ma'am.'

Casey turned to him and glowered

'Are you going to question everything I say today?'

Casey knew she was being unreasonable, and felt her cheeks burning with embarrassment.

'I'm sorry, ma'am.'

But he was quite right. Harrison had a threesome of off-the-peg thugs, crude but effective. He was, however, mixed up in some nasty stuff, which gave her an excuse, and anyway, she wanted to make him squirm after what he'd done to Liz that day, outside Notter's office. She should try to smooth things over with Harry, but she was too angry. Not with him particularly. Lord alone knows she would have got nowhere in this job if she were really that sensitive. No, it was all Fraser's fault really. She had no idea how to handle everything that was going on around him right now, and absolutely no clue how she felt about him either personally or professionally. She was as sure as she could be that he wasn't guilty of any of the things he stood accused of, but she knew he was adept at bending the rules. Sometimes he did things in his own sweet way. As far as she knew, he had never harmed anyone, although he did have a temper. She'd seen rage wash over him before, although she had never seen him raise a hand to anyone. But anyone could snap, couldn't they? And he had been through a lot lately. It was possible.

She looked up at Harry and tried to smile.

'Can you try and get hold of a car, Harry. Don't mind me. Having a bad day. And no, it's not my hormones.'

'No worries, ma'am. See you out front in five?'

'Perfect. Thanks. Oh, and Harry?'

'Yes, ma'am?'

'If you carry on calling me ma'am, I may have to hurt you.'

Harry grinned and wandered off.

Harrison's place was a large, pink concrete monstrosity on the edge of the city. It benefited from amazing views in every direction. It also happened to have been built in a zone. Casey wondered how many arms had been twisted, or palms greased. In order to get planning permission for the place.

'Barbie's palace,' muttered Harry.

'Too over the top for Barbie,' said Casey.

They both reached for their warrant cards. Harry rang the bell. They heard it echo inside the building. A few seconds later, the door swung open. A young woman stood in the doorway. She was holding a dishcloth and looked surprised to see them.

'Can I help you?'

Casey stepped closer and held up her card.

'Detective Sergeant Casey Drummond, ma'am. Wondering if we could have a word with Mr Harrison?'

'I... I could go and ask him for you?'

'That would be great. Thank you.'

The young woman looked at Casey and at Harry, as if trying to read them. Then, she seemed to snap back to the present, and looked flustered.

'Oh! Sorry, sorry... I... would you like to come in?'

She stepped aside and ushered them into a square hall. The floor was gleaming, polished granite. Fortunately, the garish pink exterior had not continued in here; however, the mirrors and paintings that lined the room bore gold rococo frames, that hinted at a similar sensibility at work. Casey had to assume that Harrison's wife and daughter must be responsible for that, since he didn't come across as a Barbie type of guy.

'Thank you, Miss...er...?' said Casey.

'Oh, I'm just the help... Rachel...Green.'

'And your real name? It's okay. It's not you we're interested in, but we do need to know.'

The woman flushed scarlet.

'I'm sorry. It's just... my name's Lorna Roberts. I have a record. Mr Harrison was... he offered me this job.'

'He doesn't know your real name?'

'Yes, he does. He... er... that is... he doesn't like me to be around his friends, so I don't usually... the other member of staff is out just now.'

'That's okay, Lorna. Could you go and see if Mr Harrison is free?'

'Oh, yes, yes, of course.'

Casey watched her scuttle off.

'See her eyes?' said Harry.

'Yes. She's wired. She's also very scared for some reason. And I saw the edge of some fairly hefty scars at her wrists.'

'Suicide?'

'I would guess self-harm. Wonder what that poor girl has been through...'

The question went unanswered as the rumbling voice of Harrison preceded his entry. Casey could not make out the words but the tone was clear enough. The young woman who had let them in was being read the riot act. For what though? Just because he could, perhaps. He was known to be a bully. When he emerged from the side corridor and into the hall, he was all smiles though.

'Well, good morning, Sergeant, and... er... Constable,' he said. 'To what do I owe this pleasure?'

173

Casey saw little indication of pleasure in Harrison's face. His smile did not reach his eyes, which seemed to fix on her, almost like a snake. Perhaps he was the inspiration for that guy's tattoo.

'We were just wanting a word with you about something that happened at the week-end. Routine stuff really.'

'Come on through.' Said Harrison, opening a door to one side of the hall.

Inside was a huge study. What looked like a reproduction of the desk in the Oval office, occupied most of the space by the large bay window. At the other end, two expensive-looking brocade covered sofas stood either side of a coffee table. Bookshelves lined the walls and were filled with leather-bound volumes. So even were the books, that Casey wondered if they actually had any words in them or if they were just mock-ups, some interior designer's wet dream.

'Do have a seat.' Said Harrison gesturing towards the sofas. 'Coffee? I could get-'

Casey interrupted him.

'That won't be necessary, Mr Harrison, but thank you for the offer.'

Harry pulled out his notebook, scribbled the date and time down, and then waited.

'So, what can I help you with today, Sergeant?'

'I'm not sure if you heard about the assault in Hadden Street on Sunday night?'

'No. Can't say I did.'

'A young woman was viciously assaulted. There appears to be no motive.'

174

'I'm sorry. I'm confused,' said Harrison. 'What does this have to do with me?'

'I was coming to that. Following her release from hospital, this same young woman was travelling by car with some friends, when it appears that a van started following them. Last night. The occupants of that van were identified by a reliable witness as employees of yours. Could you explain why your men were following this girl and what the intention was? Only I tend to take the harassment of victims and witnesses very seriously. Very seriously indeed.'

Casey looked at Harrison, who appeared to have lost his smile.

'I have no idea, Sergeant. I assume that your witness identified my enforcement team. They're not popular, for obvious reasons. Perhaps you shouldn't set too great a store on this witness's account?'

'Oh, I am aware of your men's activities and I'm sure you are right in saying they're not welcomed often by anyone, but our witness, you see, is someone who has no reason to lie. In fact, the witness's statement was supported up by others who were there at the time, including a police officer of some experience. There is no doubt that your men were following the car. The question is why, and whether, in fact, they were also involved in the assault on this young woman a couple of days earlier?'

'I have no idea why they were following the car, Sergeant. As for the assault, I am certain my men would not have been involved.'

'Nevertheless, if you could give us some idea of their whereabouts, and your own, around that time, I would be most grateful.'

'One moment,' said Harrison. His face was now a rather unhealthy shade of pink, as he struggled with the rage inside him. He got up and went over to the desk. He flipped through a large diary and ran his finger down a page. He flipped the pages backwards and forwards, and then returned to his seat. His colour had returned to normal.

'Well, Sergeant, it would appear that you have had a wasted journey. My men were away from Saturday evening 'til Monday afternoon. A job in Edinburgh. So, they couldn't have had anything to do with that girl's assault. I was away all week-end. Glasgow. Business meeting. My train got in just before eleven on Sunday night.'

'Can anyone vouch for that?'

'Always use the same cab firm, Have an account with them. I can forward you the details.'

'That would be very helpful. And you have no idea why your men were following the car the other night?'

'None whatsoever, Sergeant.'

'Well, they might want to stay away from this young woman. She has already been traumatised enough, don't you think?'

'Absolutely. Now, if that's all, I really need to get back to-'

'Of course, yes. Sorry to interrupt your routine. We'll be in touch if we need any further clarification. Just one more thing. Can I confirm the names of these men of yours? Samuel Robertson, David Gordon and Michael Clark – is that right?'

'That's correct.'

'I don't suppose they're-?'

'Out of town today.'

'Oh, well, that's a pity. We might need to come back then. We'll be in touch.'

Harrison's face was reddening again. Time to go.

'What do you mean you'll have to come back? They had nothing to do with whatever happened to that girl!'

'We still need to speak to them. Each of them. Individually. Would you happen to have contact addresses for them?'

'They've been staying here, as it happens, the last couple of months. Staff quarters. More convenient for all of us. Been a lot of work for them lately. But, as I said, they're out of town.'

'When do you expect them back?'

'Later on today. I'll send them down to speak to you.'

'That's very decent of you, sir. Saves us a journey.'

'Yes, well... happy to help.'

'Thank you, sir,' said Casey

Casey managed not to laugh. He really wasn't happy, not happy at all.

'I'll show you out then.'

The journey back to the station was upbeat. Harry was very amused.

'You rattled his cage there. Any reason other than the obvious?'

'Obvious?'

'That you think he's a piece of shit... ma'am.'

'I've warned you about that ma'am business. Only when the boss is around, okay?'

Harry chuckled.

'Probably already complaining to Notter about us,' said Casey. 'Ach, well...'

'So, why were we there?'

'Ask Liz. She'll tell you.'

'Ah... I can guess. It'll be fine, anyway. We were following a legitimate enquiry. We'll just have to get the paperwork in pronto, keep him happy, if that's possible.'

Casey smiled over at Harry.

'You took lots of notes.'

'Okay. Sarcastic wee thing today, aren't you?'

Casey laughed.

'We'll do it together. Then we can have a little look into the three stooges.'

'Good idea.'

'Reckon Notter will butt in on it?'

'I happen to know he has a function tonight. Kilgarry club. Starts at seven. I think that might be a good time for the interviews. What do you think? We should still be finished by ten. They weren't there, after all; it'll just be fun to hear them explain what they were doing tailing Fraser.'

'And she's back,' said Harry.

Casey shot him a quizzical look.

'You were acting all girly and hurt before. Not yourself at all.'

'I can do girly!'

'I know. I've seen the way you look at Fraser.'

'Piss off, Harry,' said Casey.

Harry grinned the whole way back to the station.

25

Casey was reading case notes but taking nothing in. She had read one paragraph three times and still barely registered anything. She got up from her desk and went in search of coffee.

Fraser kept haunting her. For the last few months, he had seemed withered, shrunken, devoid of life. But lately, she had seen him rally, the old fevered look returning to his eyes, that vague resemblance to a hungry eagle on the hunt. He needed to work on this case. This could be his lifeline and, without her help, he might struggle to maintain his grip on things. But she couldn't allow him to get involved, or not officially anyway.

She knew he was investigating, though. He couldn't help himself. And she could never tell anyone about that, apart from Harry of course. But even that was tricky. She liked to talk things over with him. He would often have a slightly different take on things, which was refreshing, and sometimes vital. He was almost certainly unconnected to the corruption within the force, but, even if that were true, was it fair to expect him to risk everything? He had a young family to think of, and few other interests outside his work. Losing his job would be devastating for all of them. Marriages had broken under less strain than that. She really should try to keep him out of it.

'Penny for them?' It was Harry. He'd crept up behind her but she was too weary even to jump.

'They're not worth a penny,' she replied, smiling.

They each took their turn at the drinks machine. The coffee tasted awful but it was all that was available, so it would have to do. They wandered back along the corridor towards the office.

'Did you get through to the three stooges?'

'They'll be here at seven, no doubt word perfect.'

Casey shrugged.

'Well, as long as it annoys their boss, I don't really care.'

Harry grinned

'Any more thoughts on the lassies?' he said.

'Not really. Same killer, I think. Dangerous job they were in.'

'But did you notice their histories? They must have known each other quite well, I'd have thought.'

'Not necessarily. They worked different areas. Maybe knew each other on sight but they might not have been friends. What about their histories?'

'In care. Same care home. Same time. That's what I mean by knowing each other. Small place. No more than half a dozen kids at any one time. They must have known each other.'

'Yeah... what was the name of it?'

'Oakland House. About thirty miles outside the city. Nice drive, by the way.'

Casey looked at his beseeching puppy dog eyes and laughed.

'Okay. I expect the paperwork can wait for a couple of hours. Get your coat. And maybe we could pick up some real coffee on the way?'

Oakland House was a large Victorian villa, on the edge of a small village. Set back from the road and cloaked by woodland, it appeared to be a perfect place to hide, and perfect for hiding secrets. They had phoned ahead and as they drew to a halt on the hissing gravel of the drive, a tall, imperious-looking woman emerged from the front door to greet them.

'Helen Duncan,' she said, extending her hand to Casey and then Harry.

They followed her brisk steps into a warm, bright hallway. Children's artwork, beautifully framed, hung everywhere. Ahead of them, a wide, curving staircase wound upwards, its bannisters gleaming, rich with age and wax polish. A smell of baking wafted through from somewhere.

'Smells delicious,' said Casey, smiling.

'Oh, yes,' said Helen, 'I told the girls you were coming so they decided to do some baking. Scones, I think. The young people here all seem to love baking.'

So far, so ordinary.

Helen led them through to a small front room. It was lined with bookcases and contained a large desk with an office chair on one side and two dining chairs on the other. Towards the back of the room there was an old Chesterfield suite and a low coffee table, presumably for casual or informal meetings. This was clearly considered to be neither of those and Helen moved swiftly to the desk, gesturing for them to sit on the two hard chairs opposite.

'So, how can I help you?' she said, a smile carefully plastered to her face. Casey wondered how much training that particular skill required.

'We were here to ask you about two former residents, Stephanie Arnott and Jade Clark. You have probably heard about the murders? Any information you can give us might help us track down who's responsible,' said Casey.

The woman's face grew pale and she nodded.

'Well, we don't usually give out information about residents but these are special circumstances.' She stooped and picked up two files from the floor. She opened the first. It was quite slim.

'Stephanie Arnott. Wasn't here for very long. Couple of weeks. More to give her poor mother a break, really. That woman was a saint, so patient, so grateful for everything we tried to do for her daughter.' She put that file aside and opened the other one, which was much thicker.

'Jade...'she murmured and it was plain to see that she felt this quite acutely. 'Such a sad life. She came to us at eleven. Had been in a series of foster placements. They had all broken down. Not her fault at all, poor kid. She had her problems but she wasn't a bad bairn at all. She had night terrors, would sleepwalk, often wet her bed... I suppose that made things very hard for the foster parents. Here, of course, we work shifts, so if we don't get much sleep, we can go home and catch up on it. Tricky otherwise, as you can imagine. But I really don't remember anyone having a bad word to say about Jade. She was always a people pleaser, very gentle, avoided conflict. Got very upset if any of the others had a fight. Happens a lot of course. Jade used to come and hide in here, away from it all.'

'So, why was she in care in the first place?' asked Casey.

'Her mother had problems with her mental health. Bipolar disorder. A very nice woman but could be difficult to help, if you know what I mean. If she took her meds, it was fine. She coped. But she hated taking the tablets, so she would stop, end up having a manic episode in public and getting arrested. Or she would go the other way, get really low, and try to end it all. That poor child was caught in the middle of it. Medical staff did their best to help her and social services really tried to support them both at home but, in the end, they had to take Jade into care. She just wasn't safe. Shortly after that, her mother threw herself off Union Terrace bridge.'

'Jesus... sorry... inappropriate,' said Casey. 'Poor kid. So, when did she leave here?'

'Well, that's the thing. She should have been here until last summer but she ran away. I reported her missing but nothing came of it. She phoned a couple of times. But, yeah... never saw her again...'

184

'Any reason you know of why she would have done that? Any changes in her behaviour, anything like that?'

'Well, she did mention a boyfriend. It was quite sweet really. I mean, she was fourteen. You know how it is. All very serious. True love. Et cetera, et cetera. And she would sneak out sometimes. To meet him, she said. Was missing for a few days the last time, but she always came back before, and, you know, we can't lock them in. Not allowed. Anyway, I thought it would all blow over. A few tears and that would be it... I was wrong.' The look she gave Casey was a long and anxious one, as if she were waiting to be shouted at.

'You did your best,' said Casey. 'No-one can ask for more than that.'

'But she did change. Was more secretive. And she missed meals, which wasn't like her. I thought she was maybe just pining, and then I realised she was messing with drugs or alcohol or both. Not when she was here. She never did that here. Only, when she came back... her eyes... well, you'll know what I mean. I was never sure but... I suspected, you know?'

'Did you ever meet the boy? Did she tell you his name at all?' asked Harry, who had been quietly writing things down up until then.

'Oh, no... never met him and she never told me his name. But I think I might have seen him.'

'Can you describe him?' asked Harry.

'Not very well. I was upstairs with another young person. I heard a shout from downstairs and

185

the sound of the front door, so I knew one of them was running off. I looked out the window and saw her running for the gate. And there was a boy there, waiting for her. He seemed older than I expected. Don't know why I thought that really. Didn't see his face. But he had a car, so he was at least seventeen I would guess?'

'Not necessarily,' said Casey. 'You'd be surprised how young some of the kids are that steal cars for fun.'

'Yes... I know,' said Helen. 'Just trying to... well... benefit of the doubt and all that. Anyway. He had dark hair. Skinny looking. Under six foot but not short, if you know what I mean.'

'Five nine, five ten, maybe?' said Harry.

'Yeah, probably,' said Helen. 'He seemed very big next to her but then she was tiny...'

'So how long was this going on before she ran away?' said Casey.

'Oh, I dunno... a few months, maybe. Not long. But seemed like forever at the time. So worrying for us all... and, well, turns out we should maybe have worried more.'

'There's no point thinking like that,' said Casey. 'They can be so determined. I'm not sure anyone could have stopped her doing what she did. Except maybe... well, if her mother... but even then...'

Her words hung, disjointed and sad, in the air, and their voices grew silent. A tap at the door shook them back to the present, as a couple of care workers and two young girls came into the room carrying plates of scones, dishes of butter and jam and a tray crowded with mugs, a pot of tea, bottle of milk and a sugar jar. They deposited everything on the desk.

'Wow! Looks wonderful,' said Casey. 'And what are your names? I'm Casey.'

She reached out and shook each small hand in turn.

'Shannon,' said the first one.

'Megan,' said the other.

'You must be about the same age. Are you twins?'

'Nooo,' the girls chorused, laughing.

'I'm eleven,' said Megan. 'Shannon is almost thirteen. We're not even sisters, are we?'

The two little girls giggled and ran out again. The care workers followed them.

'So, er, Miss Duncan,' said Casey.

'Oh, Helen, please. And it's Mrs actually, not that it matters, really.'

'Oh, right...er...Helen. Sorry about that. I was just wondering... this pattern of behaviour... fairly classic signs, really, aren't they?'

'What are you trying to say? That I should have known? That I-'

'No, no, no... I'm sorry. You misunderstand. I was just trying to find out, from you, if you had seen any of the other girls behaving in a similar way... then or now?'

Helen took a deep breath and seemed to focus her attention on her hands for a few moments.

''Yes, well, truth is I should have suspected... I've had the training. I should have thought about it, but, I had a bit of a blind spot where she was concerned, I suppose. I preferred to believe it was all innocent.'

Casey waited for her to go on, but a silence grew between them like an icy tumour, threatening to engulf the three of them and freeze everything. Casey looked over at Harry. He winked at her.

'Shall I be mummy then?' he said cheerily, breaking the tension.

As Casey drank her tea and listened to Harry and Helen prattle on about the weather and holiday plans, she felt that maybe she'd put the poor woman through enough for the day. She asked if she could look at the files. Helen pushed them towards her. Too much to read in one go.

'Would it be possible for us to have copies of the main background information in the file and possibly these day reports for the time period you've been telling us about?' asked Casey.

Helen hesitated. Then, her shoulders seemed to sag and she nodded. She lifted up the phone and spoke to someone on the other end to ask for photocopies to be made. She then covered the mouthpiece and spoke again to Casey.

'If you could take out the pages you want, our admin person is on her way through and she'll copy them for you. Is there anything else you'll be needing while we're at it?'

'If I could have a list of residents, staff and anyone involved in the place. Board of directors, that sort of thing?'

Helen stared at her for a few seconds, as if trying to read her mind.

'Is that really necessary?'

'It might be. Can't really know at the moment.' Casey flashed her brightest smile.

Helen smiled back and then spoke into the phone again.

'And could you print out copies of the resident and staff lists, together with information on the board of governors? That would be appreciated. Thank you, Sally.'

About twenty minutes later, Casey handed Helen her card with the usual request to call if she thought of anything else, and left the building, carrying a sheaf of photocopies. The journey back to the city was a thoughtful one. Harry tried chatting but realised very quickly that Casey was a little preoccupied. He didn't know why and wasn't sure he wanted to know. He just couldn't see how it could be connected to their time at Oakwood House. They were just pulling up outside the station when Casey broke her silence.

'She never asked for I.D. Notice that?'

'Neither she did. Obviously a trusting sort.'

'But is that not a bit unusual for someone in her position?'

'The staff probably deal with that sort of stuff all the time, and she *was* expecting us...'

'No, I'm not trying to say she's incompetent or anything, but it is a bit...unusual... for a manager of a care home.'

'I think you're reading too much into this. She seems very genuine, like she really cares about the kids.'

'Oh, I agree with you. She's lovely. Just maybe too nice, somehow, for that level of responsibility... or am I being too harsh? Yes, I probably am. Can't help but think, though, that if you were a predator, that home, with that sort of management style, would be so easy... don't you think?'

Harry looked at her, allowing the idea to seep in.

'That's a horrible, idea, Casey.'

'Yes, sorry. Just thinking out loud. Ignore me.'

'I can do that,' said Harry, though without much conviction. He was already planning to take a closer look at case files for young prostitutes in the area, over the last few years.

26

Fraser was just about to go and call on Laurie, to see how things were there, when the phone started to ring. He snatched it up, whilst trying to shrug on his jacket.

'Fraser Gilchrist. Can I help you?'

'Hello, Fraser,' said Maggie, her familiar gravelly tones forcing a smile out of him.

'Maggie. An unexpected pleasure.'

'Of course it is. You're so full o' shite...'

Fraser chuckled and waited for her to go on.

'Well,' she said. 'It's Tara. She's remembered something the dead lass told her. Wants to speak to you. You're very honoured, by the way... she barely speaks to me most days.'

'Okay. Well, I'm just on my way somewhere. Only take me about an hour or so. I could be at yours in...maybe two hours? That okay with you... and her?'

'That'll be good. I'll have the kettle on. Unless you fancied a wee drop o' something stronger?'

'Tea'll be fine. I'll be driving, Maggie,' replied Fraser.

'Och, you lot don't know how to enjoy yourselves.'

He heard her laughing.

'Okay, then. See you shortly,' he said.

Fraser wondered whether he should call Casey. He decided against it. Might have nothing to do with anything. No, he would wait and see what the lass had to say. No point dragging Casey into the firing line unnecessarily. If Notter got wind that they were still in touch, he'd try to find a way to ruin her career, small-minded little prick that he was...

Fraser grabbed his keys and headed out. It was a cold, windy afternoon, the air prickling with frost. The sharp tang of sea carried on the wind seemed to clear his sinuses. Sharp cold air stabbed at his face, making the bones ache. He was glad to get inside the car and, after a few attempts, got the engine to start. He had to scrape the outside of the windscreen and wipe the inside, before he could move off. Even as he drove, the damned thing misted up so he steered with one hand and wiped with the other, until things settled down a bit. Soon he was rattling along the familiar rutted track to Laurie's house. He loved that first glimpse of the tiny cottage as he crested the hill, and the glorious view over the rocks and out into the cold North Sea.

As usual, Laurie was expecting him. He was quickly ushered into the warmth and settled in a chair by the table. Jamie and Dod were cuddling together on the small sofa in the kitchen. They greeted him warmly and came over to join him. Laurie directed Fraser's attention to the laptop and, a few clicks later, he was watching a video clip of the demo. He wasn't sure what he was supposed to be looking at. Laurie stood next to him, reached over and adjusted the slider at the bottom to two minutes into the film.

'Oh, I see you!' said Fraser, smiling. He turned to look at Jamie and Dod who gave him forced smiles in return. He frowned in puzzlement.

'Keep watching,' said Laurie. 'The girl in the green coat.'

'It's Jade,' said Fraser pointing at the screen.

'Yes, that's her. Just keep watching.'

Fraser carried on looking and noticed how she was stealing glances at Jamie and Dod, how she followed them, and lastly, the filthy looks and stares she directed at Mark Mackenzie.

'Right... very odd... wonder what the story is there,' said Fraser, still not sure what he should be looking for.

'She was following us,' said Jamie. 'This proves she planned it, planned it all. But why? I mean, you don't expect someone to sneak stuff *into* your bag, just out of it.'

'Maybe she trusted you to look after it,' said Fraser.

'But why? And where did she get it from in the first place?'

'No idea. Listen, could you send a link for this to my e-mail address?'

'Sure,' they said in chorus, which made Fraser laugh.

'Just once would do! How are things otherwise? You seem a bit better, Jamie.'

'Much better. Laurie has been feeding us her amazing food. Her curried sweet potato soup is to die for! And it's so lovely here. She might not be able to get rid of us!'

'You're very kind, Jamie,' laughed Laurie. 'It's been great for me, having company. It's been a while. In fact, the only other person who's visited me is Fraser, and I had to find a dead body for that to happen!'

Soon, he was driving away, out onto the main road and heading for the city. He didn't notice the silver hatchback pulling out from a layby, close behind him, or see the driver hesitate at the turn-off to Laurie's. It was only as he was nearing the city limits that he saw the car. He pulled into a side road and the car sped past him, pulling into the next road along. Cautiously, Fraser pulled out again and joined the stream of traffic heading into the centre. When he looked back, he saw the car emerge and turn back towards the countryside, back the way it had come. They must be lost, he thought to himself, and carried on going, amused by his own paranoia.

The traffic was heavy, so he made slow progress, but, eventually, he was parking at Maggie's, and climbing the stairs to her flat. He rang the doorbell. A tune pealed out at him. Tacky but designed to force a smile out of you, he decided, as the door was flung open by a florid and perfumed Maggie.

'Hello, Handsome. Come in, come in!'

Tara was waiting for him. She smiled and offered him tea.

'No, no, thank you. I'm almost drowning in the stuff today.' He said. 'So, Maggie tells me you remembered something?'

'Jade left a bag here last time she came, asked me to look after it for her, said it was important.'

'Okay,' said Fraser, wondering what it was about today that was encouraging everyone to tease him with information, like a school test.

'Well, I thought I'd have a look. See what was in it. There was a notebook, a sort of diary inside. It felt a bit weird looking at someone's personal stuff like that, especially since she's dead...'

'It's okay,' said Fraser. 'I don't think she'd mind you reading it.'

'But that's the thing; it's not hers. It belongs to someone else. I didn't understand half of it anyway. Lots of numbers and letters, like a code or something.' She handed Fraser a small, expensive-looking, silk-covered journal.

Fraser opened it up and felt his belly lurch with surprise, as he read the first page. It was just a name, and a mobile number. The journal had belonged to Sarah Arnott.

'Hey, are you okay?' said Tara.

'Yes, sorry, I'm fine. Just a surprise is all. Did she ever mention this book to you?'

'Think she said it came from Stephanie. Was Sarah Stephanie's real name? Only lots of girls do that, you know, use a different name.'

'No. Her mother, I think. But how did Jade come to have it? Did she say?'

'Well, I know she stayed with Stephanie sometimes. Stephanie would get a bit... you know... kind of funny about being there, in her mum's place, after she died. Bit lonely. But they fell out all the time too, so she'd stay over for a couple of nights, they'd have a row and then she'd leave. But Stephanie always came back looking for her. I think Jade was the only one who could cope with Stephanie. That girl could be a real handful sometimes. Up and down. Real temper on her. Probably the drugs though. She was bad on it. Worse than Jade even ... not that she deserved... well... you know...'

Fraser nodded and started to leaf through the pages. The coded entries were all in the same format: four digits, two letters, four digits. Between these pages, there were scrawled addresses, or a number and postcode. At first glance, there appeared to be several addresses outside the city, plus half a dozen within it. Most of the city ones were very central or in solid residential areas. There were a couple of exceptions. This would have to be looked over and translated into English. Fraser would need his laptop and a lot of technical and professional advice.

Fraser slipped the book into his inside pocket and stood to leave.

'Oh, there were these too,' said Tara, handing Fraser a couple of notepads and a computer disc. Each had Sarah's name on. 'I was going to just chuck it all, but then I thought you should maybe see it first?'

'Well, I'm very glad you did... erm... I don't suppose you have a carrier bag?'

Tara fetched one from the kitchen and handed it to him.

'By the way,' said Fraser. 'Do you have any idea whether Jade had any connection to a local campaigner called Mark Mackenzie?'

'She didn't really know him, but she hated him. Said it was his fault Stephanie was killed.'

'Oh? Why did she think that?'

'Stephanie didn't like him. Don't know why. But Stephanie was always making a big drama out of things. It was just the way she was. Jade always stuck up for her, even when she knew Stephanie was in the wrong. They were like sisters.' Tara was on the verge of tears. Fraser patted her shoulder. thanked her, and left. So, that was it. Jade had only been given Stephanie's version of events. Fraser doubted that it was even remotely connected with the facts. But lying wasn't a criminal offence. Nor was it a compelling reason for murder.

Ten minutes later, Fraser was in his car and heading to Eddie's. He decided that switching priorities was probably a good idea. His head was swimming. It would be good to talk things through with Eddie, whose experience as an investigative reporter might prove invaluable.

27

Fraser knocked on Eddie's door for the third time and was about to give up when the door suddenly flew open and a madman in boxer shorts appeared.

'What the fuck? Might have known. Jesus!' he said and turned to walk slowly down the corridor to the sitting room.

'No, Jesus wasn't available today. I'll just have to do,' said Fraser.

He followed him into a sitting room that reeked of stale alcohol and lord knows what else. Fraser wrinkled his nose and looked around him. The scatter cushions were lined up on the floor in front of the couch. The coffee table was covered in dirty glasses, along with a couple of half-empty bottles, and a series of half-filled takeaway containers.

'Party last night?' asked Fraser.

'Had some good news for a bloody change. Been offered a publishing contract for that book I finished working on earlier this year.'

'Oh, the one on the Buttermere scandal?'

Lord Buttermere as was, was a self-made man with a title that had been bought and paid for through generous donations to a certain political party. The scandal had erupted on the internet and had involved a swingers' club and the leaking of confidential government papers. He had been a very naughty boy.

'Yeah. That very thing,' said Eddie.

Fraser watched as his friend poured himself a glass of water and downed it, before padding through to the sitting room and collapsing on the couch with a groan.

'Celebration dinner for two?'

'Sherlock strikes again... Young lass from next door. I met her just after I got the news and she joined me on my anti-liver campaign. She's young, though. So she won't be feeling anywhere near as bad as I am right now.'

'She went home then?'

'Of course she did. Jesus, Fraser, it would be like fucking my daughter. She's only about twenty, twenty-one. Sadly, I am more than twice her age... oh, God... Just thinking about that makes me feel depressed. What are you wanting anyway, and why are you here at this time in the morning?'

'It's almost three in the afternoon, O Aged One,' laughed Fraser.

'Fuck! Really? I was supposed to speak to my agent today... and that just isn't going to happen now, is it?'

'It seems unlikely, certainly.'

'Oh, God. So, what's going on, Fraser? Shit, I can't...' Eddie forced himself, apparently with some difficulty, into what vaguely resembled a sitting position.

'Shall I make us some coffee?'

'Please.'

Fraser pulled off his jacket and draped it over the back of a chair. He then started to gather up the debris from Eddie's night before. Soon, the clutter free coffee table had been wiped, the cushions replaced on the couch, the dishwasher humming merrily and a steaming cafetiere prepared.

'Fraser, will you marry me?' said Eddie, who hadn't moved a muscle in the last ten minutes.

'You are very welcome,' said Fraser. 'Just get some caffeine into your alcohol stream, and then I'd suggest you have a shower while I rustle up some bacon rolls?'

'Mmmmm.... Bacon... I like bacon. It's so salty and chewy and erm... bacony...'

'Coffee first.'

Fraser decided there was little point attempting to engage in any demanding topics of conversation until the hangover treatment regime was near its end. He therefore put on some gentle music and sipped at his coffee while Eddie filled him in on the events of yesterday, the intricacies of contracts, and the terrible injustice of the pathetically small advance he'd had to accept in order to see his book on library shelves. Listening to his friend's pretend gripes was amusing to Fraser, but, even if it hadn't been, it was a small price to pay for the benefit of Eddie's contacts and expertise in investigating what was turning out to be a multi-layered and extremely puzzling case.

While Eddie took his shower, Fraser made a start on the promised bacon rolls. With the bacon hissing and spitting under the grill

Fraser finished off making the rolls and carried them through to the table along with a fresh jug of coffee. He could hear Eddie rumbling about getting dressed, whilst indulging in some almost offensively tuneless whistling. Fraser took out the journal, the notebooks and the disc, and arranged them neatly in a row on the sofa side of the coffee table, ready for Eddie's return.

At last the door swung open and a much brighter and happier-looking Eddie appeared.

'Seriously, Fraser, I think I love you!' he said, before grabbing a roll and taking a huge bite.

Fraser smiled and waited for him to notice the stuff on the table that wasn't either edible or potable. Then Eddie's eyes drifted down towards the items.

'What's all this,' said Eddie, frowning. 'Sarah? These are hers? How did you get these?'

'I was handed them this afternoon. They had been in the possession of a young woman recently murdered.'

'Murdered? Jesus, Fraser. Think you've maybe almost achieved the impossible and put me off my bacon roll!' He took another bite.

'Really?'

'Well, I did say almost. Let's eat first, eh? Please? I can't think about her and enjoy my bacon at the same time. Real men don't multi-task, you know.'

His attitude appeared flippant and unfeeling, but Fraser, who had known him for over twenty years, recognised it for what it was, Eddie's habitual version of a displacement activity, pretending to not give a shit. Fraser knew better, in other words, so he grabbed a roll and waited until Eddie was ready to talk. He watched his friend run his fingers delicately over the items, as he chewed, as if willing Sarah to rise up out of the pages of her journal and tell him what it was all about.

'So, who had this stuff then?' asked Eddie.

'The murder victim, Jade, had left a bag of things with a friend. They were in there.'

'So, she knew Sarah?'

'Possibly, but the connection is more likely to be her daughter, Stephanie. They were at the same care home, briefly, and I gather they worked fairly close to one another. Not entirely sure how Jade came to have them but I assume that Stephanie found them after her mother's death.'

'Wonder why she hung on to these?' said Eddie, fiddling with a corner of one of the notebooks.

'I was hoping you might have been able to help me figure that out. You mentioned something before about a big project she was working on. Might these things be connected to that?'

'I suppose. Yes, quite probably. Almost afraid to look.'

'Almost,' said Fraser as Eddie picked up one of the notebooks. Eddie just grinned in response.

Fraser picked up the other one and started to leaf through it. Apart from the strings of indecipherable numbers and letters, there were a few short notes, often just a couple of unconnected words with a question mark or exclamation mark after them. Ideas she'd had, presumably, ones which would have made some sort of sense to her at the time, but which shone no light on anything for

Fraser. Each entry was meticulously timed and dated. There were a good number of crossings out too, possibly indicating theories that she had ruled out. There were also notes from some sort of surveillance she was undertaking. Opposite to the text were those puzzling strings of letters and numbers. He scrutinised the first few and suddenly saw what they were.

'Crikey, Sarah. You'd have been no challenge for the Bletchley code breakers!' he laughed.

'What?' said Eddie.

It's the strings of numbers and letters. I just figured out what they are.'

'Come on then, smart-arse.'

'Piss off, Eddie. Pretty damned obvious, really.'

'Date, initials, time. She's been taking note of who goes in and out of there, wherever *there* might be.'

Fraser looked back at the text, flicking backwards and forwards, but there seemed to be no sign of a location or, indeed, of a reason why she might be so interested in the comings and goings there. He closed the notebook and was about to set it back on the table, when he noticed a series of numbers on the bottom of the front cover: *4,5,6*.

'Do you see any numbers on the front of that notebook?' Fraser gestured to the notepad in Eddie's hands. He flipped back to the front cover.

'Uhuh... *7,8*? Does that mean something?'

'No idea.'

'Oh, hang on! Sarah was one of those sickeningly organised people. She was also ridiculously paranoid at times. Year or so ago, she sent me something. I filed it. Hang on.'

Eddie jumped up, suddenly energised, and came back through, reading over a couple of sheets of A4. He stood for a moment, quietly reading, his forehead furrowed with concentration.

'Eddie? Eddie? Hello?' Fraser reached over and jabbed Eddie in the arm.

'Ow! What was that for?'

'Och, don't be a fairy. What have you got there?'

'Not sure. Seems to be lists, addresses...'

Eventually, Eddie handed Fraser the papers and went back to his seat.

'So, my numbers are seven and eight,' said Eddie. 'What are they on those lists?'

'Er... hang on... oh, right. Seven seems to be a private address. City centre. About a five minute walk away. Eight is outside the city. Oakland House?'

'Oaklands,' said Eddie. 'I remember that, council sold off that big chunk of the gardens. Caused a big stooshie! That's why we've got demos and action groups springing up everywhere. But you know how it is - money clings to money like shit to a blanket and sod the rest of us. Luxury flats versus protected woodland? No fuckin' contest to them. Money is the winner every time. A few activists aren't ever gonna change that'

'Don't think it's connected, but then I'm not officially involved with the case. You'll have to give

Casey a ring in the morning, let her handle it from here. Was thinking a pint might be in order?'

'Oh, God, do I want to go there again?' groaned Eddie.

'Yes. Yes, you do. Hair of the dog and all that.'

Fraser looked down at the list again. Number four was council offices, number five, some private club in leafy suburbia and six was, of all things, the police station. Why the hell would she be watching the station? And where was the notebook for numbers one, two and three?

28

Casey and Harry looked down at the three files on the table.

'Fine bunch of specimens,' said Harry.

'Agreed. Don't fancy our chances really, but at least they'll know we're watching them.'

Harry laughed.

'Can't see that worrying them.'

Casey looked round as the door opened and four more police officers wandered across to join them.

'So who's taking Sammy Robertson?' said Casey.

An arm reached forward and grabbed the folder, and two officers headed back towards the door.

'Davie Gordon?'

Another arm reached for the second folder, and the other two disappeared through the door. Harry picked up the remaining file.

'So that leaves us with Mickey Clark, then,' he said. 'Such a charmer. I remember arresting him when he was still at the high school. Vicious brat even then.'

'I don't suppose the others are any better,' said Casey, as they walked towards the door.

'No, indeed,' said Harry. 'They were all at school together. All went to the young offenders together too, a sort of finishing school for them. Came out more fucked up than they were when they went in

'Not a believer in the short, sharp shock approach?'

'Let's just say I remain to be convinced, although, having said that, I reckon a hot backside from time to time when they were younger might have helped. Don't quote me on that, by the way.'

'None of them had the greatest start though,' said Casey.

'What do you mean? Plenty of folk have a tough time growing up and don't turn into thugs. Must be in them to start with, I reckon.'

'I know what you're saying but being surrounded by pimps and pushers doesn't help either. There's a difference between being hard up and being neglected almost to the point of death. Sammy was on the 'at risk' register at six months old. That's pretty sad.'

'Maybe a mixture then. Nature *and* nurture. I just simply don't accept that being kind and gentle with kids necessarily predisposes them to being kind and gentle themselves. Lost count of the number of heartbroken, decent parents who've ended up having to come down here to collect their little darlings. Felt like clipping the wee buggers round the ear myself.'

'You may be right, but I still can't help but wonder how some of them might have been if they'd had a different upbringing.'

'Och, don't mind me. I'm turning into a dinosaur.'

Casey laughed.

Mickey was sitting in the waiting room, fidgeting with his collar and looking distinctly uncomfortable.

'Mickey?' said Harry. 'Want to come through?'

Mickey gave him an evil look and then got to his feet as slowly as he could manage without falling over. Casey watched him and couldn't help being amused. If he thought that would get a rise out of Harry, he really didn't know him very well. Mickey was in his mid-twenties, slim and athletic, with a livid scar that ran from the edge of his left eyebrow down almost to his jaw. He also appeared to have an almost total lack of either manners or good judgement. Didn't he realise that being as rude as possible was likely to make the interview even longer?

They found an empty interview room and went in. Harry shut the door, as Casey took a seat at one side of the small table.

'Who's the bird, Harry?' said Mickey, and smirked at Casey.

'Detective Constable Thomson to you, sonny and this is Detective Sergeant Drummond. Now, sit down!'

Mickey did his slow-motion routine again, whilst Harry and Casey waited. It made no odds what he did. They knew they had little or nothing to hold him on and they were reasonably certain that he knew that too.

'So, Mickey,' said Casey. 'What exactly is it that you do for Mr Harrison?'

'You got a boyfriend, Inspector?' said Mickey.

'Answer the question,' said Harry.

'He looking after you, Inspector? That's nice. Touching, like...'

Casey said nothing and Harry pretended to be writing.

Mickey lost the smile.

'Why do you want to know?' he said.

'Just routine,' said Casey. 'Please answer the question.'

'I'm an enforcer. That's what Mr Harrison calls us. We go and enforce the rules, get people to pay their bills.'

'And how do you go about doing that?'

'Bit of persuasion. Me and my mates can be very persuasive, Inspector. Bct you can be pretty persuasive too, eh?'

Casey could almost feel Harry bristling and hoped he wouldn't rise to it.

'So, this persuasion... does that involve hurting people?'

'Oh, no. That would be against the law, wouldn't it, Inspector?'

'So, where were you working last week-end?'

'We were out of town until Monday.'

'You sure about that, Mickey? Because we can easily check.'

'I'm sure. Next question.'

'Two nights ago, you and your colleagues were seen following another vehicle. Could you tell us something about that?'

'No idea what you're talking about, Inspector. Free country, isn't it? Can drive where we want on public roads. No law against that, far as I know. We weren't following anybody.'

'According to the driver of the other vehicle, your van was following them for about twenty minutes, during which time, that driver deliberately drove in a circle, more than once, in order to verify that you were, in fact, following them. Why would that be, Mickey?'

'We were just out for a run around town. No idea what your driver's talking about, Inspector. Coincidence, maybe?'

'We both know that's not true.'

'What I know or don't know doesn't matter. What matters is you've got nothing on me or my mates. We've done nothing wrong. Just three mates out for a drive around town.'

'Did your boss ask you to follow the car that night?'

'We weren't following any car. Why would Mr Harrison want us to do that?'

'Perhaps you could tell us?'

'I don't think so, do you, Inspector?'

Casey turned to Harry and raised her eyebrows.

'Well, Mickey, you're usually the driver. Is that so?' said Harry.

Mickey turned and smiled.

'That's right, Detective Constable. Give that man a chocolate watch.'

'So, you've moved on a bit then from taking and driving away? How old were you that first time – fourteen?'

'I was a kid. Can't get me for that.'

'I seem to recall, you were also in a gang a few years back. Liked to play with knives back then, eh? Not good for the complexion I see...'

Mickey scowled, said nothing.

'I'm wondering, you see, why it is that three young lads like you consider yourselves hard men, when you only get into fights you know you can't possibly lose. I mean, three against one isn't very sporting, is it?'

'That's not what we do,' said Mickey. His eyes flashing with ill-concealed temper.

'I suppose it's understandable really. After all, the one and only time you got into a fight on your own, you ended up in ARI getting stitches, eh? Weren't very brave that night as I recall.'

'I was a kid.'

'What age were you then – fifteen? Not that long ago, kids that age were working on the trawlers, or digging coal. Dangerous jobs those. Took a lot of courage. Facing possible death every single day. Bit easier nowadays, isn't it? I mean, judging from your designer clothes and stuff, you make a fair income from being a coward, eh, Mickey?'

Mickey leapt out of his chair.

'Fuck you!'

Harry stood up and loomed over Mickey.

'Sit down!'

Mickey did as he was told. Staring at Harry with a look of pure hatred.

'Well, I think we're about finished here', said Casey. 'Unless there's something you'd like to add, Mr Clark?'

Mickey said nothing. Casey and Harry stood up. Harry walked over to the door and opened it, ushering Mickey out. He and Casey accompanied Mickey to the reception area.

'So nice to catch up, Mickey,' said Harry. 'See you again very soon.'

'Fuck off,' said Mickey and then stormed off outside.

'Well, that was fun,' said Casey. 'Wonder how the others got on.'

'Much the same, I'd imagine,' said Harry. 'Although none of them have my gift with words.'

'Sheer poetry,' said Casey.

'Glad you appreciate it.'

Harry checked his watch.

'Way I see it, we just have time to get the paperwork done before ten. I doubt that will be anywhere near as much fun.'

Casey followed him back up the stairs, and her mind wandered back to the nature-nurture debate from earlier on. If there was a truth to be found, she had no idea where it lay. She just felt that being exposed to cruelty could make it more likely that it became normalised. What she wasn't so sure about was whether she would manage to be a decent parent, or if she would repeat the mistakes her own upbringing had taught her. It was an uncomfortable thought. She wondered if she would ever get the chance to find out.

29

The shift had begun with an unexpected phone call from Eddie. Unfortunately, it only went downhill from there. Someone had obviously overheard her mentioning Fraser's name and, office gossip being what it was, had leapt to the conclusion that it was Fraser she was speaking to. Somehow, it had filtered through to Notter, presumably through another half-heard conversation. There was no point telling him what had actually happened, since whatever it was that Eddie wanted her to see, had to be kept quiet for a while, apparently. She just hoped it was worth the ear-ache.

Casey could barely look at Notter. He had been pacing up and down pontificating at her for at least half an hour. She did not want to look him in the face for fear her contempt for him would be too obvious. Instead she kept her eyes focused on the floor, which had the added advantage of making her appear, to Notter at least, penitent and submissive. Had he known her better, he would not have been so easily fooled.

'So, do I have a firm undertaking from you that you will not be allowing Fraser Gilchrist to worm his way into this investigation?'

'I will be strictly professional. Sir.'

'Is that a yes, Drummond?'

'I'm sorry sir, I'm not sure what you mean: yes, I will be allowing him or yes I won't?' she looked up with wide, innocent eyes. Almost fluttering.

Notter coloured immediately, and cleared his throat.

'Will you or will you not be allowing Fraser to take part in these investigations?'

'I will not, sir,' said Casey. Of course, she wouldn't be *allowing* Fraser to do anything. He did exactly as he pleased. She was relieved that Notter had not asked whether she would share information. Much easier to give a partial truth convincingly than an outright lie.

'Very good. You may go now. When are you back on duty?'

'Day after tomorrow, sir.'

'Well, enjoy your time off, Drummond.'

'I will, sir.'

She left the office and sighed. Things never got any easier. So difficult to control your temper around that sod. She walked back to the office, tidied everything away into a drawer, locked it, grabbed her stuff and left. She brooded about her boss as she walked. It was only a matter of time before someone lost it with him and bloodied his nose. Problem was, they'd be the ones in trouble then. It didn't seem fair. They should allow everyone on the team one small punch, just as a reward for their forbearance. The thought made her laugh to herself as she headed for the stairs.

In her car, Casey texted Eddie, to say she was coming now and to get the kettle on. A few minutes later, she parked her car, tucking it into a small space behind Eddie's on the main road. Might be a bit awkward to move it if someone parked behind her, but there wasn't much space, anyway. And they could tackle that problem later on. Eddie buzzed her in, with a cheery 'Coffee's ready!' which was good to hear. Then, she climbed the cold, concrete stairs to his lovely flat. Every time she came here, she felt that painful swell of envy, but she loved visiting anyway. The door swung open before she had a chance to knock. Eddie waved her inside with a flourish.

'Entrez, mademoiselle,' he said. His French accent was atrocious. Always made Casey laugh.

'So, what's all this about?' asked Casey.

'Patience, chérie!'

Eddie refused to tell her anything at first. He poured coffee and pulled a second chair towards his desk.

'Sit,' he said.

She did as she was told. Eddie showed her the documents in one of the files, talking her through all the implications.

'Where did you get this?' she asked.

'Jamie had it. Didn't know she had it though. Looks like this is what the guy was after. This is why she was half-killed.'

'Who does it belong to?'

'Did. It *did* belong to Sarah Arnott.'

'Oh,' said Casey, and frowned. 'Arnott...any relation to Stephanie?'

'Sarah was her mother.'

'What happened to her?'

'Car crash, about six months ago,' said Eddie. 'She was an old friend of mine from college. A journalist, freelance like myself.'.

'So, what was she working on? Is it relevant?' said Casey.

'I think so. She had told me that she'd been offered a private job. Said it was a bit hush hush. Something to do with that new development, I'm pretty sure, although she wouldn't say. She refused to tell me who was paying her but I have my suspicions. I reckon that campaigner guy, you know, the posh boy, plenty of money... reckon he was paying her to dig up some dirt about the planning applications and all that. Back-handers and threats. That kind of thing.'

'Campaigner guy?'

'Can't remember his name. Think he was speaking at that march the other day. Didn't pay much attention to be honest. Been too busy working on the second book and finishing articles for the nationals.'

'Mark Mackenzie,' said Casey. She leaned back in her chair with a snort of disgust.

Eddie looked at her, waiting for her to go on. She looked back at him and shook her head.

'I caught him following me. He came into the station. Said he wanted to help Jamie. Was all concerned about her because she'd been on his sodding demo, or so he'd have us believe. But we know why now, don't we? Bastard was looking for this.' Casey waved her hand at the screen.

'Makes sense. Wonder if he knew about the other stuff though? Those pictures... that video footage...'

'What other stuff?' said Casey.

'I'll show you. But I have to warn you it's sick, perverted crap,' he said. 'If it's all connected, then I think you might be dipping your toes into a major investigation.'

'Guy strikes me as fancying himself a bit too much for my liking but I didn't get any pervy vibes off him,' said Casey. 'Not always obvious though, eh? But anyway, I have a feeling the guy is pretty fixed in his thinking. I reckon it's all about that planning permission stuff. Probably trying to get back at his filthy rich parents and their snotty friends.'

'Careful,' said Eddie. 'Inverted snobbery is just as unattractive as the traditional variety.'

Casey smiled.

'You're right, of course. But I just didn't take to him. I reckon the guy's a prick but not a perv.'

'Are you seriously claiming to have a built-in perv-detector?' said Eddie. 'You could be on to a money maker right there if you do!'

He laughed, but his gaze did not waver from looking into Casey's eyes. He won. She had to break eye contact.

'Okay, okay, it's just a hunch. Probably worthless. But I just don't think he's involved in anything like that. So, why are the two things together on the flash drive?'

'I often have a lot of different files on a lot of different flash drives. Means nothing.'

'Fair enough. What else did she tell you about what she was working on? Any indication that there was more going on than she thought?'

'Kind of... I met her on the street one day and we went for a coffee and catch up. She was still gorgeous, you know. But anyway, soon realised there was no chance there. She had a girlfriend by then. Anyway, she told me that she had started on the investigation for posh boy, and had stumbled on a story, a big story. She seemed wired. Really excited, but angry, all at the same time. That make sense?'

'Yes, perfect sense,' said Casey.

'Anyway, she said she was worried, thought that someone might try to shut her up, destroy her research. The usual paranoid bullshit. I told her it all sounded a bit "President's Men"-ish. She got a bit annoyed. Then she said that she would send me something. That it wouldn't mean much on its own, that it was a key. She didn't want anyone else to have it. Asked me to file it away. Made no fucking sense to me at the time but, hell, it was only two bits of A4. Wasn't going to kill me to store it for her.'

'So,' said Casey. 'She didn't tell you anything about this story?'

'No, just that it would be big and that it involved some powerful people. I made her promise to fill me in on the details soon, and to keep me informed. I didn't want to steal her story or anything. I was just a bit worried that she might be losing it, to be honest. What, with that nightmare daughter and mounting debts. No-one could have blamed her for having a bit of a melt-down. I thought if she knew she could talk to me, she might be okay, might let me know if she needed help. She said "Some people are not who they say they are". No idea what she meant. She had to rush off before she could explain, but she seemed to be talking literally if you get me, that she'd found something, or someone, who had a false identity. All very Jason Bourne, but there you go. I did wonder about her sanity at the time, but after what happened, I wasn't so sure. She was onto something. I guarantee it.'

'What's with all the film references? Been watching too much T.V.?'

'Probably...anyway, that's it really...'

'And did she?' asked Casey. 'Stay in touch that is?'

'She phoned to check I got her e-mail. Never heard from her after that. Few months later, she was dead. They said she'd been drinking. She never drank. Had a bit of a problem with it years ago. I figured she'd gone into that meltdown. Now, I'm not so sure.'

Casey gazed at the screen. How had Sarah managed to get all this information? Did the wrong person find out about it? Was her death really accidental, or was it just made to look that way?

'Her girlfriend... would she have any idea where Sarah got all this stuff?' said Casey.

'Never met her,' said Eddie. 'Name was Kelly, I think. Yeah, Kelly Sullivan. Sarah showed me a photo. Pretty girl. Worked in an office somewhere. I did phone her. Sarah gave me the number, just in case... fuck, you know me. All that paranoia. Thought she was losing it. Seriously. Anyway, I did what she asked and filed it away with the rest of the stuff. So, when it happened, I thought I'd better ring the lass, see if she was okay. She sounded devastated. They'd only split up a week or two before. No idea why, but obviously she still cared about Sarah. She told me she was moving back home. Fresh start or some such bollocks.'

Casey pulled out her notebook and scribbled the girl's name down, wondering why it was that when Eddie got emotional, he swore so much more...

'Don't suppose you know where home was?'

'She was Irish. She told me the place but I honestly don't remember. Bally-something. It'll come to me. I'd never heard of it before, anyway, but then I've never been to Ireland, oddly enough. Always planned to go but never did. Hang on, though...think I might still have her old number from here somewhere if that would help? You could maybe check that with the dates or something, get a proper check done on her, find out that way?'

'If you could, that would be great,' said Casey, wondering how on earth she would find the time to follow up on everything associated with this case.

She'd have lean on poor Harry. She waited until she was out of the flat and then gave him a call.

30

Next day, the office was quiet. Most folk were out at lunch or were in a meeting that was taking place in the boardroom upstairs. Casey decided she would be happy to mind the phones and let some of the other staff go and find out about the new policies and procedures. They could tell her later. It gave her a valuable window to carry out searches she didn't want certain people to know about.

The images that she'd seen last night were seared into her brain. There had to be a connection with Oaklands. She just had to find it. Eddie had promised to hand everything over, once Casey decided it was safe to do so. She hated this secrecy, but if they were right and someone here had been covering this crap up, she didn't want there to be any possibility of their getting away with it. Even if it meant sacrificing her career. She owed it to those poor kids...

A shadow fell across her desk. She looked up, startled.

'God, will you stop doing that to me? I never heard you at all!'

Harry chuckled.

'I *am* quite god-like sometimes,' he whispered and handed her a sheaf of papers.

'What's all this?'

'Those print-outs you asked for. The documents? Interesting reading.'

Casey looked at the address. Ballynahinch. That's the place Eddie was trying to remember.

'There's also the first few disclosures for staff at Oaklands. Plenty more to come but to be honest with you, care workers are pretty heavily vetted nowadays, so you're unlikely to find anything on record against them. Off the record, on the other hand... I've been reading through those case files again and all those poor lassies had been away from the place a while before they were murdered so whoever it was harmed these girls, it's pretty unlikely to be the staff.'

'Right. Okay... Problem might be higher up the chain. Could get a bit tricky... If you want to back out now, Harry, you can. I don't want you falling foul of anything.'

'Like Fraser did, you mean?'

'Exactly,' said Casey. 'You've got a family to think of.'

'That's why I'm sticking with it. My eldest, Sophie, is fifteen next birthday. Not much different from some of these poor wee sods when they went off the radar. Soon as you told me about all this, I was on board, and there is no fucking way I'm backing off now! Ma'am.'

Casey smiled up at him.

'Did I ever tell you how much I love you, Harry?'

'Not often enough, my little goddess.'

Casey looked at him as if she were a shocked headmistress.

'Too much?' said Harry.

'Just a bit,' said Casey, grinning. 'Come and see what I've found.'

Harry dragged a chair over and sat next to her. She typed a file name into the computer and opened a document file. It consisted of a list of case numbers with names and dates.

'I did a search on murder victims, using search details taken from our two girls. And see, these four were the ones Fraser was revisiting just before all that shit... before they accused him.'

'So why was he looking at old cases?'

'Oh god, who *ever* knows *anything* with Fraser? One of his famous "feelings" maybe?'

'Must have seen some connection.'

'Well, to begin with, I thought there wasn't any. We're a coastal city. The sea is an obvious dumping ground. The street women are high-risk. Strangulation and sex often go together...'

'Not in my house!'

Casey laughed.

'You know what I mean though. Nothing unusual to connect them really. But here's the thing... they were all killed *exactly* the same way. I looked at the reports and spoke to Tony. And on top of all that, they all spent some time in care, although not all of them at Oaklands.'

'Okay...'

'I can see it now. I can see what Fraser was driving at. All of them, apart from Jade, the lass in the park, were dumped at sea. They washed up along the coast. Not even weighted down or anything, just dumped like dead fish off a trawler, as if they were worth nothing, as if they didn't matter to anyone.' Casey felt her eyes starting to prickle. She sniffed and coughed to cover it up but there was no fooling Harry. He patted her back but said nothing.

She spread out seven print-outs of photographs, and laid a copy of Eddie's list down next to them.

'Eddie e-mailed these to me this morning. Now this is the postcode for the Kilgarry club, the one that raises funds for charities, including our own community projects. It corresponds to this photo.' She flipped the photo over to display a series of letters and numbers. 'You get the picture. So, it's obvious Sarah was watching these places for some reason. I'm getting a bad feeling about all this.'

'Me too,' muttered Harry. Casey looked over at him. She could see a redness spreading upwards from the collar of his shirt. His mouth was a thin line. He was raging.

'We'll have to go slowly, Harry. Not a word to anyone else yet, until we have the full picture. I don't want these sods getting a chance to wriggle out of it. And they would. We're talking power and influence. We're talking people who could destroy us. Who might already have destroyed other people. It's going to be a sensitive job. Are you up for that? Can I trust you not to blow up over it, before we get the names?'

Harry swallowed hard.

'I was on some of those earlier cases,' he said. 'Don't worry, Casey. Whatever it takes, lass. I want to see those bastards sent down. And worse.'

It was Casey's turn to offer support. She patted Harry's back. He didn't seem to notice.

'Also,' said Casey. 'There's a wee job I'd like you to do.'

'I'm listening.'

'Fingers MacNamara.'

'What do you want me to do to him?'

Casey chuckled.

'Harry! I don't want you to do anything to him. It's just... only I heard a rumour that he wasn't where he said he was that day. Also, there's a couple of other folk claim to have seen him in a bad way a couple of days before Fraser supposedly attacked him. People apart from Toomey, that is. If that's the case, Fraser's off the hook.'

'He could have got the dates mixed up. I do it all the time. It means nothing.'

'Oh, it means a lot in this case, Harry, believe me.'

Harry looked puzzled. Casey seemed suddenly on edge and appeared to be struggling with what to say next.

'Well, we could hardly go to the bosses with only Toomey's statement. They would just say that he was trying to get his own back on his old pal for stealing. And there was always the danger that he'd change his story later. But it is important, because...shit, okay. I'll have to tell you, I suppose, but you're not to breathe a word of this to anyone. Clear?'

'Sure. Whatever.'

'It's important because if it happened a couple of days earlier, Fraser couldn't have done it, because that week-end he ended up in the hospital getting his stomach pumped.'

Harry stared at her, a frown creasing his brow.

'What? I never heard about that. When did that happen?'

'No-one knows except me. I found him. It would have been his son's tenth birthday. I knew that, so I went to check on him. So, you see, he couldn't have done it that week-end. Couldn't have done it the day he was supposed to have either. He was still far too ill. Don't you dare let him know I told you.'

'But why wouldn't he tell them that himself? It might have got him off the hook.'

'It was attempted suicide, Harry. I know it was. And more to the point, he knows that I know it was. But he'll never admit it, not even to himself. You know he was on painkillers for a while, for that knee injury. Fraser claims it was just an accident, that he was drunk, that he forgot he'd taken them earlier so took too many by accident.'

'Well, isn't that possible? It's not unheard of.'

'I was there, Harry. He'd emptied the bottle. I found it in the bin. Deliberate.'

'Fuck! Okay. So what do you need?'

'I've written the details down for you,' said Casey, handing Harry a brown, A5 envelope. It was sealed shut. 'Get statements from the witnesses. If we have those, I think we can persuade Jimmy to admit he might have been mistaken about it being Fraser. Failing that, we'll ask the medical staff if they can corroborate things. I would rather avoid that though. He'd be raging.'

'His priorities are all fucked up if you ask me.'

'He doesn't want it on his record.'

Harry pressed his lips together and gave a short nod.

'Okay. Leave it with me,' said Harry, turning away to head back to his own desk.

'Also...'

'There's an also?'

'A couple of them. Could you speak to one of your colleagues and ask them to get me some information on the Kilgarry club. Public domain stuff only. Brochures and such. Tell them it's for a newsletter article or something. I'll be digging a bit deeper, see if I can't get hold of a membership list, links to other organisations. I get the feeling there's a lot more to that club than meets the eye. Be interesting to see the contrast between the actual work they do and the PR stuff.'

'Can do. You said a couple of things?'

'Yes. Could you manage to look through those other cases and give me a short paragraph on each? I'm not going to have time to read them all and I know you were involved in a few of them.'

'Do I get overtime?'

'No. Maybe a pub lunch and a pint?'

'I'll see what I can do.'

'By the way, I'm meeting Fraser tonight for a drink, if you fancied joining us?'

'I'd love to but I'm on Daddy duty tonight. The wife's going to a henny.'

'Some other time then?' said Casey, as the office door opened and other voices filled the room.

'Sure,' said Harry and nodded towards the computer screen.

Casey folded up the sheet of paper with Kelly's details on it, and stuffed it into her pocket. Then she shoved the other papers into a drawer, closed down the offending page on her computer, and went back to the report she was meant to be completing. As she typed, she wondered how much longer she could keep all this a secret, and what would happen to them all if she messed up. She closed her eyes for a moment and tried to drive that thought away.

31

As soon as she got home, Casey fished out the paper with Kelly's details on it. Almost six o'clock now. If she were still doing office work, she should be home by now. She tapped in the number on her phone. It rang a few times. Then a male voice answered.

'Hello, could I speak to Kelly Sullivan please?'

'Hang on a moment. I'll give her a shout. Could I say who's calling?'

'My name is Casey Drummond.'

There was a low, warm chuckle at the other end of the phone.

'Okay then, Casey Drummond. One moment.'

She heard him shouting Kelly's name., and what sounded likc a confused conversation. Well, the poor girl would have no idea who she was, after all, and Casey wasn't sure she wanted to tell her male friend or relative that she was from the police. Might freak them both out.

'Hello? Kelly Sullivan here. Can I help you?'

'Hello, Miss Sullivan. Sergeant Casey Drummond here, from Police Scotland. So sorry to disturb you. I'm calling in regard to the death of your friend, Sarah Arnott. Just wondered if you would mind answering a few questions for me?'

'But I don't know anything. Why now? I don't understand.'

Casey could hear an edge of panic in the girl's voice and realised she would have to go slowly if she wasn't going to frighten her off completely.

'It's nothing to worry about. Just all very routine stuff. You were close friends, I understand?'

'Very close for a while.'

'I am sorry for your loss. I really don't want to upset you. It's just that some new information has come up and I was hoping you might be willing to talk to me for a few minutes. Would that be all right with you? It really won't take long.'

'I... er ... I suppose so. If it would help.'

'It would. Thank you so much. Could you tell me how long you knew Miss Arnott?'

'Erm... we met at a protest meeting. I didn't know she was a journalist or I probably wouldn't have been talking to her at all, to be honest with you. But she was really friendly, and we ended up going to the pub with a few friends of mine. That was about two years ago, and we were together for just under a year... until just before...'

Casey heard Kelly's voice breaking. She waited for a moment.

'So, what was this meeting then, the one that you met her at?'

'It was a group that was set up to support residents that had been harassed by a local developer. He was trying to force them out of their homes. He already had a big bit of land there, but he wanted more. Hateful man.'

'Where was this development? Do you remember?'

'Oh, yes, I'll never forget it. Oaklands, it's called. Just south of the city. Used to belong to the council I think... do you know it?'

'Yes, I do know it. Thank you that's very helpful. I understand you yourself were working in an office here at that time. Could you tell me where that was?'

There was a long pause at the other end. Casey was worried she might have lost her but then the voice answered again, a little hesitant but there nonetheless.

'I worked for the local council, as a P.A.'

'Who in particular did you work for at the council?'

'Well, a few people. They did move us around a bit. But mostly it was Councillor Robert Priestley. Am I in trouble?'

'I don't know, Miss Sullivan. Are you?'

The soft noises at the other end of the line told Casey that the girl was weeping.

'I told her it would happen, that you would blame me, but I didn't do it!'

'Could you start at the beginning?'

'There's not much to tell. I sometimes took work home. Sarah was around a lot. She must have got my password somehow, for the secure site. I was feeling really ill one night, full of the flu or something. Sarah was really sweet. Made me hot drinks and ran me a bath – bubbles, candles, the works. Had a long soak. It was great. But when I came out of the bathroom, I heard her printing something off. I thought it would be a booking or something. We'd been talking about a city break somewhere. So, I went through to see, and she wasn't on my desktop; she was on the works laptop. She'd gone into the e-mails, the minutes, everything, sent it all to her own computer. We ended up in a screaming row, but she wouldn't delete any of it, said I didn't understand, that it was more important than any stupid job. But it was easy for her to say. I handed in my notice the next day. Thought I would have to go before I was pushed or I'd never get another job. I left soon afterwards. I had holidays due so I didn't have to work the full month's notice.'

'I'm so sorry to hear that.'

'You won't tell my boss here?'

'No, of course not. And, if it's any consolation, I think Sarah was trying to do something very important. I think she was trying to get the evidence to convict some very, very bad people.'

'Thank you... I did love her you know...'

'I'm so sorry, Miss Sullivan. And thank you for agreeing to talk to me. You've been a big help. And don't worry, I don't think we'll be bothering you again.'

Casey put the phone down. Well, that was one mystery solved. It was a really shitty trick Sarah had played on her lover, but she was choosing her daughter over everyone else. A lioness protecting her cub.

32

The bar was noisy and the music loud. They had to shout to hear one another. The drink was going down well, though. At the interval, Fraser checked his phone, as he usually did, and saw a series of messages, at roughly five-minute intervals, starting about two hours previously. They were all from Laurie.

Hi Fraser, Strange car outside with two guys in it. Did you send them here?

Hi. Car still here. Afraid to go outside. Have locked the house. Please respond!

Fraser! Please call me. Car still there. Getting dark. Don't feel safe.

Fraser cursed and stepped out of the pub onto the street, where it was quieter. He moved away from the huddle of smokers, so he wouldn't be overheard, and called Laurie. She didn't respond. He tried a couple more times and then ran back into the pub. Casey and Eddie were laughing about something as he came in. They turned to look at him and stopped laughing. Fraser slid into a seat and spoke quickly.

'Laurie texted earlier but I missed it. They're in trouble. I can't drive, none of us can now. Casey, could you...?'

Casey looked at him.

'Forward the messages to my phone. I'll go and speak to the guys. We'll get someone out there,' she said and grabbed her coat to leave.

'Where are you going?' asked Fraser.

'I'm going to get us a driver, someone who owes me a favour. Wait ten minutes. Meet me outside.'

When she'd gone, Fraser hastily forwarded the messages. Then he downed the last couple of inches of his pint. He felt completely sober. And more worried than he'd felt for a long while.

'You okay?' said Eddie.

'Yeah. Just feeling like a prize klutz. Those fuckers must have been watching me and I missed it. Stupid bastard that I am. Just have to hope we get there in time.'

'I'll come too.'

'No!' barked Fraser.

Eddie looked startled.

'Sorry, Eddie. I don't want you dragged into all this. I need you to be safe, someone I can rely on to hold it all together for me, someone to make sure that evidence isn't destroyed. And I don't want to make things worse for Casey. I can say that I forced my way into this case but, if you're there too, it will look much more like she's been speaking outside, and that's a career breaker.'

Eddie nodded.

'Understood. Do you want me to carry on trying to make sense of Sarah's stuff?'

'Yes. Please. That would be brilliant. It's what you're good at. You'll be much faster than us. No red tape to slow you down,' said Fraser, smiling. 'Best go. Can you make a start tonight? And make sure everything's copied, backed up, whatever you geeks call it.'

'Sure thing, my Luddite friend. Best get out there and watch for her. I'll stay on here for a while. If anyone's been watching, they'll hopefully follow you, not me,' said Eddie, with a wry smile.

Fraser grabbed his coat and hurried out. A couple of minutes later, a sleek, grey Beamer drew in to the kerb. Casey was in the front seat, so he dived into the back and buckled up as they drove off quickly.

'That was quick,' said Fraser.

'Hope we're quick enough,' replied Casey, and then gestured towards the driver. 'Meet Derek. Old acquaintance of mine.'

Fraser met Derek's eyes in the rear-view mirror. A grunt issued from his large frame. Obviously a man of action, not words.

'Pleased to meet you,' said Fraser. He didn't expect a response, so he wasn't disappointed.

Derek was a confident and capable driver, but that didn't make Fraser feel any better as the small car raced madly over the icy roads out of the city. He knew they were at or above the speed limit, despite the road conditions, and wondered if they were going to make it there in one piece. Soon there were no streetlights to offer a sense of security, no housing schemes offering some semblance of civilisation, no human sense of safety in numbers. The skeletons of winter trees, silvered by moonlight, blurred past, as they drove. He was vaguely aware of Casey straining to spot the turn off.

'Where that tree is,' said Fraser. 'The turning is right there!'

The driver hauled on the wheel, the tyres squealed and a metallic scraping noise let them know that the chassis had kissed tarmac. Fraser was thrown into the door by the momentum and felt his heart racing with genuine fear. Casey looked back at him and grinned.

'You all right back there?' she said.

'Funny. Very funny,' hissed Fraser, thinking that he was getting way too old for this.

The road climbed the hill, swiftly becoming a rough track, and the driver had to slow down in in order to retain the exhaust on the car. When they crested the hill, they saw the house. The lights were all on and the door lay open, spilling warm light out into the cold night. A police car was parked over to one side. A uniformed policeman was standing by the gate. He was talking to someone in plain clothes, someone horribly familiar, who was holding a bloody handkerchief over his face.

Derek drew up just behind the police car and Casey and Fraser climbed out.

Notter pulled the handkerchief away from his face and dabbed at his nose, from which blood slowly trickled. He wasn't happy.

'Drummond! I thought I told you-'

'I was off duty, sir. Having a drink with friends. I got a message from Laurie. She wanted Fraser here.'

Fraser had to make an effort to prevent his eyebrows from rising in astonishment. Casey was getting much better at lying to her boss. And was it his imagination or was Notter a little less hostile today?

'Hmph,' said Notter, clearly finding Casey's explanation hard to stomach. 'Well, your friends are inside, Fraser. Their visitors have made a bit of a mess of the place, but no-one's hurt.'

Fraser struggled not to laugh.

'What happened to you?' he said.

'One of the guys swung a punch at me. They got away.' As he said this, he glared at the uniformed officer, a very young constable, who appeared to be suddenly fascinated by his own left foot. Fraser decided not to ask...

'You should maybe get that looked at,' said Fraser, quietly, and then walked away into the house.

He was welcomed by a trio of relieved smiles.

'Hi, guys,' he said and looked around at a sea of devastation. Drawers had been hauled out and emptied on the floor. Laurie's artwork lay crumpled on the floor. It was, essentially, a mess.

'So glad to see you,' said Laurie. The disapproving glance she shot out of the window told Fraser all he needed to know about what she thought of Notter.

'This is my fault,' said Fraser. 'I must have led them right to you.'

'No, Fraser. You didn't do this. They did. You mustn't blame yourself,' said Laurie.

'Did they hurt you?'

'No. They were scary. Broke a few things and shouted a lot. But, no.'

Fraser looked over to the couch, where Dod and Jamie were cuddled up and shivering. Fright, he thought, and then remembered that the door was still lying open. He went to close it and then realised that it was broken.

'Ah. I wondered why you hadn't closed it.'

'I just propped it up there. They broke the door in. It was like something out of the wild west. We wouldn't open the door so they just knocked it down.' Laurie was fiddling with the fringe on the shawl she was wearing. She was speaking softly but Fraser suspected that there was a lot of noise going on inside her head.

'Did they say anything?'

'They were looking for something. Seemed to think it must be here, that Jamie had it.'

Jamie looked up at Fraser. Red-rimmed eyes told him she'd been crying. He noticed red marks on her arms and throat.

'They hurt you?' he said.

'It's okay. It's nothing,' said Jamie, but her voice shook as she said it and her eyes began to fill. Dod drew her into his arms and held her close. His face was a white mask, bleak with the familiar combination of shock and shame. Fraser had seen that look often. Guys who were unable to protect their loved ones often wore that same haunted expression. Fraser felt a lump in his throat and couldn't think of anything useful to say to them.

Casey appeared at his shoulder.

'They are sending a van,' she said. 'They'll get you back to the station to take statements and then on to somewhere safe, probably a B&B, but better than nothing.'

'I'm not going anywhere,' said Laurie.

'You can't stay here,' said Casey.

'Yes, I can. This is my house and I'm not going to some B&B, just because…'

Her voice cracked and faded and she turned her face away.

'How's about you come to my place,' said Fraser. 'Just for tonight. We'll get someone out to fix the door tomorrow.'

Laurie did not turn round or speak. She just nodded.

'Is Derek still around?' asked Fraser.

'Yes. I'll tell him,' said Casey and went out again.

'Will you two be okay to go in the van when it arrives?' said Fraser to Dod and Jamie.

'Yeah, no worries,' said Dod, still cuddling Jamie and stroking her head, as if she were a frightened child.

'Laurie, if you wanted to grab a few things, I'll be waiting for you outside?'

'Okay. Thanks,' she said, without turning round.

Fraser wandered outside. Notter was sitting in the car with the young constable. There was no chatting going on. Each appeared to be stuck inside his own dull thoughts. Fraser approached them. He leaned into the car.

'I'll be taking my neighbour to my place for the night. I gather you've been making arrangements for Jamie and Dod?'

'Not me,' said Notter. 'Sergeant Drummond's handling it.'

'I see. How's the nose?'

Notter glared at him and Fraser was amused to notice a twitch in the young constable's mouth, and a glint of laughter in his eyes. He managed to suppress it. He'd do okay, thought Fraser. An icy silence hung in the air.

'Okay,' said Fraser. 'Well, it was lovely chatting with you but I must get on. You know, can't stand here yapping all night.'

'You're on thin ice, Fraser,' said Notter.

'Yes. Very cold tonight altogether I think. See you!'

Fraser walked over to where the equally chatty Derek was sitting, glowering, in his car. The world was full of cheery buggers tonight, thought Fraser.

Casey was perching on the bonnet of the car, reading something on her phone. She looked up as he approached.

'All sorted?' she said.

'Getting there. Some mess they made, the bastards. How long will it be before they figure out who's got it? We should try to make sure we get multiple copies of everything.'

'I already suggested that to Eddie.'

'Well, if we need to contact him again, it might be safer for me to phone.'

Fraser looked puzzled.

'Just in case someone's put a tap on your phone.'

'Now you're getting paranoid.'

'Talking of paranoid, I was out at Oaklands the other day. Interesting place,' said Casey. 'Our two most recent victims stayed there at the same time. Stephanie was only there for a few weeks, but Jade practically grew up there. Just so you know, I've told Notter that you're not involved in these investigations.'

Casey smirked at him, then seemed to notice something happening behind him.

'Oh, here she is,' said Casey.

Fraser turned to see Laurie walking towards him. She had a large cloth shoulder bag, of ethnic design and epic proportions. He wondered what on earth she had in there and then realised that she had probably packed her laptop and sketching materials in it. He smiled a welcome and helped her manoeuvre herself and her bag into the back of the car. Then, he got into the front seat and prepared for what he hoped would be a much less anxious drive home. As he fastened his seat belt, he felt his phone vibrate, telling him he had a message. He fished it out of his pocket and peered at it. It was from Eddie.

Fraser. Just had a look at that disc. You'll want to see these. Too much for an attachment so uploaded them. Sent you a link. Check your e-mails. Text me back when you've seen them, so I know it's working. Eddie.

Fraser glanced into the back seat. Laurie was gazing, sightlessly, out into the dark night. She wouldn't sleep for a while. He'd have to hope she wouldn't mind him checking his computer. He wondered what was so urgent that Eddie would text him now. What was it that couldn't wait until morning?

Fraser shoved his phone back in his pocket and prepared to navigate for Derek. He could have driven it himself, blindfold, if he'd not been drinking. He only wished he could be as confident about where Sarah had been going with all this stuff and where her investigations were now leading him.

33

Fraser wandered through ahead of Laurie, switching on lights. The stove was still warm, so rescuable. Fraser opened the door and carefully added tinder, before placing a half-log in and closing the door again. Within minutes, small, hungry tongues of flame were licking rapidly round the wood.

'Should keep the place warm, anyway,' he said. He turned and watched as Laurie settled herself down on the couch and pulled her laptop out of her bag.

'I'm surprised they didn't destroy that too,' said Fraser.

'I'm sure they would, if they'd found it. I always keep it under my bed. Force of habit. Couldn't bear to lose what's on it. And they destroyed three weeks' work, so I'm going to have to crack on to hit the deadline now.'

There was no anger in her voice, only sadness, and Fraser was struck by her passivity, almost as if this treatment was what she was used to, as if she had never been entitled to peace in the first place.

'Can I get you anything? Tea, coffee, glass of malt?'

'Tea would be nice. Malt would be nicer but I can't drink just now.'

Fraser resisted his curious impulses and did not ask. If she was on medication, she might not want anyone to know about it. Anyway, tea seemed like a good idea. The terrible drouth was upon him, from early evening beers. He would need to get as much fluid inside him as possible, if he were to function tomorrow.

Fraser puddled about in the kitchen and came through with two large mugs of tea. Laurie looked up and smiled.

'On you go and do whatever it is you have to do. I'll be fine here.' She said.

Fraser was stunned again. He'd just been about to ask her if she would be all right for a little while, that he had to check his e-mails, but she seemed to know already. Must be something in his body language.

'If you're sure?' he said.

'Quite sure. Got a few things to check myself.'

Fraser carried his tea through to the bedroom, where his desktop was. He was glad to be able to close the door. He wasn't yet sure if what Eddie had sent him was suitable for Laurie's eyes.

Eddie's e-mail was the last one he'd been sent, so was easy to find. There was a short message:

Hi there. You won't believe who's on these! I've put a few notes on, just thoughts that occurred to me. Ignore them if you like. Between us we'll maybe be able to name them all. Got an appointment with the GP tomorrow morning but I'm home all afternoon if you're free? Speak soon.

Eddie

P.S. Text and let me know if the link is working!

Fraser clicked on the link. It brought him to a secure section of Eddie's business website. He'd been busy. Obviously had the same worries Fraser had. He'd scanned all the notebooks and they were suitably titled and ready for him to download. Fraser rummaged about in the desk drawer and found an unused flash drive. He plugged it in and saved the scanned documents. He then clicked on the last file, which Eddie had called 'Photos, S.A., research'.

There was a series of photos, 247, to be precise, each dated and timed, and with a single digit appended, as on that list of places, the one Sarah had sent to Eddie. In each photo, people could be seen entering and exiting the particular building or standing in a huddle, chatting and laughing, in the doorway or outside on the street.

What struck Fraser immediately was that there were no women in the photos, no wives, no female colleagues, no-one remotely feminine. He recognised a few of the faces, some of which Eddie had sussed too, judging by the notes underneath. They were prominent people. The sort of people who only ever socialised with each other, people for whom paying income tax was an option rather than a necessity. There were names, too, which he did

247

not recognise but which Eddie had added. They would need to go through them all together.

He was about to go to save and quit when he spotted a very familiar face, not coming in or out of the house, but sitting waiting in a car outside. It was a tiny detail in the photo but Fraser was certain. It was Notter, obviously the driver for someone. He let his eyes travel back to the people around the doorway. Two faces he didn't recognise but the third, half hidden behind the others, was one he knew. From the stance, the body shape and that hint of a smug expression on the section of face that was visible, Fraser knew; it was Notter's father-in-law, Dougie Harrison.

He had to warn Casey. If Notter was involved in any of this stuff, he might be a real threat to her. Having said that, he could be quite gullible when it came to people with money and status. He might not even know what his father-in-law was mixed up in, but any threat to his image, that farcically engineered veneer of the perfect family, would be completely shattered, and it was difficult to predict how he might react. Notter's career might well suffer too, even if he were entirely innocent. Much as he hated Notter, Fraser wouldn't want to do that to him, although he, as yet, had no idea how that could be prevented.

Fraser reeled himself in, back to the problem in hand. He reminded himself that his first priority must be the safety and welfare of those kids. Any adults caught in the crossfire would have to look after themselves. After all, they only had themselves to blame for any damage they might suffer. There was only one solution. He phoned Eddie.

'Fraser?'

'Yes, it's me. I got the stuff. Need to ask another favour.'

'What sort of favour?'

'The pictures with Notter in them. They can't go forward with the rest. Any way you could store them elsewhere?'

'I could make a copy that doesn't include the offending pictures. But why would you want to protect him?'

'It's not him I'm protecting, it's Casey. I don't know yet how involved Notter is in all of this. I don't want it getting buried and I don't want anyone getting hurt. Plus, I might need a little leverage later on.'

Eddie's low chuckle indicated approval of the last remark.

'Always knew you had a dark side, Inspector!'

Will it be ready tomorrow? Sooner we get this stuff off our hands the better. Have you made copies? Just in case... you know...'

'Hey, you're speaking to someone that once lost twenty thousand words through not having a back up. Consider it done.'

They ended the call and Fraser fired off a quick text to Casey.

Hi. Something here I think you need to see. Meet you at Eddie's tomorrow afternoon?

The reply came back almost immediately.

What time?

Fraser fired off a reply and then closed everything down. He hauled some blankets out of the top shelf of the wardrobe and went through to check on Laurie. She was curled up on the couch, reading a book. She looked up and smiled.

'Like your house. It's so cosy!'

Fraser piled the blankets on the arm of the sofa.

'Yeah, it is now,' he said. 'Had to put in a lot of insulation; Uncle Jim never felt the cold, thanks to a diet of porridge, soup and whisky, and a lifetime of working outside in all weathers. Believe me, this place was Baltic before.'

Laurie gave a low chuckle.

'You can be very intense sometimes,' she said. 'Shall I put the kettle on?'

'I can do that.'

'Let me, please?' said Laurie, getting to her feet.

'Okay,' said Fraser. 'I'll get some bedding organised. You can take the bedroom. I'll crash here.'

'Oh, no you won't,' said Laurie.

'I don't mind. You look like you need some sleep.'

'And I'll sleep fine in here. I mean, what height are you? Six one, six two?'

'About that, yeah.'

'And I'm five-five. So, who do you think will sleep better on this little couch - you or me?'

Fraser laughed.

'Okay, okay. There's a bossy streak in you!'

'You bet there is,' she laughed. Then she grabbed the mugs and went through to make more tea.

Fraser fed the stove again and closed the vents, to keep the fire on a slow burn until morning. Laurie seemed like a different person tonight. She clearly felt safe with him now, really safe. Fraser was glad and hoped her trust was warranted. While he waited for Laurie to bring through the tea, he sent a quick text to Eddie.

Hi. We'll be there about three tomorrow. Take care. Lock your doors. F. x

A response came back almost immediately.

Isolated a few more weel kent faces. See you tomorrow. M. x P.S. I'm always careful. Perhaps, given all the young women around you right now, you're the one who needs to be careful? See ya!

Fraser grinned. Very Eddie, cocky bugger that he was. Then Laurie came through with tea and serious subjects were off limits for the next hour. Sleep came easily to both of them that night; in Laurie's case, high adrenaline followed by relief enabled her to relax into unconsciousness, whereas Fraser slid into sleep on a wave of post-hangover exhaustion. Both snored horribly. Neither of them noticed.

34

Fraser and Casey arrived almost simultaneously at Eddie's place, and parked next to one another. It was an overcast day, with a chilly, ice-promising, drizzle. They both ran for the doorway, with merely a nod to acknowledge one another, before they rushed into the relative warmth of the unheated entrance hall. They started to climb the stairs together.

'Jeez, it's cold!' said Casey. Shaking the rain off her jacket as she climbed.

'Agreed. Dod and Jamie all right?'

'Yeah. Little B& B out of town. Safer for now, I think?'

'Probably.'

'And Laurie? How did it go last night? She's used to being alone. So are you, come to that.'

'Oh, it was fine. We had a long yap about art school and the daft stuff we got up to as students. It was... yeah, nice, actually. She's a really nice person.'

'Is she back home now?'

'Not yet. The workmen couldn't get there until late afternoon. I said I'd run her home when I get back. She seemed okay with that, surprisingly.'

Fraser knocked at the door of the flat. A muffled voice from inside the flat indicated that Eddie had heard them. They waited. And waited.

There was a scrabbling noise on the other side of the door. When it opened, Fraser and Casey gasped in shock. Eddie slid down the door. He was covered in blood and was having difficulty breathing. Fraser rushed forward to support him. Casey took the other arm, as they half-carried him through to the sitting room, which was looking almost as bad as Eddie was. Fraser and Casey helped Eddie onto the couch, propping him up with cushions to help with his breathing.

'Call an ambulance,' said Fraser.

Casey pulled out her phone and punched in numbers.

'What the fuck happened here, Eddie?' said Fraser, kneeling down next to his friend.

'He...Heavies... three... fuck... can't breathe...'

'Don't try to talk,' said Fraser, and looked around the room.

The notebooks and disc were gone and Eddie's computer lay smashed on the floor. Shelves had been swept clean, their contents scattered across the floor. Whoever had done this had meant to make sure that there was nothing left. Shit! Still, at least there were copies on Fraser's computer.

He looked back at his friend. Eddie's face was reddened and swelling rapidly. One eye was swollen shut already. A cut above the other eye oozed blood that trickled in a sticky line down the side of his face, His nose looked like it might be broken; it was swollen and tilted to one side. His lips were split and bleeding and every painful breath released a fine mist of blood over his chin and chest. Fraser felt guilt heavy on him. It was his fault this had happened, his fault his friend had been beaten half to death. What else were they looking for?

'Th...they...couldn't find it,' said Eddie, with a weak and crooked smile. 'Coffee jar. Kitchen.'

Fraser got up and went straight to it. The jar was half full of coffee. He tilted it and shook the coffee downwards. The corner of a small plastic bag came into view, Fraser grabbed it and pulled. A shower of coffee grains tumbled out over the work surface as he hauled out the bag. Inside was the flash drive.

A noise outside told Fraser that the ambulance and, no doubt, the police were here. He dropped the bag into his jacket pocket and cleared the coffee from the surface. As he wandered back towards Eddie, his friend managed a smile and tried to wink.

'Ow... Bastards!'

Fraser grinned. Eddie would be okay. He reckoned. But a cold, hard fear began to grow in the pit of his stomach. Someone must have been watching them. But he had been so careful. How was it possible for anyone to know what they had here? Were they still watching?

A glance over at Casey's white face told him she was having similar difficulties, similar unsettling thoughts. Their solemn thoughts were interrupted by a hoarse voice, rich with pain.

'Just got... that... fuckin' laptop!' gasped Eddie. Almost immediately, all three started to giggle, to the astonishment of the ambulance workers and police officers who, at that exact moment, came pouring in the door.

35

Casey was almost home when she noticed a car following her. As she pulled on the hand brake, she watched the car park up a little way further along the road on the opposite side. She noted the number plate, phoned the station and asked a colleague to give her the registered owner. The answer did not come as a surprise. She called in a favour. Ten minutes later, Mark Mackenzie was cuffed and sitting in the back of a squad car on his way to the station.

In a small interview room, Casey sat across from Mark Mackenzie once again. Beside her, a constable sat waiting to note down any answers Mackenzie might give.

'Well, Mr Mackenzie' said Casey, irritably. 'You'll know why you're here?'

'I'm not sure what you want me to say,' said Mark. His silky vowels did not have the soothing effect he had hoped for.

'I would like you to explain, if you can, why you keep following me?' Casey's voice was low, even and measured. If Mark Mackenzie had known her better, he'd have realised that she was livid.

'I was not following you. Why would I be following you?'

'Look,' said Casey, reasonably. 'Either you tell us what you are up to, or I will take steps to have you charged with interfering in an ongoing investigation' Or stalking and harassment perhaps.'

'Oh, come on!' cried Mark, turning red with anger.

'Well?' said Casey.

'Okay. About a year ago, I hired someone, to do some research for me. About the development at Oaklands...'

'Sarah Arnott,' said Casey. 'Yes, I know.'

Mark looked up at her in astonishment.

'But, how -?'

'So, what did she find out?' said Casey.

'Erm... she... er... she managed to get copies of certain documents. I don't know how and she said not to ask. She knew someone on the inside at the council, someone who was not happy with certain things, certain... arrangements being made.'

'Corruption,' said Casey.

Mark nodded.

'And what were you planning to do with this information?'

'Leverage. That's all. Let them know that we knew what had happened and would make it public, if they didn't back down.'

'Blackmail,' said Casey.

'I suppose... But have you seen what they are planning to do? Those trees have been there for hundreds of years. It's a small remnant of ancient woodland. Loads of wildlife, rare plants, you name it. It's a site of special scientific interest. It should have been safe.'

'Why does that bother you so much?' asked Casey.

'Oh,' said Mark, sitting up straight, anger glinting in his eyes. 'I see. I'm some posh git who likes to dabble, to interfere. I should think of all the jobs the project will create, eh? It's all bollocks! I have an interest because it is my life's work, I have an interest because my doctorate was on this very area of land. I have an interest because I am a fucking human being who would like this planet to still be viable a hundred years from now!'

It was Casey's turn to look embarrassed.

'Still doesn't explain why you were following me.'

'Okay... Just before Sarah died, we argued about it. She wanted to publish and be damned. I tried to make her see how dangerous that would be, that there were a lot of vested interests, and a lot of very powerful people with connections who would willingly destroy her to protect their investments and their reputations. She wouldn't listen. She said there was more, that she'd discovered some connections between the people involved in the development and a spate of unsolved murders. I told her to stop. I really did. But she seemed wired. She thought she could make a reputation for herself, make enough money to take care of that disaster of a daughter of hers. I told her she should just cut her off. Tough love. She told me I would never see the stuff she'd found, refused to give me the evidence. I fucking paid for it!'

'Then what happened?'

'I begged her to reconsider. I tried to emphasise the importance of the land there and how terrible it would be... everything... She just laughed in my face. Laughed! I said I'd paid for her time, paid for the information. She said it was worth more. It was her work. Once she sold the story, she'd pay me back, and, anyway, once it hit the news, the project would be killed stone dead. Wasn't that what I wanted? She simply wouldn't listen to reason.'

'Blackmail is so much better, is it?' said Casey.

Mark glared at her but said nothing.

'Did she tell you anything about the other stuff she'd found?' said Casey.

'Not really. Just hints. Big names, she said. Sex, money and power. She said it would be explosive. Rock the whole establishment. But still she didn't get it. If it were that big, it would never be allowed to happen. And for an experienced investigative reporter, she could be remarkably naïve. She was so sure she could do it. She was cocky, you know?'

'Or desperate. If she was in a hole financially, she might have needed the money.'

'I suppose... but... She did say she might meet me half-way, give me a couple of things to use, things that are in the public domain but well hidden. Most people wouldn't make the connections. She reckoned that might shake them up a bit but it wouldn't put her source in danger and they wouldn't know about the leak until it was too late.'

'Not stupid, then.'

'No. Never that. But she was taking big risks. We spoke on the phone, arranged to meet up again, but she didn't show. Then I heard about the car crash.'

'The accident that killed her?' said Casey.

'Accident?' said Mark, with a sardonic smile. 'Yeah, sure, an accident...'

'You don't think it was.'

'No. I do not.'

'There must have been an investigation?' said Casey.

'Tell you what, sergeant,' said Mark, an edge of anger in his voice, 'You find that report. You go and look at who signed it off. Then you'll have your answer. Now, if you don't have any more questions for me, I would like to go now.'

He stood up.

'Sit down!' said Casey, almost losing it. She was exhausted and really wanted to go home but not before she had sorted him out once and for all.

'You still haven't explained why you were so keen to get this stuff.' She said.

'You really don't get it, do you? It's only a matter of time before someone makes the connection between what she was investigating and the person paying her. Me. And I don't want to end up like her, especially for something I never even asked her to investigate.'

'So you intended to destroy it all?' said Casey.

'Of course I did.'

'Even if what was in it was evidence of crimes far worse than some planning irregularities?'

261

Mark stared at her.

'Look. I have no fucking idea what she found out. I don't want to know, either. I just know that I don't want to end up with my car wrapped round a fucking tree. Okay?'

'So, where were you last Sunday night?'

'Last Sunday? Oh, yes, I was at my sister's. My nephew's birthday and – Good God, you're not seriously accusing me of attacking that girl?'

'You had the motive and quite possibly the opportunity as well. At your sister's you say? Your sister can corroborate that?'

'Of course. I have her number in my phone. You can call her right now if you want!'

Casey took the number and handed it to the constable.

'One last thing.' said Casey.

Mark sighed theatrically and leaned back in the chair.

'Where was it you followed me from?'

'Outside that reporter's flat.'

'And how long had you been watching the flat?'

Mark shifted uncomfortably in the chair.

'Couple of hours,' he mumbled.

'So you witnessed it all?' said Casey, in a low and carefully controlled voice.

'Yeah.'

'And it didn't occur to you to call for help?'

'I...I thought about it but-'

'But what? He could have died!'

'There's something you have to understand. Something Sarah told me.'

262

'What?'

'That there are some people involved who are high up, beyond suspicion.'

'So?'

'So, if I *had* called the police, you might *all* be dead by now.'

The truth, so apparent in what he was saying, the seriousness that imbued these few short words, fell like molten lava, heavy, burning and inescapable.

'So, can I go now?' said Mark, getting out of his chair. The smug smile was firmly back in place. Casey bristled.

'You can go, of course.' She said. 'But, just so's you know, if I ever catch you following anyone involved in this investigation, you'll be in the cells so fast...'

As he was going out the door, Mark turned back and looked at the young constable. He nodded towards Casey.

'She always like this?'

'Oh no,' said the young man, with a smile. 'You've caught her on a really good day.'

Mark Mackenzie had to laugh.

36

Casey was trawling through her e-mails, when a call came through to her.

'Sergeant Drummond. Can I help you?'

'Casey?'

'Dod? What's wrong?'

'Jamie just saw the guy that attacked her. He just walked past the café we're in. I don't know what to do.'

'Tell me exactly where you are.'

'It's the café on the main street here, "The Linty Tea Shop".'

'Okay. Stay right where you are. I'm on my way!'

'Please hurry. He might have seen her. He might come back.'

'I'll be as quick as I can.'

You sure you know where this place is?' said Harry.

'I told you; I went with them that night. I noticed the wee café at the time. Very quaint. All china tea sets and home bakes.'

Harry didn't respond. He was wondering how Dod and Jamie were. It was worrying. From her description, the guy that attacked her was not one of the ones who'd targeted Eddie. No, this guy worked alone, knew what he was doing, was far more dangerous. Harry wondered who'd hired him, and realised it had to be someone who had access to serious money. People like him did not come cheap.

Harrison had money, but he was notoriously tight-arsed; he'd go for the cheap option, every time. His men were pretty hopeless but there were three of them. Eddie had spent his entire working life at a desk, and he didn't work out. He'd stood no chance against three younger, fitter men. Harry had met Eddie a few times. He liked the guy. He felt his jaw tighten with anger when he thought about the cowardly attack. He'd like to catch them, give them a taste of what they'd put poor Eddie through.

Casey had to slow down as they entered the village. There was a strict speed limit because of the small primary school there. Harry watched out the window as Casey drove slowly down the narrow main street. She stopped in front of the café, where an elderly woman was waiting. Harry rolled down the window on his side of the car and the woman leaned in.

'Sergeant Drummond?' she said,

Casey showed her ID and the woman pointed into a small alleyway at the side of the café.

'You could park in there, off the street,' she said.

Casey reversed into the space, carefully, to ensure that there was room enough on both sides for the doors to open. She and Harry then got out of the car and followed the woman in through a side door and along the corridor to the cosy sitting room. Dod stood up as they came in. He smiled but his bony frame was stiff with anxiety.

'Hi. Glad you're here,' he said.

Harry and Casey just smiled and sat in the two chairs pointed out to them by their host.

'It's really good of you to look after them,' said Casey. 'Mrs... Miss...?'

'Oh, sorry, dear. Terrible manners on my part. I'm a Mrs, widowed now. Ellen Gilbertson but you must call me Ellen.'

'Nice to meet you, Ellen. This is my colleague, Harry Thomson.'

'We've met before,' said Ellen, with a sad smile.

Harry looked at her and then his eyes brightened as he remembered.

'Gosh, yes. It's been a while, Ellen,' he said.

'Harry was one of the policemen who came when... my daughter... He was so kind to us both. And him so young himself at that time...'

Casey glanced at Harry but he wasn't paying her any attention, so she didn't ask. She was wondering why he'd been out here, so far from the city, and what had happened to the daughter.'

'Anyway,' said Ellen. 'I expect you need to talk, so I'll go and rustle up a fresh pot of tea, shall I?'

'Not for me, thank you,' said Harry.

'Nor me,' said Casey.

'Oh... oh, well, in that case... I have paperwork to be getting on with. Just let me know when you're for the off.' Ellen scurried out, pulling the door closed, softly, behind her.

'So, Jamie,' said Casey. 'Do you think he saw you in here? I'm only asking because, if so, there is a risk to Ellen.'

'Oh, no!' said Jamie. 'I mean... I don't know. Dod was standing up, so maybe, if he did look in, I was hidden from him? I saw him though. He had the same jacket on. It's low on the neck so you can see that snake tattoo he's got.'

Harry rummaged in pocket and brought out his notebook and pen. He flicked through to the notebook pages and started to scribble things down.

'Well', she said at last. 'Looks like we'll have to find you somewhere else'

'But where?' said Dod.

'No idea. Harry. Let's just get these two to the station and then we can sort it.'

'No problem,' said Harry, putting his notebook away again.

'So,' said Casey. 'Is there anything else you need, stuff we can stop by a shop for?'

'Might need to get some clothes. Lost everything, nearly, and what I have with me needs washing.'

'Okay. Well we might have to make do with one of the wee towns round here, so I hope you're not fussy? I can take your laundry home with me and do it at mine's.'

'Oh, but you don't have to do that.' Said Jamie.

'Who else will do it?' said Casey with a shrug. 'It's no bother anyway.'

The door to the living room slowly swung open and Ellen popped her head around.

'Would you like some tea now?' she asked. 'And I've some lovely, fresh made lemon cake?'

The drive back to the city felt soothing and inevitable. Casey drove much more slowly, aware that any perceived hurry on her part might be interpreted as panic by those in the back seats, and they had been through enough lately. Harry had put himself on what he called 'rear window duty', checking for any cars that might have been following them.

'Any chance of some music?' said Jamie.

Harry flicked on the radio. A thin, high, whining voice filled the car. It was a local radio station that specialised in pop music. Definitely not Harry's scene.

'I have this on when I'm coming in to work, for the local news bulletins,' said Casey. 'You can change the channel if you want.'

'Is this okay?' Harry said to the back-seat passengers, hoping for a negative.

'Yeah,' said Jamie. 'Love this song.'

Harry said nothing, and went back to checking the road behind them.

'Could we call in on Fraser?' asked Jamie.

'Oh, well, I don't think –'

'Please! Just want to see Laurie.'

'Harry,' said Casey. 'Would you phone Fraser and check if it's all right? We can't stay long mind.'

'Brilliant. Thanks, Casey,' said Jamie. 'Oh, Harry? Tell Fraser not to tell Laurie. I want to surprise her!'

Twenty minutes later, Casey pulled in behind Fraser's car, right beside his cottage.

'We can't stay long mind, if we're going to catch the shops,' said Casey.

'Supermarkets are open late,' said Harry, and he looked into the back seat of the car, where Dod and Jamie were.

'What do you think, guys?'

'Yeah. That would be cool,' said Jamie.

Laurie stood up when they came in. She smiled broadly to see her two erstwhile lodgers. They crossed to her and each of them hugged her.

'Could I use your phone, Fraser?' said Harry. 'Not managed to get a B&B yet for these guys.'

'I'll do that,' said Fraser. 'You guys have your coffee. Looks like you need it.'

'I'll stick the kettle on,' said Casey.

'There's no need,' said Laurie. 'Fresh pot of tea and a pot of coffee, all ready to go.'

Harry looked confused. Casey raised her eyebrows at Fraser.

'Don't ask,' he said. 'Listen, Case, could you sort the drinks if I go and make some phone calls?'

'No bother,' said Casey, peeling off her jacket.

Fraser grabbed a phone book and searched for accommodation options, a B&B that could take all three of them, just for a couple of days hopefully.

'I really need to get back home,' said Laurie.

'I know,' said Fraser. 'Just a couple more days, okay?'

'No. Tomorrow. I need to speak to my publisher, or I'll lose the contract.'

Fraser stared at her.

'I understand. I'll run you home in the morning. But, first sign of trouble-'

'I have your number,' said Laurie and smiled. 'And it's not me they're after, is it?'

'No, but-'

'Please. I need to be home. Don't worry so much.'

Fraser attempted to smile at that. She really had no idea. Fraser could feel sweat forming on the palms of his hands, as he grappled with the pages of the directory, and decided that, like that ageing police officer in the famous action film, he was getting 'too old for this shit'.

37

It was always at this point, when the immediate crisis was over, that Casey would start to resent having been called in on her day off. She would be embarking on the first of a ten-day run of shifts soon. Just the way the new rota worked. On the plus side, she had a long week-end at the end of it, which meant she could go away somewhere if she wanted to. Not that there was anywhere to go right now. But the principle remained.

'Fancy a pint, Sarge?' It was Eric Brown, a fellow sergeant. He had also been called in on his day off and looked as if he was searching for an excuse to go and get hammered,

'Might come for one but I'm working tomorrow, so I can't stay long.'

'Fair enough. Usual place. What'll you have? I'll get them in.'

'Just lager. A half pint. As I said, just the one I think.'

At that moment, Harry wandered past.

'When do you get off, Harry?' asked Casey.

'I'm here until ten,' he said and mimed suicide by hanging, crossing his eyes and sticking his tongue out.

'Never have a camera when you need one, eh?' laughed Jane, another colleague. She slapped

Harry's head gently with the cardboard file she was carrying.

'Oy! Assault!' cried Harry.

Casey was just about to leave, when all the phones began to ring.

The car had clearly been going at speed. Tyre tracks showed an erratic path towards the eventual crash site. Casey walked over to Harry.

'Is it true?' she said.

'Yes, ma'am.'

'Where's Notter?'

Harry nodded his head towards the ambulance. Casey looked over and saw Notter sitting in the doorway of the vehicle. Someone had draped a blanket around him. One of the crew was crouched down in front of him, speaking to him in a low, calming voice. Casey wandered over, not knowing what to do, but aware that she had to step up to the plate somehow.

'Sir?' she said. 'I am so sorry.'

Notter looked up at her. He was ashen and trembling, all his usual bravado gone.

'Thank you, sergeant.'

The paramedic made himself scarce. Casey perched next to Notter in the doorway of the ambulance.

'So, what happened here, sir?' she said.

'I... I'm not quite sure. When I heard... I mean, I recognised the number plate, obviously...'

Casey waited.

'It's my father-in-law's car,' he continued. 'My wife borrowed it. Hers is in for a service. She was going on a shopping trip. She was always going on shopping trips...'

Casey looked over at the car. It looked like they were getting the bodies out now.

'Where are the children, sir?'

'They're with their grand-parents.'

'Good. They're safe then, sir,' said Casey.

'It's just my wife and the chauffeur. My wife...'

Casey followed his gaze. Two stretchers lay on the grass, next to the car. Two body bags were being zipped closed. She looked back at Notter. His lips were trembling, his eyes bright and unblinking. She stood up with him, took his arm, and guided him gently towards one of the squad cars. She felt her phone vibrate in her pocket. A message from Fraser, probably. She helped Notter into the car, nodded to the driver and closed the door. She watched as the car slowly drew away, then pulled out her phone.

Heard on the radio. Harrison's car? F x

Casey thought for a moment. It would be on the news later, anyway.

Notter's wife and the chauffeur dead. No others involved. C x

Another text.

Please pass on my condolences, and if there's anything I can do etc. F x

Case smiled. Very Fraser. He might not like the guy but he would be there for anybody under these circumstances.

Will do. X

Casey put her phone away and crossed to where Harry stood at the side of the road.

'Would you tell Notter that Fraser was asking after him?' she said. 'And maybe make a note if anything comes back from forensics, to go and speak to Mark Mackenzie and his pal, Len. Doubt it'll be necessary, but you never know. Belt and braces on this one I think.' Casey nodded back towards the car that was carrying Notter away from the scene.'

Harry raised his eyebrows.

'Can do. Condolences from Fraser? Full of surprises, isn't he, nowadays?'

38

Fraser stood in front of Eddie with a can of beer in his hand.

'You sure beer is wise?' asked Fraser. 'With the pain-killers, I mean?'

'Stop it, Fraser. You sound just like my mother. Thanks for picking me up, by the way. Much appreciated. They weren't keen on me leaving by myself.'

Fraser looked at his friend's swollen face and its multi-coloured bruising.

'No worries,' said Fraser and handed him the beer. 'Think I'll stick with coffee though. You do realise it's not even eleven o'clock yet?'

'Yes, mummy, I do. Now, what's this I hear about another car crash? Harrison? Surely that's no accident?'

'I wouldn't know.'

'You've heard of car-hacking in the CIA and all that?'

'Conspiracy theories, Eddie. That's all they are.'

'So far, my friend, but what if it's true? If it has happened there, you can bet your life it's happening here too. Modern cars are packed with electronic gizmos. It's not beyond the realms.'

'Let's just wait and see, shall we. But if there was an attack of some kind, it's likely that Harrison was the real target. Not sure his daughter would have done anything to merit an assassination plot.'

'Exactly! Hard to prove though.'

'We'll not be told anyway. Unless there's a witness. Might get leaked out to the press if there was something odd happening, and someone saw it.'

'That would be nice… to know, I mean. I'm nosey. I like to know things.'

Fraser laughed.

'I'd noticed. How's the book coming on?'

Eddie groaned.

'Huge pile of edits to get through. How can that be? I went through that damned thing umpteen times and it's still a hot mess. So depressing…'

'They still want it though, Eddie. That's what matters.'

'Fifteen spelling errors. Can you believe that? Fifteen!'

'That's not bad out of…. How many words?'

'Just over a hundred thousand… but still…'

'You find anything else in those documents – anything that might have provided a motive for an attack on Harrison?'

'You're coming round to my way of thinking?'

'Reserving judgement for now.'

'Don't do that.'

'What?'

'Make me feel like some sort of suspicious nut-job.'

'But you *are* a suspicious nut-job. As am I, if I'm being honest. After all, if I wanted to commit a murder and get away with it, I would probably choose a car as my weapon, make it look like an accident.'

'Should I be worried?'

'Always,' laughed Fraser.

'Seriously, though. Sarah, and now this?'

'Car crashes are pretty common, sadly. Means nothing by itself.'

'Will they be checking the car?'

'Naturally. Forensics will be all over it. Might not find anything though. And if your conspiracy theory is true, then we probably never will.'

'That's a comforting thought.'

'So, I'll need to go and get some stuff done. You need anything?'

'Thanks for the shopping, and tidying the place up a bit. I'm beginning to think I really should marry you. No, I'll be fine. Beer in the fridge and pizzas in the freezer. And they should be delivering a new laptop to me later on tonight, so that'll keep me busy.'

'Okay. I'll let you know if anything else turns up about Sarah. You keep me posted about anything you find on Harrison, okay?''

Fraser wandered out, still mulling over the possibility that Eddie might be right. He'd have to find out more about car-hacking, but, for now, he needed more background information on Notter's father-in-law. What he was into. Who he was in contact with. Sex. That was a good place to start, and Maggie's place was only five minutes away.

Maggie seemed surprised to see him but ushered him with her usual effusive charm.

'Can't stay away from me nowadays, eh, Handsome?' she chuckled.

'Sorry about that. But you make such a good cup of tea, Maggie.'

'How disappointing. Please tell me you never use *that* as a chat up line. No wonder you haven't nabbed that young sergeant of yours yet.'

'I will bow to your greater knowledge on these matters,' said Fraser.

'So, what can I do you for? The girls are out but I can still offer a half-decent therapeutic massage.'

'I'm sure you can, but I just want to pick your brains for now.'

'Another terrible chat-up line... what about?'

'Dougie Harrison.'

'Him! Utter bastard. But then you know that.'

'I do, but is there any information you can give me about him, other than his dodgy dealings? What he's into, who his friends are, all that sort of thing.'

The smile left Maggie's face.

'This is about that accident, isn't it? His daughter. It was on the news.'

'Sort of. But not directly. Just trying to get a picture. You know I'm not officially on the case? But friends of mine have been getting hurt, so I'm doing a little digging of my own.'

'Of course. You'll be back at work soon, Honey; I just know you will. Anyway, yes. He is a violent sod. I've seen the mess he makes of some of these girls. Poor kids. Took days to recover after he'd been at them.'

'He likes it rough then?'

'Not for him. He's a control junkie. Likes role play, so long as he's always the one in charge. One lass I knew... she's long gone now... overdose... he had her tied up for eight hours. Whip marks. Sodomised her with objects. Torn to bits, she was, poor kid. Private doctor patched her up so there were no records, and she was warned to keep her mouth shut.'

'By Harrison?'

'No, dear. By his buddies at the club. Didn't happen there so I don't know why they were involved. All one big, happy family though, aren't they?'

'You say this happened to her, but was it a one-off?'

'Well, I never saw another, but the girls said that there were others before that. He loved to make them scream. None of them reported it, of course. They just avoided him. He goes for the new girls, ones that don't know him yet. Turns on the charm, apparently. Didn't know he had any.'

'Why didn't you say anything before?'

'Me? You think anyone would listen to me? Against that lot? Anyway, it was just stories, hearsay...'

'All right... true enough...'

'I mean. I was okay reporting that nutter before, but he was just a nutter. He didn't have an army of powerful friends. I prefer to keep breathing if it's okay with you.'

'Okay. Okay. I'm sorry. Stupid question.'

'He likes to strangle them too. A lot of the girls say they quite like that but not with him. He liked to hurt them. Got his jollies from seeing the terror in their eyes. Bruised them badly, sometimes. Some of them couldn't speak for a week or so after it.'

Fraser tried not to show how he felt. He swallowed hard.

'Did it ever... I mean, did he ever...?'

'What? Go too far? Kill them? I don't know, Fraser, but it would not surprise me.'

'Did he ever use a rope or anything to strangle them with?'

'Not that I heard. Just his hands. Think that was bad enough.'

'Listen, if I tell Casey about this, would you speak to her? Tell her everything you just told me?'

'Off the record?'

'I'm not sure. But, as you said, it's hearsay. It's just that it might really help build a case against him, if he has done that.'

'Okay, Fraser. For you.'

'Thank you. You've been great, as usual.'

'Now, that is a much better chat-up line! You sure you wouldn't like a massage?'

He could still hear her laughing as the lift doors closed.

39

Casey was in work early. Sleep had been a little fugitive the previous night, so she'd eventually given up and hit the caffeine instead. By the time nine o'clock hit, she was buzzing and light-headed.

The entire station was shocked by news of the crash. People had been talking about having some sort of collection for Notter, until an e-mail came from him to all the staff, requesting that they did not do anything of the sort. When he turned up at work at the usual time, they knew he was serious about wanting everyone to carry on as normal. The staff couldn't help wondering about what really happened though. The chauffeur was an experienced driver and there had been no ice on the road. Given the connections to both Notter and Harrison, Casey was guessing the technicians would be very thorough in their examination of the car.

Casey had skipped breakfast and the combination of too much coffee and low blood sugar was making the words on her computer screen dance in front of her eyes; she was glad that most of the information she'd been looking for now lay in her desk drawer in a crisp, neat pile of fresh print-outs. This might be a good time to make some phone calls. She started with Suzy at the centre.

'Hello again,' said Suzy. 'What are you looking for this time?'

'It's about Oaklands.'

There was a short, tension-filled silence.

'The development?'

'No. The children's home.'

'Ah. How does four o'clock sound? I can give you about half an hour. That be okay?'

'I hope so. See you then.'

In front of her on the desk was a reporter-style notebook. It was open to a page with another list of women, all victims of murder over the last three years, all with a history of prostitution and drug abuse. However, the manner of their deaths did vary, so there was nothing that obvious to tie them together. Being attacked was almost accepted as an occupational hazard. Most assaults on working girls probably went unreported. Those that were had a very low solve rate for reasons that are fairly obvious. No witnesses and an activity that rarely took place in the open. However, all seven had one thing in common. They had all spent time in care. And they were all late teens or early twenties, way too young to die. All seven displayed evidence of a serious beating, a violent rape, or both. Fraser had been investigating the first four when he was suspended, following what everyone now knew to be a bogus allegation of corruption. The fifth girl was attacked and killed after Fraser left, just a couple of months before Stephanie was killed. As she looked at the list, she wondered how many more there might be, how many were never found, hidden in shallow graves or lying at the bottom of the ocean.

She opened her desk drawer and leafed through the print outs. The list of locations tied in neatly with the photographs. She reached for a cardboard file and put these, plus the notebook into it, before locking it all away in a drawer. It would be good to have Suzy's take on things. Casey was as certain as she could be that there would be no more hard evidence to be got from Suzy, but there was always a chance that one of the clients might agree to speak to Casey, and perhaps even give her a statement. She glanced at the clock. She had a couple of hours before her appointment. She reached for her jacket and called over to Harry.

'Harry, I need to go check something out. You fancy driving?'

'Is the pope a Catholic?' Harry grinned and grabbed his coat.

They walked out and down the stairs.

'So, where are we going then?' asked Harry.

'Just a wee visit to Oaklands.'

'Did you phone?'

'No. Thought I'd try to catch them on an average day.'

'Okay, but you know what that means, don't you?

'What?"

'No cake!'

Casey laughed and crossed the car park.

'We'll just take my car. Bit less obvious.'

The drive down was uneventful. As they drew into the drive at Oaklands, they noticed a couple of expensive looking cars parked up ahead already.

'Hmmm, they have visitors.' Said Casey, pulling into a space well away from the front of the house. 'Let's just wait and see who it is.'

'They might be there for the duration and we'll have wasted our time.'

'Can you read those registrations from here?'

Casey pulled out a notebook and pencil, while Harry read out the numbers. The door opened and they watched as two men came out the front door. They stood at the top of the steps for a few minutes and appeared to be having some sort of heated discussion.

The smaller of the two men seemed quite agitated, and stormed off to his car. Casey made a quick note of descriptions of the two men and drew arrows to the cars. Then she shoved the notebook back into her bag. The small man drove away at speed, appearing not to notice Casey's car. The other man strolled towards his vehicle and got in. A minute later he too drove past. He glanced at them as he drove past, his face impassive.

'Okay,' said Harry. 'Are we doing this?'

'Let's go.'

They walked quickly up to the door and pressed the buzzer. The door was opened by a young woman, mid-twenties, in jeans and t-shirt. She smiled at them.

'Can I help you?'

'Police,' said Casey, holding up her I.D. card. 'I was wondering if we could come for a little chat?'

'Oh... I don't know... the manager isn't here just now.'

'Oh, it doesn't have to be the manager. In fact, it might be better to talk to the people on the floor. You're the ones who really know these kids, yeah?'

'Erm, okay. I suppose that would be all right...'

She stood back to let them in.

'I'm Sergeant Drummond but you can call me Casey.'

'Alice Shaw. I'm a care worker here.'

Another worker came out of a side room. She was slightly older and seemed puzzled by their presence.

'Erm. These people are from the police, Barbara. They just want a chat?'

'Office might be best then,' said Barbara. 'I'll stay out here, so there's someone around for the girls.'

Alice led them into the office, the room they had been in before, but, instead of steering them towards the desk, she led them further in, to where two overstuffed chesterfield sofas flanked a low coffee table, in front of the large bay window. Casey and Harry sat together on one sofa. Alice took the other. She seemed nervous, wringing her hands and pulling at imaginary threads at the bottom of her t-shirt. Harry took out a notebook and Casey began.

'So, how long have you been working here, Alice?'

'Four years, roughly. Came here for a placement when I was at college. And I really liked it. So, when a vacancy came up, I applied and got taken on. It's only part time but I love it,' she said, with a nervous smile.

'So, did you ever work with Stephanie Arnott or Jade Clark?'

'Erm… yeah… I heard about… such a shame. Nice lass, Jade. Stephanie was too, don't get me wrong… just a bit more… challenging.'

'I gather Jade had got herself a boyfriend, had started sneaking out at nights. That happen a lot here?

'Well, you know. I mean, they're teenagers, most of them, and we're not allowed to lock them in.'

'So what do you do if they run off?'

'One of us will go and drive around, see if we can find them, try and persuade them to come back, but, well… we don't usually find them and even if we do, they don't want to leave their friends.'

'So, then what?'

'We do call you guys sometimes, when we're worried for their safety.'

'Are you not always worried? I mean, these are kids, right?'

Alice flushed.

'We've been told not to call the police too often. That the place might get closed down if that happens too much. But it's difficult to be sure. Some of their friends can be a lot older and that's not good. Trouble is, by the time the police get there, they've gone again.'

'So, how old are the girls you have here just now?'

'The oldest is fifteen. We have three girls with us just now. There were four but one of them has gone back to her mum's. There'll be another one coming in next week though. There is always someone who needs a bed here.'

'So, this girl who's gone home. What was her story?'

'Oh, she wasn't here long, just a few weeks. Her mum's a single parent. Was in hospital for an operation. Breast cancer. Really sad for them.'

'Will she be all right?'

'They don't know yet.'

'And how old is the girl?'

'She's only twelve. Nice kid. Hardly spoke. Really distressed by it all.'

'That must have been difficult. Anything worrying you about the ones that are left?'

'The oldest, (she's also the one that's been here the longest), is fifteen. Fell out with her last foster parents, so she came to us.'

'That happens a lot?'

Alice sighed and looked off into the distance.

'Yeah,' she said. 'She had a bad start in life. Abuse or neglect or something like that, I'm guessing.'

'You don't know?'

'We don't need to, really. Social Work have all her records. All we need is the basic stuff, to help us support her properly, not that she wants our help a lot of the time.'

'So, does she sneak out?'

Alice stared at Casey. Her eyes were full of sadness.

'I worry about her. I've seen her boyfriend. He's older than me by the looks of him, and he has a mean face. That sounds so stupid... sorry...'

'Sometimes first impressions are the best,' said Casey. 'Do you have his name? Can you describe him?'

'No name. About five nine, dark haired, thin... nothing remarkable about him.'

'And the other two girls?'

'Oh, they're fine. No problems there. Well, apart from a few tantrums but that's to be expected. Great pals. Almost like sisters.'

'Okay. Well, thanks, Alice, that's really helpful. Do you think Barbara might come to speak to us? She's been here longer, I'm guessing?'

'Oh, yeah. She's been here since it opened ten years ago. Part of the furniture. I'll go and ask her.'

'Oh, Alice, before you go? There were two guys leaving when we arrived. Who were they?'

'Think one was from the council and the other one's an MP or something? Not sure but Barbara was dealing with them, so you can ask her about it.'

Alice left the room.

'Those guys keep turning up,' said Casey.

'Something on your mind?'

'Those same guys were at the station talking to Notter the other week. Also, I'm thinking that description of the boyfriend... could have been Jade's guy.'

'To be fair, it could be half the young male population!'

'True. There's something going on here though, something rotten.'

'I don't think so, Casey. Alice seems completely genuine to me.'

'Oh, yes. She's very sweet and seems to actually give a shit as well. I suppose she'll get as cynical as the rest of us eventually.'

'You are a ray of bloody sunshine today.'

The door opened before Casey could respond, and Barbara walked in. The distant and vaguely superior look on her face told Casey that she was not going to be so easy to talk to as her younger colleague. Casey got that old, familiar sensation. The hairs on the back of her neck told her that she was getting very close to an unpleasant truth.

Casey invited Barbara to sit.

'So, can you tell me about your visitors?' said Casey.

Barbara's eyebrows rose a fraction. She stared at Casey and smiled. It was neither warm nor humorous.

'Visitors?' she said.

'There were two men leaving as we arrived. I gather one was from the local council and another was the local MP.'

'That's correct.'

'So what were they here for?'

'Paperwork. Nothing that could be of any possible interest to you.'

'Try me.'

'You must understand that certain things are confidential. It is a care home. There are some politically sensitive issues.'

'Indeed. Like girls disappearing at night? Like their bodies turning up years later? Do you realise how many of your ex-residents have ended up dead?'

'We can't be held responsible for every damaged child who passes through here, especially after they have left.'

'True, but you are responsible for what happens while they are here.'

Casey saw Barbara colour slightly. A twitch at the corner of her eye indicated she was tense, despite her outward calm.

'By the way,' continued Casey. 'There are seven that we know about, seven in the space of three years. But perhaps you know all this already?'

A flash of anger brightened Barbara's dull stare, but she said nothing.

'Is it not a little... unusual... for those people to come here when the manager is not here?'

'She trusts me to deal with things when she's not here.'

'So, they didn't make any arrangement to visit then? No appointment? Phone call?'

'They are on the board. They like to make unannounced visits to check things are working properly.'

'Very wise.'

Casey could almost hear Barbara's hackles rise.

'I'm sorry but do you actually have any questions for me. We have a lot to do, and the children will be here soon from school.'

'How long have you been working here?'

'About ten years.'

'Since it opened?'

'That's correct.'

'And how long has the manager been here?'

'There are two. About eight or nine years, I think. Previous manager took early retirement, I think. Ill-health or something.'

'So why is there no-one here today?'

'Job-share. Both part-time. Only cover four days a week. Admin and floor staff manage fine the rest of the time.'

The way she said this seemed to indicate that, in Barbara's view, they would cope just fine without management.

'So, what can you tell us about the late night disappearing acts these kids get up to?'

'Happens a lot. Nothing we can do, really. This is not a secure unit.'

'No, it's not, is it? Not very secure at all.'

'I don't like your –'

'My tone? Yes, I get that a lot. From crooks mainly. Are you a crook, Barbara? Do you know something about what's going on? Something you're not telling us?'

'I have answered your questions, but now I think you should leave,' said Barbara, standing up suddenly.

'Sit down,' said Casey. 'Unless, of course, you'd prefer we cuffed you and took you with us back to the station?'

Barbara sat down. Casey slid a piece of paper across the table towards her.

'Do you recognise these names?'

Barbara nodded.

'Did you work with any of these girls?'

'All of them.'

'I see.'

Barbara reached down and touched the document. Her hand was trembling.

'Are th...they...all...?'

'Dead? Yes, that's right.'

Casey watched as all the colour seemed to drain from Barbara's face. Her shoulders drooped. She looked up at Casey. There was no trace left of the cool defiance of earlier. She looked terrified.

'I can't help you. You must know that.'

Casey said nothing, and waited.

'If they find out you've been here asking questions...,'said Barbara. Her mouth trembled over the words.

'We can arrange protection,' said Casey, deliberately softening her tone.

Barbara looked at her and slowly shook her head.

'You really don't get it, do you? You take this to the station, you sign my death warrant.'

As she said this, her eyes slid downwards towards the list of names.

'Is there someone you could go to?'

Barbara shook her head, her eyes scanning the room as if looking for an escape route.

'You don't understand. They're everywhere. They'd find me. I'm sorry. I can't help you.' She looked at Casey again. 'You have to close this place. If you do that, then I can disappear. But you have to close it.'

Then she stood and headed for the door. When she got there, she gripped the door handle, and, without looking at them, she murmured her final words.

'You'll find the answers at their private club.'

Then she turned the door handle and opened the door. She waited for them to take the hint, which they did. Casey patted Barbara's arm on her way past. As they crunched over the gravel towards the car, Casey and Harry happened to glance back. At an upper window, two young girls began to wave. They seemed to be giggling about something. Casey and Harry waved back.

'Why are they not at school?' asked Harry.

'Why indeed,' said Casey. 'Let's hope they are out of here before anything happens to them.'

40

Casey was relieved to be back in the city, back on familiar ground. Harry parked her car and waited for her to speak.

'Harry, I need you to dig up anything and everything about Oaklands. Specifically, find out who the previous manager was and exactly why they left. I'm going to go down to the centre on my own. A casual approach might work better with Suzy. She's a wee bit prickly sometimes.'

'Okay. Anything else?'

Harry climbed out of the car and Casey slid over into the driver's seat. He'd warmed it up nicely for her. Casey fished out her phone and called Fraser. She wasn't even sure why she was doing it. Habit? The need to hear his voice? It went straight to voicemail, so he was already on a call or had switched it off. Casey suspected the latter. She sent a text.

Hi Fraser. Need to talk. Usual place, back of five? C x

Worth a try.

Suzy already had a pot of coffee made when Casey got there. Just the smell of it was enough to put a smile back on Casey's face.

'So, you had some more questions for me?' said Suzy, as she poured the coffee.

'Erm... more a sort of discussion, I think. Let's see how it goes, eh? Thank you so much for the coffee. So tired of instant.'

'We have about forty minutes', said Suzy, pointedly. 'Then I'll have to get sorted for opening again at five.'

'Oh, sorry. I know you're busy here. It's about a connection there might be between some murders –'

'A connection to this place?' Suzy's voice was sharply accusatory.

'No, no, no... sorry. Got my stupid head on today. I was going through some old cases, to see if what happened to Stephanie and Jade was... well... there were others. Over the last year and a half, there are seven that might be connected.'

Suzy leaned back in her chair and stared at Casey.

'So, what do you want with me? You should be out there catching them!'

'I'm sorry, but, I need to ask you to look at a list of names, see if there are any you knew, who maybe came here? And, also, if anyone of them mentioned being afraid of someone?' Casey pushed the list of victims across the table to Suzy.

Suzy read down the list, her facial expression hard to read, then laid her hand on the paper and looked up.

'I knew all these girls, all of them... I thought they had moved on somewhere. Makes you think, doesn't it? People in this life, they disappear every day, and no-one pays the slightest bit of attention because that's just what they do.'

'Sorry, Suzy. I realise this might be upsetting for you, but –'

Suzy looked at the list again, her face creased in concentration.

'These first two were friends, I think... yeah... And I only have vague memories of the next two. Weren't here long, either of them. Then, there's this lass, Hayley. Bit highly strung. Bit of a drama queen. Harmless, but.... Think her boyfriend, or minder, or whatever, could be a bit of a coarse bastard sometimes. Always a few bruises. Mind you, that's not unusual. Same for most of them. And no-one would report it. They know better than that.'

Casey nodded. She knew that Suzy was right; the girls would never have reported any abuse. Too risky.'

'So, how old were these girls, roughly?'

'These ones were all pretty young... teens or twenties, so hard to tell with make-up and stuff. I suppose some might even have been underage. They would cover it up, get false ID, before they ever tried coming here for anything. They know the score, that we'd have to report it. Child safety concern. If we didn't do that they'd close us down, for sure. But the fact that we do... I mean, the kids know... it's why some of them don't come near here. They're on their own. Way it's always been though,' said Suzy. Casey saw a glimmer of anger flash in Suzy's eyes. Was it anger? Defiance? Casey suddenly realised that Suzy knew these things first hand. She had been one of those kids.

'I was wondering,' said Casey. 'If I write down these names and give you my card, could you have another think later on and let me know if you come up with anything else? Might be really useful.'

'It's unlikely, but sure, you can do that.'

Casey watched as Suzy trotted over to a drawer and took out a ring-bound notebook. She passed it to Casey, who quickly scribbled down the names and handed it back.

'Must be a difficult job,' said Casey.

'Has its moments.'

'Why do you do it?'

'Why not?' said Suzy, with a laugh. 'You know, it's never going to stop. All we can do is try to make them as safe as possible.'

Casey watched her, wondering what it was she wasn't saying.

'Safe from who? Punters or pimps?'

'If only it were that simple. These girls find danger everywhere. No-one gives a shit, anyway, do they?'

'Some of us do,' said Casey. 'Anyway, I'd best be off. Hope you have a decent shift.'

'It'll be easier when Jamie's back. Any word on how she's doing?'

'She's getting there. Still a bit shaken up and not really fit for work yet.'

'Poor kid. Lucky to be alive though.'

'Lucky? In what way? Do you know the guy?'

Suzy coloured.

'Er, not really. But I've heard about...I know you don't mess with him.'

'Don't suppose you know his name?'

Suzy shook her head.

'That's all I know.'

She gave Casey a look that could have been either rage or fear. Suzy was pretty hard to read. Suzy got up and started to gather the cups. The conversation was clearly at an end.

'Okay. Well, thank you so much.' Casey dug in her pocket and came out with a business card.

'If you do hear anything...?' she said laying the card down on the table.

As Casey stepped down, she heard the door being securely locked behind her and thought how vulnerable Suzy must feel here on her own and how she might be able to use some help. She phoned Maggie and explained the situation.

'So, I was wondering if maybe you knew someone who might be able to help out, just until Jamie comes back?'

'Of course... Hadn't thought... I tell you what, I'll give her a ring, and, if she's agreeable, I'll go down there myself. Could do with a change of scenery.'

'Thanks, Maggie.'

'No bother, dear. Actually, your lover boy just left here. Said he was coming to see you. Hope you shaved your legs this morning!' Maggie let out a peal of laughter and Casey had to laugh with her.

'You are incorrigible, Maggie,' she said.

'Flatterer!' Maggie's earthy laugh boomed out of the phone.

Casey walked down the lane towards her car. As she did so, she called Fraser and arranged to meet at their favourite coffee shop. Not that she really needed more coffee; Casey was already buzzing with caffeine. As she neared her car, she noticed a man standing in a shop doorway. He leaned forward to drop his cigarette, and she saw a large tattoo coiled around the side of his neck. A snake. Casey quickly retreated into a side street, heart racing, her mouth suddenly dry, hoping against hope that he hadn't seen her. Then, almost tearful with terror, she turned and ran, running faster than she'd ever run before and not really caring where to.

41

Fraser had almost finished his coffee and was considering giving Casey a call, when the door opened and she came stumbling in. She almost ran to him and slid round to the back of the table, having not uttered a word yet.

'What the hell...?' said Fraser.

'He was waiting for me. By my car.'

'Who was?'

'The heavy...snake guy...'

'Shit!'

'Exactly. Whoever he's working for seems to know exactly where we are. I mean, he must have known my car... What's happening, Fraser? I'm freaking out here.'

'Where were you earlier?'

'At Oaklands... do you think...?'

'Who did you see? Who were you with? Did something happen there?'

Casey gave him a quick run-down of events. Fraser listened quietly.

'So... the only people who might have called him, or called someone else who then called him, were the two care workers, Harry, the councillor, the MP or Suzy. Unless of course, he's been following you all day.'

'If we could get phone records... but you need a court order...'

'Not necessarily. I have a few friends in... low places.' He laughed briefly, until he noticed the expression that fell across her face. 'Kidding Casey... for God's sake... you going to be okay?'

Casey nodded, marvelling at how his low, almost emotionless voice, was beginning to calm her down.

'Two questions,' said Fraser. 'What sort of coffee would you like, and would you like to crash at my place until we've got that joker off your tail?'

'Latte and yes but I'll need to fetch some things from my place.'

'I'll get the coffee and you can buy essentials on the way. I suspect your flat might be out of bounds along with your car. Not worth the risk right now.'

While Fraser was up at the counter ordering the coffees, Casey thought back over the last couple of weeks. There were other occasions when snake boy had shown up. How had he appeared at that wee village for example? Who had told him where Laurie was? Who else knew? There was only her and Fraser. No. There were others. Anyone at the station could have found out. It wasn't a happy thought. She watched Fraser coming back with a tray. Coffee and cake. How civilised. He set it down on the table and sat down.

He was about to tell her what Maggie had said, when he realised she was staring at him.

'What?' he said.

'What if it's someone at the station. I saw those guys there one day, with Harrison and Notter.'

'What guys?'

'The councillor and the MP.'

'Oh... right...But you don't think Notter would be involved? He's an arse but he's a pretty straight arrow.'

'No, I don't. Harrison's too cheap to have paid for a professional.'

'So why were those three at the station together?'

'Not sure but Notter wasn't too happy about them being there, by the look of him. He did mention something about the Kilgarry Club. They raise money for good causes.'

'Oh, yes,' said Fraser and his voice had a sneering edge to it, as he said the words. 'The great and the good. I remember Tony talking about that club. He was invited to speak at their annual dinner. He said he was surprised to realise that he didn't know a single person there. Well, you know Tony. He seems to know everyone! It was a puzzle at first, he said, but then he added that when he got talking to them, he understood why he didn't know them.' Fraser chuckled.

'Barbara said we'd find the answers at their private club. It has to be that place.'

'Certainly worth exploring.'

'One thing I must do first.'

'What's that?'

'I need to look at those mug shots. See if we can get an ID.'

'Okay. I can wait for you in the car.'

'Where is your car?'

'Station car park. Figured it would be safer there.'

'That's handy... but Notter won't like it.'

'No. I don't suppose he does. Shame.'

'I get the feeling you were about to tell me something back there, by the way, before I started on about folk at work. What is it? Do you have something for me?'

'I've just come from Maggie's. She told me some interesting things about Harrison. He likes to hurt the girls. Gets off on it. He also has a thing for strangling them during sex. Might be worth hauling him in, although with Notter around, you probably need more evidence of that before you do it.'

'Jesus... I should talk to Maggie myself. Do you think she'd be willing to go on record? Would she speak to me about it?'

'I already asked. She'd be happy to speak to you but strictly off the record. Powerful people are involved. They've been protecting Harrison for years.'

'Maybe that's the problem. The crash seems a bit suss to me, although we're still waiting for forensics to come back with a report. Maybe Harrison's powerful buddies are sick of covering for him...must have been him they were after. His daughter is, from all accounts, a bitch, but it's unlikely anyone would go that far to deal with her.'

'I think you're right. But I'm also fairly certain that forensics won't find a thing. Even if they do, I imagine that evidence will be quietly buried. It'll never get through to you guys.'

Casey understood what he was trying to tell her, and knew he was probably right, even though the thought of that made her feel deeply uncomfortable. She watched through the window, feeling calmer but still alert for any indication of danger. She looked back at Fraser.

'What about you? Are you still being followed?' she asked.

'I don't think so. Harrison's guys are amateurs.'

'They can still do damage.'

Fraser nodded, frowning in thought.

'Absolutely. I'm more worried about the professionals, though. That attack on Jamie. The guy who did that seemed to be more... well, high-end... And if Eddie's right about Sarah's car incident, well, that's even more sophisticated... professional hit. Maybe even government-level stuff. Maggie did mention something... parties with high up people, people who could call on secret services.'

'Oh, come on, Fraser! That's a bit far-fetched.'

Fraser didn't even look at her, as if he didn't hear her at all.

'Best check on Laurie.'

Fraser took out his phone. Casey watched the street outside. It started to rain. Casey watched the slow trickle of water down the glass, and tried to stay calm.

'That's funny. Went straight to voice mail. She must be on a call. I'll try again in a minute or two.'

'So, what exactly was Maggie saying today?' said Casey.

'Not much, to be honest. Kept going on about some important people and how it was best left alone. Didn't seem to know anything about the kids' home but she said a lot of the girls had sad stories, that she'd probably heard them all. Still, she does make a decent cup of tea and excellent shortbread.'

'She bakes?'

Fraser laughed.

'I suspect there's a lot about Maggie we don't know. Yeah, the baking surprised me too. Some kid...'

'Hardly that. She must be in her fifties.'

'Not quite. Late forties maybe, at a pinch. Looks older, I'll grant you.'

Fraser tried Laurie's number again and frowned when he still got no answer.

'Still no answer?' said Casey. She frowned and looked around her. 'What about a back door?'

Fraser grinned.

'That's my girl. I'll go and speak to that pretty young thing behind the counter.'

'How many non-pc things can you cram into one sentence?'

'That a challenge?'

'No.'

Casey smiled and watched Fraser's easy stroll over to the counter, the quiet way he persuaded the young woman to move away from her colleagues for a private conversation and the way her face flushed pink as he was speaking. There was no escaping it. Fraser was almost always an instant hit with females. He might be old school but he had

305

something, some strange ability to persuade you that you were the only woman in the world he wanted to talk to, at that moment. Casey couldn't help but wonder if he ever meant a single word of it, or was it always just an act with him, a habit he wasn't even aware of. And why did that bother her so much? She saw him turn and amble back.

'Well?' said Casey.

Fraser sat down and took a sip from his mug.

'When we finish our coffee, we'll go. There's a door marked private, right next to the counter. See it?'

'Yeah.'

'It's fob-locked.'

Fraser dropped his hand onto the seat between them and uncurled his fingers, revealing a small oval of plastic on a metal ring.

'It's a spare one. Once we are through that door, there is another fob-locked door going out the back, onto Aitken Lane. We're to throw the fob into the corridor as we leave. She'll collect it.'

'But we'll be seen.'

'Not from outside. And we'll just have to pick our moment, wait for a rush at the counter. Yeah?'

'Okay.' Casey felt that there were a hundred ways this could all go horribly wrong but what choice did they have?

They watched as the customers came and went. It was just a trickle. Casey could feel herself growing more and more tense by the minute and fought to stop herself jiggling her legs up and down with impatient anxiety. Fraser tried to keep her calm, by asking lots of boring questions about work, and squeezing her hand under the table. She kept looking outside but there was no sign of the snake man. But perhaps he was hiding in a doorway close by. Or maybe he was in here. She kept scanning the room, looking for him.

'Casey, stop it,' said Fraser.

'Sorry. Can't help it. Should have called it in.'

'It'll be fine. Almost there. People will be coming for their coffees to take on the train home. You'll see.'

And, of course, he was right. Five minutes later, a queue began to form, one that obscured them from view for anyone outside. Quietly, Fraser stood and gestured to Casey. They quickly crossed to the door. The faint beep of the fob was masked by urgent voices calling for Lattes and Americanos.

They slipped into the corridor and closed the door behind them. A grey-carpeted corridor led to an outside door. It looked solid and probably was. There was no shortage of desperate people in this area, who would take any opportunity to break in. All the local businesses could do was to ramp up security, by replacing the old, flimsy, wooden doors with steel-reinforced ones.

Fraser deftly slid back the three bolts, twisted the door lock to open and applied the fob. Another beep and they were out. Fraser tossed the fob inside and pulled the door closed, as quietly as he could. They headed towards the station.

42

Casey tried not to think about the possibility of one of the crooks being inside the ranks and hurried to keep up with Fraser's long strides. Every step took her further from the café, further from her own car and further from the freedom she used to enjoy. If the snake man was out to get her, what was she supposed to do about it? She couldn't hide forever. She had a job to do. She kept looking around her as they went. They were almost there, when Fraser grabbed her and dragged her into a doorway.

'Shit! He's there,' he said.

Casey followed Fraser's gaze and saw the one person she had hoped never to see again. Snake-man was standing by the entrance to the police car park, within sight of Fraser's old car. How had he known where to look for them? It was clear he was after both of them now.

Casey looked at Fraser.

'What do we do?' she said.

'Call Harry.'

'But he'll be off duty now.'

'Just call him.'

Casey fished out her phone. She scrolled through to Harry's private mobile number and pressed the button.

'Hi, Harry?'

'Casey? Hope you're not inviting me to do an extra shift because the answer is no!'

In the background, Casey could hear the sound of people laughing and children shouting. She was interrupting family time.

'No, not at all. I... we.... Fraser and I need a favour.'

'Oh-oh. That likely to cost me my pension?'

'No. We just need a lift. There's someone after us so we can't use our cars.'

There was a brief silence, followed by a short, somewhat muffled conversation in the background.

'Look, Kelly wants me to pick up some things from the supermarket, so if you could get yourselves to the Bon Accord Centre, Schoolhill end, in the next ten minutes?'

'That would be great. Thanks, Harry.'

Fraser looked at Casey as she pocketed her phone.

'He'll pick us up at the Bon Accord. We just need to get out of here without being seen.'

Like a gift from the gods, at that moment, a large group of revellers came tumbling out of a nearby pub. Casey and Fraser slipped into the middle of them and stayed there until they reached the shopping centre. They didn't walk this time; they ran.

The centre was busy. Fraser and Casey walked in and stood in a shop doorway eyes peeled for any sign of Snake-boy. When people approached, they feigned interest in the goods on display in the shop window all the time casting frequent, furtive glances at the automatic doors, watching for Harry. Eventually, they saw his familiar haggard face, with its crown of close-cropped, sandy hair. They watched him scanning the crowds and then his face splitting into a grin as he spotted them. He weaved through the crowds towards them.

'Hi. Just got to nip and get milk. Always running out of that… Just be a tic.'

Fraser and Casey nervously scanned the crowd, half-expecting to see their pursuer appear again, like some psychic phantom. Then, Harry was back and they headed outside and round the corner to where he'd parked his car. Without further explanation, Casey and Fraser climbed into the back of the car, both thinking they'd be less visible there. If Harry thought this strange, he didn't say so; he just started the engine and asked where to.

'Could we check my car?' asked Casey. 'He can't be in two places at once, can he?'

Exchange Street,' said Fraser.

Harry drove off.

The lane was deserted when they got there. No sign of Snake-man. Casey and Fraser jumped out and checked the car for obvious damage. There was none. Casey got in and turned on the engine. There was almost a full tank of petrol. She waved to Harry, who nodded and drove off.

'I.D. will have to wait until tomorrow,' said Casey. 'Hope I still remember his face well enough.'

'I saw him too, if you need back up.'

'Thanks. Hoping I can leave you out of it. No offence. Just can't face the thought of trying to explain it all to Notter.'

Fraser chuckled.

43

The drive north was uneventful. Neither of them spoke for a while, each lost in their own heads. Soon they were within a few minutes of the turn-off to Laurie's. Casey glanced over and saw Fraser checking his phone.

'Did you want to check on Laurie?' said Casey.

'Yes. Not like her not to answer. She's not tried to phone back, either. Hope nothing's wrong. Only dropped her off this morning.'

Fraser shoved the phone back in his pocket, his eyebrows lowered, his mouth set in a thin line. He grunted and gestured when they got near to the turn-off. Casey glanced at him before indicating right and turning off into the narrow lane.

A light smirr began to cloud the windscreen. The steady pulse of the windscreen wipers seemed amplified in the car, as they drove silently towards God-knows-what. Casey's mouth felt dry and her eyes stared out, scanning the horizon constantly for any signs of danger. Fraser was quiet and still beside her. Suddenly, he touched her arm and pointed to a small side lane, edged by a row of trees. She turned in there and parked up, facing towards the cottage, which they could see in the gaps between the trees. Fraser leaned forward in his seat. Casey followed his gaze and saw a van parked up ahead, next to the house.

'Shit, Fraser... what are *they* doing here? Thought they'd stay away, after our little chats with them. Cocky wee shits.'

'It'll be Harrison. Still looking for those damned files.'

'We have to do something.'

'Fuck... You wait here, Casey,' said Fraser, unclipping his seat belt.

'I'm coming with you.'

'No. I need you to stay here. If something kicks off, I'm relying on you to call for help.'

He slipped out of the car. Casey watched as he crept along the tree line towards the beach. The land sloped downwards and soon he was out of sight. She cursed under her breath, her every muscle fibre taut with tension, her hands repeatedly opening and closing into fists, as she waited, wanting to act, itching to do something. Call for help? Who was she supposed to call? Harry was on leave, wasn't he? Some sort of family do... terrible that she couldn't remember what he'd said. She'd have to contact the station. But who? There was only one option. Pain in the arse he might be but, according to Fraser, he was a 'straight arrow'. Notter. It was laughable really. Casey just had to hope it wouldn't come to that.

Casey continued to watch the house. It was frustrating not being able to see Fraser. How would she know if he got into trouble? Maybe she should just get out of the car and follow him. He'd be livid but he wasn't in charge of the investigation. He wasn't her boss at the moment. She was about to go when she heard a buzzing noise. Fraser had left his phone on the seat. She picked it up. Maggie. Not like her to phone. She clicked the green button.

'Fraser? It's Maggie.'

'Sorry, Maggie. Fraser's a bit busy. Anything I can help you with?'

'Oh... really need to speak to Fraser.'

'I'll tell him to call you back,' said Casey and quickly rang off. She could see movement near the house and rolled down the window to get a better look. She saw three figures coming from the cottage. They got into the van and started to turn it.

Shit, they'd see her here. Casey looked around and then quickly reversed in to the side of the small barn. Hopefully, they wouldn't notice the car here. She watched the road and saw the van whizz past. They were doing a fair speed. What was the rush?

She glanced towards Laurie's house and saw a flickering brightness in the window and a cloud of black smoke spiralling up from the roof. And then she was out of the car and running, heedless of any watching eyes, focussed solely on the need to find her friends. As she neared the house, she heard a loud crash and the tinkle of broken glass and saw Fraser clambering in through a downstairs window. Then she heard him screaming, shouting Laurie's name over and over.

Casey clambered in after him. The air was thick with acrid smoke from the burning timbers. Casey pulled her sweater up over her nose and mouth, but could do nothing to prevent the stinging in her eyes, which streamed with tears, rendering her almost blind. She followed the sound of Fraser's voice and then she saw him, kneeling on the ground, clearing fallen debris from a small, still body. Casey moved quickly forward and, without a word, they worked together to lift Laurie up and carry her. They used the door this time and walked a safe distance from the blaze before laying Laurie down on the grass.

Outside, in the light, it was easy to see that she had taken a beating. Her soot-streaked face was swollen and bleeding. Casey watched as Fraser loosened the neck of Laurie's shirt and checked her breathing.

'Phone... fire... police... ambulance,' croaked Fraser, between bouts of coughing.

'Is she...?'

'She's breathing... but... just phone.'

Casey fished her phone out and dialled. She ran through the basic details and gave directions to the cottage. All the while, she watched Fraser, as he draped his jacket over Laurie, talking to her softly, even though she probably didn't hear him. Casey wondered how Fraser would cope if Laurie didn't make it. After what had happened before, this small incident might be the proverbial straw.

As if he had read her thoughts, Fraser glanced over at her; his face was impassive but Casey was convinced that the tears running down his cheeks were not all due to smoke. He looked away again quickly and she watched as he wiped his face on his shirt sleeve. Glass shattered noisily behind them and they could hear the roar of the fire. Casey looked over and felt herself grieving for the little house, so lovingly cared for by Laurie, a little house with a big heart, to match its owner but which now lay in its death throes. Poor Laurie. She might well survive the beating and the fire but she'd have nothing left.

'The turn off isn't easy to see. I'll go up to the main road and guide them in,' said Casey.

Fraser nodded in response, never taking his eyes off Laurie.

Fifteen minutes later, Casey was standing by her car waving a procession of emergency vehicles in towards the turning. She followed them along the narrow track, aware of a pulsing glow on the horizon and a thick pall of smoke snaking into the sky. It was unlikely that the fire brigade could do anything now to save Laurie's little house. She just hoped that Laurie herself was still breathing. Casey left the car in the side road they'd hidden in earlier. There wouldn't be much room with all the services there and she knew better than to get in their way.

The ambulance crew moved in quickly. Casey watched as Fraser stood and backed away to let them in. He looked bewildered. As she was approaching him, she heard her name being called and looked around. It was Notter, and, for once, he did not look irritated. He actually appeared to be genuinely concerned. She walked over to him, glancing back towards Fraser as she went.

'Drummond, are you all right?'

'Yes, sir.'

'The two of you need to be checked out. Smoke inhalation-'

'Yes, I know... sorry, sir,' said Casey, horrified to realise that she was weeping. She wiped her face on her sleeve.

'Of course. Excuse... do you think you could tell me what happened?'

'We met in town. Came out to visit a mutual friend. There was a van here. It sped away just as we arrived. That's when we saw the fire and went in...'

It wasn't a lie, exactly, just a highly edited version of the truth. At least that's what Casey told herself. If he asked for more details, she would have to give them. She just hoped he wouldn't ask, not yet anyway.

'Okay,' said Notter. 'As soon as you've been checked over, I'll need statements from you both.'

'Yes, sir.'

'And, Drummond?'

'Yes, sir?'

'Well done. Not many people would have gone into that fire the way you two did.'

'Will she be okay?'

'Not for me to say. But they're loading her into the ambulance now, so you could go and ask.'

Notter walked back to his car and Casey crossed to where Fraser stood, talking to the crew at the door of the ambulance. He spotted her approaching and managed a smile.

'Looks like she's going to be all right,' he said. 'You have to get them, Casey, Harrison's men. They can't get away this time.'

317

He broke into a fit of coughing. They hugged each other. Then, Fraser climbed up into the back of the ambulance. Casey returned to her car and followed them to the hospital. Half way there, Fraser's phone started to ring again. This time, Casey didn't even glance at it.

44

The next morning, Casey, still a bit wheezy from the events of the night before, was back at her desk. Harrison's "enforcers" were safely locked up in the cells. Uniform picked them up last night, along with Harrison himself. Unfortunately, none of them were talking, so they had to let Harrison go again this morning. Casey hoped that, with a little pressure, the three idiots downstairs would drop Harrison in it. She would love to get him put away. Pity there wasn't enough to keep him, but it was just a matter of time; he was sure to slip up.

She pulled up the photographs she'd shown to Jamie, of possible suspects in her attack. To her delight and surprise, it was an easy pick. Stefan Wasilewski. Last known address in Brixton. Long history of violent crime, including several which had been dropped when witnesses suddenly developed amnesia or even disappeared off the face of the earth. A nice guy. And still wanted in connection with a violent assault on a young woman in Streatham. So, what was he doing this far north? Stupid question. He went where the work was. Killer for hire. Made people's problems disappear, no questions asked, provided he was paid enough.

It was as she was leaning back in her chair to stretch her back that she caught sight of an envelope lying on the floor near her feet. Must have fallen out of her overcrowded in-tray. She retrieved it. It was marked private and had her name handwritten on it in Harry's familiar scrawl. What now? She tore it open. Inside were two sheets of A4 stapled together. The first page was a print-out from a small newspaper article, and was dated 9 years ago. She read it, feeling increasingly uneasy.

Local Care Home Manager Seriously Injured in Car Accident

Local woman, Claire Johnson, manager of the local authority children's home, "Oakland House", was in hospital last night following a serious road accident. Staff have expressed their shock at the news. Mrs Johnson, a well-respected member of the community, is well known as a champion of children's rights, both locally and nationally. Police are looking into the incident but there appear to be no suspicious circumstances.

Casey flipped over to the next page. It was a death announcement, dated three years later. The similarities to Sarah's death were all too obvious. Casey felt a chill ripple through her. The poor woman had hung on for three years, but Casey believed that she, too, was murdered. It was unlikely, however, that they would ever know for sure. It seemed likely that she had stumbled across information she wasn't supposed to have, maybe confided in the wrong person. Casey sighed and put the sheets back inside the envelope, before shoving it into a drawer.

She went back to the mysterious Mr Wasilewski. A search of the electoral roll for the area turned up nothing. No real surprise. Probably using a different identity. Annoying. But at least now they had a name and a half-decent photo to put out there. She picked up the phone and spoke to Notter. With a bit of luck, they could get it in that evening's paper.

She heard the ping of a text message arriving on her phone. It was Fraser.

At Maggie's. You'll want to hear what she has to say. F x

Well, it would be nice to get out for an hour or so. And she was supposed to have finished her shift an hour ago. She closed down her computer and grabbed her jacket.

The atmosphere at Maggie's was strangely tense. Fraser was pacing, always a bad sign. Casey took a seat and waited for him to sit down.

'Maggie has been asking around. Apparently, all the girls were recruited by Rat. Can you believe that? *All of them.* They didn't know it at the time, of course, poor kids. They thought he was their boyfriend. The usual story. Anyway, it seems that he was being paid for his services and, thanks to Maggie and some slightly dodgy information gathering by Sarah and Eddie, we now have proof of a link between those payments and an organisation that's a known subsidiary of the Kilgarry club. Maggie, could you give Casey that e-mail?'

'This from the pen drive? asked Casey.

Fraser nodded. Although he was sitting now, he was clearly agitated, his leg jiggling up and down as he spoke.

'I returned Maggie's calls. She was trying to get hold of me yesterday. I was at Eddie's. He made the connection. Read it.'

Casey looked down at the paper. It seemed to be a payment notification of some sort.

From: Alpha Corporate Entertainment
To: Mr D. W. Wilson (Independent Contractor)
Hire of three units @ £5000 per unit
TOTAL: £15,000
(Paid in full)

'Shit,' said Casey. 'I'm guessing he wasn't selling fruit machines...'

'It gets worse,' said Fraser. 'Eddie did a little digging. Illegal but I'm sure you could get a warrant and go the proper route. It seems there have been four of these types of payment made in the last twelve months. Rat has been a very busy boy. I suspect other homes in the area being targeted, apart from Oaklands.'

'Why do I get the feeling there's something else?'

'Parties,' said Fraser, his voice dripping with disgust.

'What do you mean?'

'The Kilgarry Club hosts parties for its members. Invitation only. Supposedly for networking and fund-raising purposes.'

'Oh, yes. I saw that in their brochure. It's normal though, isn't it? High flying businessmen expect to be entertained before they offer donations to charity. Sickening but not against the law.'

'Oh, I think you might not say that once you hear... Most of the parties are exactly as you describe. A few, however, are not. Eddie has been looking at dates and places over the last week or so. The photos Sarah had taken at the club were date-stamped. These were from the parties held on the first Friday of each month. They link in with the dates on the more sickening images and videos on that pen drive, evidence of regular molestation and rape of very young girls. You remember those?'

'I'll never forget them,' said Casey, her voice distorted by the rage now swelling in her throat

'Look, I didn't know about that other stuff, okay?' said Maggie. 'The girls here always go, so I assumed it was all kosher. Don't have to do much. Just pretend those dipshit rich buggers are absolutely fucking fascinating... well, they're so far up themselves, they believe they're irresistible, anyway. The girls are well paid for their company... and that's all they get, believe me. I make sure of that. And there's never been any trouble, so they're happy to do it. It's like a night off for them really.

None of us have ever seen any young ones there, none of this crap you're on about.'

'Jesus, Maggie!' said Fraser.

'Look, we all have to survive, okay? Judge all you fucking want but this is the real world. If we don't go tonight, they'll know... they'll come after us. Party's tonight. We have to go.'

'Yes, yes... you have to go,' said Fraser. 'But I wish you'd told me about this before.'

Maggie stared at him. Her face softened, and she turned away.

Fraser crossed over to her and pulled her round to face him.

'You *did* know, didn't you? Go on, admit it! How long? How long have you known, Maggie? Do you have any idea what you've done? Girls are dead because –'

'You still don't get it, do you, Fraser? These bastards control everything – the police, the courts, the whole fucking city! I didn't know for sure, just heard rumours, and if I'd said anything, I'd be dead right now. So, I'm sorry I'm not some fucking heroine for you to feel proud of. I'm just the same grubby little bitch I've always been... how do you think I've stayed alive all these years? Fucking stupid...'

Maggie tore herself away from him and turned away. Fraser stared at her, his face white with rage. The room felt heavy with silence, the only sound an occasional sniff from Maggie.

'We have to do something, Fraser,' said Casey.

'Agreed. We have to check out the party.'

Maggie turned and stared. She shook her head.
Y...you can't! You can't do that,' she said.

'It can't go on, Maggie,' said Fraser. 'We have to stop this.'

'You don't know what you're getting into,' said Maggie. Her voice was trembling.

'High time I did, then, eh?'

'I can't help you,' said Maggie. Anger flashed in her eyes.

Fraser turned to Casey. His expression told her that caution hadn't been so much thrown to the winds as discarded and trampled underfoot.

'Can you get me into the station. I need to speak to Notter.'

'But –'

'Just trust me on this, eh?'

Casey flushed and nodded, her lips pressed together tightly as if fighting back some unruly words.

Fraser turned back to Maggie.

'What time are you leaving and where is it happening?'

Maggie stared at him, her mouth trembling with rage or fear.

'Come on, Maggie. I need to know. I could, of course, just get someone to follow you, or make a few phone calls and have you arrested.'

'Bastard!'

'Well?'

'Fuck's sake... you're going to get us all killed.'

'If you don't, I'll hold you personally responsible for the next corpse that washes up along the coast.'

Maggie looked at Casey and then back at Fraser. Her chin was wobbling and her eyes glittered

'Oh, shit... all right, all right... Jesus... it starts at eight. They send a car for us about half seven. Now, you have to go!'

'Kilgarry Club?'

Maggie nodded. Fraser glanced at the clock and then headed for the door.

'C'mon. Casey,' he said. 'We don't have much time.'

45

Casey nodded to the desk sergeant, who simply raised his eyebrows when he caught sight of Fraser, but there was no time to explain.

'Notter in?' asked Casey.

'Yeah. He has a meeting at four though...'

'This won't take long,' said Casey, giving Fraser a look which said that it had better not. Fraser pretended not to notice.

As they were going up the stairs, Casey's phone went off.

'Drummond. Hello... yes... oh, shit... well, I'm on my way up.'

'Anything I shouldn't know?' he said, with a smirk.

'Harrison's disappeared.'

'Ah, I was half expecting that. Very wise, I would say.'

The corridors were deserted. A background murmur of voices grew and then faded as they passed each open doorway, their quick footsteps muffled by thin, industrial carpeting. As they reached the door of Notter's office, Fraser wheeled round and stopped Casey.

'I'll take care of this. Alone. If it all goes tits up, you still get to keep your job.'

Casey swallowed her protests. The gleam in Fraser's eye told her there was no point.

'Okay. So, what do I do then?'

'Maybe you and Harry could pay a visit to that councillor. I doubt if he goes to the parties, but he might know about them. Squeeze as much information out of him as you can. Emphasise the effect this sort of shit can have on people's lives and career prospects.'

'You are a bastard, Fraser,' said Casey, with a smile.

'I know. It's a gift.'

'You are remembering that I'm not on shift just now?'

'Am I working?'

'Fair point.'

'If this goes well, you'll get time owed, I would think.'

'And if it doesn't?'

'Then I'll owe you dinner.'

'I'll hold you to that,' said Casey.

Fraser watched her walk away and hoped that she would come for dinner either way. He rapped on the door but didn't wait to be invited in. Notter was on the phone. He told whoever it was that he would phone them back.

'Fraser. What do you think you're doing?'

'Had to speak to you. Sorry about your wife. Surprised you're here at all today.'

'I had to... one or two things to clear up.'

'Didn't want to be at home?'

Notter nodded, and Fraser knew he was remembering the arguments they'd had about Fraser coming back to work after the fire. It had been a bad idea, Fraser conceded now. He wondered if Notter would feel the same way.

'What is it you want, Fraser. Only, it's not a good time for me just now, after... after what happened. You must understand.'

Fraser let out a bitter bark of laughter.

'Oh, I do, Eric. I understand only too well, or are you suffering from amnesia as well as grief?'

'Look, I really am sorry about –'

'No bullshit, please. We don't have much time.'

'What? Where's this "we" coming from, all of a sudden?'

Fraser stopped pacing and marched over to where Notter was sitting. He loomed over him, bringing his face as close to Notter's as possible.

'Listen, Eric. The shit is rapidly approaching the proverbial fan. I foresee a situation in which some fairly prominent people in this city might get put away for a long, long time. Do you want to join them? Only, I've heard that ex-policemen don't do very well inside.'

'Wh...what are you talking about?'

'I'm talking about a group of well-off, well-connected sicko fucking perverts, the kind that like to play with children, like to hurt them. I'm talking pictures, videos, really obscene stuff, Eric. I'm talking very, very sick shit, and we have it all organised in a nice, neat package, ready to hand over to the right people. And I mean the *right* people, people who know how to deal with scum like that, no matter how much money they give to charity. I think you must have had an inkling. You were far too close not to know that something was wrong, but you said nothing. You, Eric, you did fuck all about it, which makes you just as guilty as they are. More so, even, since you're supposed to be a police officer, or had you forgotten that?'

'I…what are you talking about? What children? How dare you march in here and –'

Fraser slammed his hand down hard on the desk. The sound echoed in the almost empty room.

'Listen, Eric, I know exactly how I was forced out. I even have scientific evidence to back me up. Then there's that signature that isn't mine, on that fake invoice, and you know what? The handwriting on that was very fucking familiar. All I have to do is lift that phone…'

'Okay, okay… look, I can't… I… what do you want from me?'

'That's better. Ready to listen now?'

Fraser walked around the desk and sat down in one of the chairs facing Notter.

'There have been some very odd planning decisions recently. Don't you agree?'

Notter looked puzzled by the sudden switch of subject.

'Where are you going with this?'

'Your father-in-law seems to have some hold over the local council… or is it perhaps a little higher up than that?'

'I… don't know-'

Fraser reached for the phone. Notter covered it with his hand and sighed.

'That's not fair and you know it. I've suspected... but with no proof... anyway, that's how the world works, the real world. I'm not responsible for that.'

'But you are responsible for forged documents that helped put me on suspension. You may even have something to do with that trumped up assault charge. People are going to be looking into that too, believe me. I think you can probably kiss that pension of yours good-bye, wouldn't you say?'

'Fraser, please. I don't know anything about that assault. Nothing to do with me. Please be reasonable. I've just lost my wife.'

'Reasonable? *You* want *me* to be reasonable? Coming from you, that's... well, a bit rich, wouldn't you say? That little stitch up you and your friends did on me happened not long after I lost the two people I cared most about in the world. Where was your pity then, your fucking compassion?'

'I had no choice. I felt terrible...'

'Oh boo fucking hoo!'

'He had me over a barrel. Said he had photos. Said he'd sell a story to the papers about me with prostitutes. Not true but it wouldn't matter. I'd lose everything.'

'So, instead, you arranged for me to lose everything!'

'Please, I'll vouch for you. You'll be reinstated.'

'No, no, no, no, no. That won't do. That won't do at all. But listen, I'm not interested in crucifying you the way you crucified me. I can now prove it's all nonsense. I can get my life back without your help thank you very much. Because I still have friends here, friends who have scientific proof that those papers are bogus. You can put it behind you. Lesson learned. But you'll owe me big time. And now you need to pay. We need a raid on that club.'

'You can't be serious. On what possible grounds?'

'Photographs, films, e-mails... we have copies of some very interesting documents. I suspect your father-in-law does too. It's been a profitable few years for him, hasn't it? And then there are all those fringe benefits... you know, a few disposable teenagers. Who cares about them? No-one gives a shit, right?'

Notter had grown quite pale by now. A faint sheen of sweat appeared on his forehead.

'I... don't know anything about that. Just a few planning decisions. Thought he was just bribing people, calling in favours, that kind of thing. Wasn't right but didn't really hurt anyone... I didn't... are you sure? No...no... can't be true... I wouldn't have... oh, God...What do you want from me? Do you realise...?'

'Oh, yes... what a can of worms I'm opening here? I do indeed. I have seen the vile photographic evidence, watched some sick fucking movies. I'll never get some of those things out of my fucking head... And I also know that there is someone out there who is killing girls, and going after anyone else who becomes an inconvenience to them, gets too close to the truth. Courtesy of an experienced killer who is particularly efficient.'

'Fraser. Please believe... I had no idea. I was going to... He's gone too far.'

'Damned right. I don't know what he has on you and I don't even fucking want to know. That's not important any more. But this is. This ends now.'

'What do you propose?'

'Do you know where Harrison is?'

'I'm not sure. He should be at home just now. Should I -?'

'He's gone. Vanished. Left you to mop up after him, like the good little son-in-law you are.'

Notter's face had drained of colour.

'But he can't have...'

'Yes, well, I'm afraid that is exactly what he's done. Oh, dear, Eric. He's become a bit of a liability, hasn't he? Not just to you, although I'm sure it's been no fun this last few years. No, he has made enemies in high places too. Still, I'm sure it's something a neat little car crash might have solved. Just a pity your wife picked that day to borrow the car. Of course, that kind of approach would take an expert, wouldn't you say? Someone with a bit more finesse than the rent-a-thug types he employs. A professional. Maybe even special-ops type professional. You crapping yourself yet? 'Cause you should be. After all, you could be next on that list. Guilt by association.'

'Christ... what are you saying? What do you want me to do?'

'Oh, I *had* thought we might join the party. Only I'm not exactly invited, you see. Hence the need for a raid. You might also want to send a couple of uniforms down to Oakland House. I would do that now if I were you. There are a couple of little girls that don't need to get dragged into this. They probably aren't involved yet, but Casey's going to talk to your councillor friend. I suspect he might want to find somewhere else for them.'

'Jesus Christ! I didn't know about that. Harrison and... they are on the board. Fundraise for the place. I thought that, at least, was genuine. But won't they know?'

'No, I don't think so. The councillor will have to be told of course, but the arse-holes that have been treating the place like some sort of pervert's sweetie shop, they won't know for a while. Bit of a surprise for them. I love surprises, don't you?'

'Shit... oh, fuck...'

'Tsk, tsk, awful language that. So, anyway, you'd best make a start. There's a lot to do. Just get that raid organised. The party starts at eight. That only gives you a few hours to get everything in place. Your one and only chance to save those kids, and redeem yourself. And if you don't, I'll make damned sure you go down with the rest of them. Got that?'

'Shit...'

Fraser watched Notter slump down in his chair, staring at Fraser in disbelief. Fraser turned and walked away, quite unable to mask the spring in his step.

46

Fraser hurried down the stairs and out into a bitterly cold day. He raced to his car, regretting the thin jacket he'd thrown on that morning. He was about to start the engine when his phone rang. It was Eddie.

'Hi Eddie. Everything okay?'

'Oh, I'm fine. Listen, I saw the article in the Evening paper. You seen it yet?'

'No. Not had time.'

'There's some info on snake-man, Wasilewski. Anyway, I was curious. After all, he's a long way from his usual patch. So, I did a search online. Found a photo from a few years back. Him coming out of court. In the background, you can see his girlfriend. I'm going to send it to you. Hang on.'

Fraser could hear the click of Eddie's fingers on the keyboard. A picture appeared on his phone. The hair was a different style, different colour. But there was no mistaking who it was. Fraser felt his insides turn to ice.

'Suzy!' he said.

'Yes. Except it's not Suzy. It's a woman by the name of Michelle James, or Mickey-J, as she was better known. High-class call girl turned expert blackmailer. Suzy, the real Suzy, disappeared from her home and her job several years back. Never been found. Doubt she ever will. She was Mickey-J's probation officer.'

Fraser felt like he'd been punched. He had to warn Jamie. Get her away before anything else happened to her.

'Thanks, Eddie. Need to go. Speak later.'

'Take care, pal.'

Fraser wondered which call to make first.

He called Jamie. It rang a few times and then he heard her low chuckle, as she spoke to someone else.

'Jamie?'

'Hi, Fraser!'

'Who's that with you?'

'Just Dod and Suzy.'

'Suzy's there?'

'Yeah. We're friends, Fraser. It's what friends do, you know? Talk... and have a wee glass or three, eh?'

She began to giggle again. There seemed little point in reminding her that her location was supposed to be a secret, even from her friends.

'Where are you?' said Fraser.

'Oh, don't be such an old woman, Fraser...'

'Where-are-you?' he repeated, feeling an edge of fear and frustration seep into his voice.

'Awww... fuck's sake. There's this cool wee bar on the main street. Suzy suggested it. Her friend's gonna pick us up.'

'What friend?'

'Oh, shit... don't remember his name. What's his name again?'

'Jamie! Jamie, listen!'

'Yeah, okay, okay, I'm still here.'

'Listen. Stay exactly where you are. I'll send someone to pick you up.'

'It's okay, we're gettin' picked up soon, eh, Dod?'

'Jamie!'

'It's okay. Suzy's said she'll look after us.'

'No! Jamie!'

But she had hung up.

'Fuck!' said Fraser.

He phoned Casey.

'Hello? Fraser?'

'It's Suzy,' he said.

'Something happened to her?' said Casey.

'No. Quite the reverse, in fact. She's the one.'

'What?'

'She's Jamie's friend, so Jamie's been telling her everything. It's Suzy. Suzy's the one who's been leaking information. She's Wasilewski's partner.'

Fraser waited for a response.

'Casey?'

'Oh, shit. Do you want her picked up?'

'Too late for that. She's with Jamie and Dod and there's someone else coming for them and I think we can guess who that is.'

'Oh, Christ, I'm at the council offices just now. Can you ...?'

'Jamie's wasted already. Hung up on me.'

'Fraser, calm down. Let me think.'

'How did you get on with the councillor?'

'He's on his way, along with a couple of social workers. If necessary, they'll stay here with the girls overnight, until other arrangements can be made. Notter's been calling everyone in, including me. I should really... no, look, hang on, I can be with you in two minutes. We'll do this together.'

'You sure?'

'No, but... well, Harry will explain it all to Notter. Just don't move. Okay?'

'I will be as still as a... a still thing...'

There was a muffled laugh at the other end and then Casey rang off.

Three minutes later, Casey's car pulled into the car park. Fraser got out of his car, waved at Harry's disappearing figure and then jumped into the front passenger seat.

Casey handed him an envelope. Just got these through from Eddie. Persuaded our councillor to print some off. Not a happy camper but if anything, he seems relieved it's all over. I doubt he was directly involved but he was being leaned on, along with several others, and all for the sake of Harrison getting certain planning refusals overturned.'

Fraser had a quick leaf through the papers. He whistled.

'Holy shit! There's some pretty big names on here.'

'I know. The really big ones will slip through, as usual. But, yeah. Makes you wonder if there's anyone left up there, at the top, who *isn't* involved,' said Casey. She started up the engine and swung the wheel hard right towards the exit. Fraser phoned Eddie. Put it on speaker.

'This stuff was not on the pen drive, Eddie. How did you come by it?'

'Well, hello and thank you to you too. Yes, of course, it's no bother, you are most welcome. Come on, pal. So, I accessed some e-mails...'

'You *accessed* e-mails... that a euphemism?'

'Kind of... but it's not that important.'

'Well, it might be, actually,' said Casey.

'Do you want this info or not? I've got a lot more stuff here. A hell of a lot.'

'It's okay, Eddie,' said Fraser. 'Fire away.'

'Okay. Well, there have been some extraordinary planning decisions, as you know. Most of them relate to Harrison's developments, although there are others. Evidence of bribes paid and blackmail, as well as all the names of people they want silenced, by any means necessary. There are some big names involved here and not just local either, not by any means. It's much bigger than we thought. Much.'

'Christ, Eddie,' said Fraser.

'Thing is, I might only have access to this stuff for a limited time.'

'Understood.'

'I've had to save it all multiple times of course.'

'Of course.'

'By the way, one of the names on the hit list is Jamie, along with Dod, Laurie, and you.'

'I'm flattered,' said Fraser. 'I don't suppose you got print-outs?'

'Of course I did,' said Eddie. 'As I said, big names.'

Fraser sighed. This was going to be some mess to clean up. The general public would lose all faith ... but of course, that would not be allowed to happen. The powers that be would trot out all the usual excuses for keeping certain things quiet. Public order for one. National security for another. Could be a shit storm otherwise...

'Eddie, you've not sold any of this?' said Fraser.

'Of course not. Running it past you first, like I always do.'

'Please just keep a lid on it for now. I'll let you know what you can use, as soon as... well, you know.'

'Understood.'

'And thanks.'

'Hope it helps.'

'And Eddie?'

'What?'

'If I catch you doing anything like this again, I *will* shop you!'

'Of course you will.'

Fraser snorted with laughter. Casey flashed him a disapproving look.

'Casey. Anonymous informant left this for us, okay? This might be the leverage we need to get *all* this shit closed down.'

Casey knew he was right but he wasn't the one who was risking his job, was he? As she thought this, she felt guilty. Hadn't this whole episode already cost him precisely that? They drove the rest of the way to Eddie's in silence, each of them lost in thought.

They found the wee bar easily enough. It was just around the corner from the B&B. It was fairly standard issue. Dark wood everywhere, lumpy walls covered in the dreaded woodchip and magnolia. Small windows and low lighting meant that it was quite dark, so Fraser and Casey had to walk right round to make sure they didn't miss them. They weren't there. Casey walked over to the polished counter and flashed her ID.

'Hello there. We were trying to track down a couple of young people. They were in this place with one or maybe two other people, just having a few drinks. They're not in trouble. We just need to trace them.'

The young woman behind the bar smiled.

'Oh, yeah. Think I know who you mean. Young couple and they were with an older woman. Left about five minutes ago. Think some guy came to pick them up. He didn't come in, just waved from the doorway, so I didn't really see him. They all seemed to be having a good time, though.'

'I don't suppose they said anything about where they were going?'

'Not really. But the girl, the young one, was shouting about a party, I think. Sorry I can't be more help.'

'Thank you. You have been very helpful, I assure you,' said Casey, with a forced smile.

Fraser and Casey hurried outside.

'Party,' said Casey.

'Yes, I heard. Phone Notter. Might need backup.'

'We're going in?'

'Fucking right we are. Bastards. Ten minutes earlier and we'd have got them.'

'What will they do to them?'

'I don't know but whatever it is, it won't be pleasant.'

47

The journey into the city and out to the west, was fast and uneventful. Casey stopped the car in a little side road close to the club.

'How are we going to do this?' said Casey, already feeling convinced that this was a very, very bad idea.

'Carefully, I would suggest. Come on,' said Fraser.

He beckoned her to follow him into the small patch of woodland that bordered one side of the large front green.

'Jesus, Fraser, you're not Richard Hannay, you know!'

Fraser smiled and carried on. They walked until they were level with the front steps.

'What now?' she said.

'Let's just watch for a while, see if there's a pattern.'

Two men were walking around the building, in opposite directions, as if looking for intruders. Other than that, there seemed to be little in the way of security.

'Right,' said Fraser. As soon as that guy disappears round the back, we run. You ready?'

'No.'

'Come on. Where's your sense of adventure?'

They watched in silence as the two men crossed in front of the house, walked down the side and then vanished.

'Now!' said Fraser.

They took off and sprinted across the lawn and up the three stone steps to the door. It was lying open. A murmur of voices to their left told them where the main bar was. But where were Jamie and Dod?

Fraser heard steps approaching and pulled Casey into a dark corner by the stairs. They squatted there together, scarcely breathing, as a couple of middle aged men sauntered past, each with a young woman hanging on his arm. One of the girls spotted them. She stared briefly, and then made a big gesture at the door. God knows what she said, but it did the trick. No-one looked in their direction.

'Do you know her?' said Casey.

'Barely. Name's Ivy. One of Maggie's lodgers.'

A short time later, Ivy reappeared. She looked all around and then approached them. She looked terrified.

'The young ones are downstairs. I have to go.'

Fraser grabbed her arms.

'Is that where Jamie is?'

'Jamie? No, no, no... she doesn't come here.'

'She's here tonight. With Suzy.'

'Oh, dear God. She'll be downstairs. You should look downstairs.'

She wrenched her arm away and hurried off.

'Downstairs?'

'Must be another staircase,' said Fraser.

He walked under the stairs and pointed to a door. Casey crept over and opened it. Stone steps led downwards, lit by a flickering strip light.

Fraser and Casey walked forward, closing the door quietly behind them. They stepped carefully downwards, listening for any sounds. In the distance, they could hear voices but couldn't make out what was happening. At the bottom of the stairs, was a corridor which met the staircase at right angles.

'Which way?' whispered Casey.

Fraser put a finger to his mouth, urging her to be quiet. He looked right and left. The corridor on the right was shorter. He and Casey hurried to the end and then walked back, listening at each closed door they passed. Nothing. They carried on going. A sudden cry rang out and made them both jump. It had been distant and muffled. Presumably, these rooms were sound-proofed.

Casey was listening at the first door, when she noticed the door number was loose. She examined it and realised that it was held in place by one small hinge at the top. By lifting it, she was able to look through a small peep-hole into the room beyond. There was a plain little room, with a single bed covered in cushions and a small chest of drawers next to it. Another door, to the left, appeared to house a bathroom. She could just make out the edge of a shower cubicle. There was no-one in there.

She stepped across to where Fraser was listening at the door and reached up to lift the door number. Fraser gave her a thumbs up. He leaned in to look. Similar set up inside but no-one there. The last two rooms were different. In one, a young girl, who looked about fourteen, lay sleeping fitfully, low moans issuing from her intermittently. She was, presumably, the source of that cry. In the other room, were Dod and Jamie. They lay, bound and gagged, on the stone floor next to the bed. They appeared to be unharmed. Fraser tried the door. It opened inward. Casey pointed to the door, to where a door handle should have been. Clearly, you weren't supposed to let yourself out.

'Can you stay here with them? I'll close the door so it's less obvious. Just want to check up the other end, now we know how to see in,' whispered Fraser.

Casey nodded and crouched down next to the young couple. They seemed to be out of it. She hoped it was only alcohol. Their wrists and ankles were bound with cable ties. Casey dug in her pocket and found her nail clippers. For once, her having crappy nails had come in handy. She went nowhere without her clippers. Their mouths were covered in tape. Shit. If she tried to peel that away, they would wake up fighting. She had to wake them up first. She tried shaking their shoulders, but all she got was a groan or two. Their eyes never opened. Shit. Where was Fraser? Almost as if he had heard her, Casey heard the door opening. She turned, smiling.

But it wasn't Fraser.

48

Fraser had checked every room at the other end before he found what he was looking for. He knew there had to be more than one. The two furthest rooms were occupied. In each, a young girl lay sleeping or drugged. They looked to be about fifteen but it was hard to tell with all the make-up. He tried speaking to each of them but there was no response. He was about to come out of the second room, to check on Casey, when he heard the sound of footsteps on the stairs. He froze, listening. The footsteps receded. They were going to the other end, where Casey was.

Fraser tried his phone. No signal. He peered out, just in time to see two men entering the room where Casey was. Shit! He stepped out into the corridor and moved quickly towards the stairs. Casey was right. He was no Richard Hannay. No hero. And those guys were big. He had to get a signal, had to get outside.

He took the stairs two at a time, no longer concerned with the noise. He was pretty sure they wouldn't hear him anyway. At the top of the stairs, he peered out. There were lots of people milling around, but they all seemed to be moving to the right. The dining room. Of course. He cautiously emerged and peered around the staircase until there were just a couple of elderly men chatting near the dining room door. He'd just have to brazen it out.

Fraser walked towards the door, looking straight ahead. He was almost at the door when a shout rang out.

'Hey! Hoy! Young fella? Where... come back here!'

Fraser never looked back. He just ran for the door and down the steps. The two goons circling the building had just crossed the front and were about to round the corner when he emerged. Fraser took off and headed for the trees. He ignored the shouts behind him and ran, hoping that neither of the two guys at the door was a sprinter. He was pretty sure he could beat them on stamina. Eventually, he stopped and listened. Nothing. He fished out his phone and called Notter.

'We're on our way,' snapped Notter, by way of greeting.

'They've got Casey,' said Fraser. 'And Dod and Jamie. Plus, there are three girls in there that are almost certainly underage. Possibly drugged.'

'And where are you?'

'Outside. Couldn't get a signal in there.'

'So, you just left Casey?'

'No. I needed to check I had back up,' Fraser said. 'I'm going back now.'

'What?'

'There has to be another way in. Round the back.'

'But they'll see you.'

'Possibly, but I have to get back, in case they move them before you guys get here. You got a warrant?'

'Thought it best not to try, since we don't know who the others are.'

'Okay. Fair point. So –'

'But I do have something that looks very much like a warrant.'

'Eric, I'm surprised at you... good man!'

'Five minutes.'

Fraser rang off and started to move back through the trees, more slowly this time. He was suddenly aware of every crack of twig and rustle of leaf. Now and then, he was sure he heard someone, but it was his imagination. He reached a spot level with the front door. Through the trees, he could see a huddle of men on the steps and on the lawn at the front of the house. They were almost all smoking. He hoped it was just a cigarette break.

He carried on moving towards the back of the house. The woodland formed a soft arc around the back of the house, petering out just before the edge of a large car park and turning area. A couple of small vans, with the club logo on the side, and half a dozen modest cars, presumably belonging to staff, sat around the fringes of the tarmac.

A few seconds later, he saw a young man, wearing a white apron, emerge from a small door he hadn't previously noticed, at the back of the building. Fraser watched as the guy started puffing at a vaper, clouds of steam rising from the small brass object and drifting upwards in the cold air. Fraser wondered what flavour it was supposed to be. He hated being caught in a cloud of that stuff. Almost preferred the smell of stale tobacco. But that was by the by...

The kitchen was in the basement. Must be directly behind the area where those bedrooms were. Was there a connecting door? Probably not. But the food would have to get upstairs somehow. There must be another staircase. Fraser waited until the young guy went back in. The security guys crossed a few seconds later. Once they were gone, Fraser sprinted across the tarmac towards the back door, which stood slightly ajar. Warm air radiated out. Must be like working inside a sauna.

He could hear the clattering of plates and a constant burble of voices, shouting orders, shouting responses. They were obviously busy. Fraser pushed the door a bit more open. The kitchen was to his right, bright lights and the flickering of gas flame lit up the doorway. He could make out a whole horde of people in white. Rushing about. Then he spotted a flight of stairs ahead of him. Had to try.

He edged his way in and then ran to the stairs. If he could get back to the ground floor, he'd be able to find them again. He ran up the stairs, grateful for the rubber treads that deadened the sound. He reached a half landing and another flight of steps to a set of swing doors. He pushed one side and realised it opened onto the dining room. To his left, he spotted another door, marked 'staff only'. He slid forward as quietly as possible and went to the staff door. It wasn't locked. He went inside and hurried to the other end. He had hoped there might have been another door, opening onto the entrance hall; there'd been a staff only door there too. No such luck.

He looked around him and spotted a set of shelves with newly laundered staff overalls of various kinds and colours. There was a brown boiler suit, about the right size. It was stained with oil and had a workshop smell about it. Close by was a toolbox. Perfect. He quickly donned the boiler suit. It was a bit short in the leg but the body of it fitted fine. Fraser collected the toolbox and walked out into the dining room. He ignored the gasps and rumblings of disapproval. A tall, smartly dressed waiter grabbed his arm and marched him quickly towards the entrance hall.

'If I've told you once, I've told you a thousand times, no maintenance people in the dining room during meal times!'

Fraser looked up at him.

'Sorry, I'm new.'

'Yes, well... bear that in mind in future.'

Fraser watched the man flounce off and thanked all that was holy that he had never had to work in hospitality. The entrance hall was deserted. Fraser hurried over to the basement door, hoping he wasn't too late. He walked down the steps, holding the toolbox steady to avoid it rattling.

At the bottom, he looked both ways. Nothing. He put the toolbox down on the bottom step and crept to the right, to check on the two young girls. They were still there, exactly as before. Fraser walked back along to the stairs and squatted next to the toolbox. He opened it and removed a few small tools, which he shoved in his pocket, just in case. He looked at a claw hammer but decided against it. Then he started to move along the corridor towards the room where Casey and the others had been. He slid the number across. The room was empty. Fraser felt something somersault somewhere deep in his guts. Where the hell were they?

He crossed to the opposite room. Nothing. He worked his way back along the corridor. At the fifth door, he found them. Relieved, he opened the door. Casey was sitting up on the floor, facing the door. She stared towards him, her head quivering. What was she trying to tell him? He was half way to her when a blow to the back of his head launched him forward onto his knees. Fraser turned to see who had hit him. It was snake man. Fraser watched helplessly, as the thug walked over and hit Casey too. She fell sideways, her head hit the bed-end with a sickening thud and she slid to the floor, moaning. A familiar voice made Fraser wheel round.

'Nice of you to join us, Fraser, I knew you'd come,' said Suzy. 'Unfortunately for you guys, the party is now over.'

She was sitting on a chair to one side of the room, not visible via the peep-hole.

'How could you do this?' he said.

'Money. I needed it. They had it. It's that simple.'

'But they're just kids.'

'I was too. You survive.'

'Stephanie didn't.'

'Stephanie was stupid. Stupid people don't.'

Rage took hold of him and Fraser lunged towards her, but he was too slow, still clumsy from the blow to his head. Wasilewski yanked him backwards. Fraser felt a hard blow smash into his back. He fell forward onto the floor, gasping for breath. Then, Wasilewski kicked him in the stomach, knocking any remaining breath from him, and leaving him gasping as pain flooded in. Fraser felt as if he were drowning in it.

The light seemed to be fading, everything becoming more dim, harder to understand. He forced himself to calm down, to regulate his breathing. Then he lay and watched as Suzy rolled back a thin rug to reveal a trap door. She gestured to her partner, who came over and hauled the door open. Below lay a spiral staircase.

'You go down first. Get the car,' said Suzy.

Snake man said nothing but did as he was asked.

'Does he always do what you tell him?' croaked Fraser.

'What can I say? He loves me. We met through a certain wealthy man I used to know, who didn't want his wife hearing about the parties. Stefan solved a problem for me. Been doing that ever since.'

'You're worse than any of them. You choose to do this. Fact that you know first-hand what the kids will go through... makes you a monster. Even more of a monster that Harrison.'

'Harrison? That's one sick bastard. I'm telling you... but under all that, he was just another cheap conman.'

'Was?'

'Is, then.'

'Is Harrison dead?'

'How the fuck should I know? All I know is he went too far, with the wrong fucking people It's only a matter of time for him.'

'Yes... I assumed that.'

'Well, assume something else then. Harrison suddenly disappears, clears out his accounts, abandons everything. I'm sure that's what he was planning to do, but do you think that the people who really control all this, the ones you'll never find, do you think they would let him get away?'

Fraser thought for a moment. Even if Harrison had managed to get a plane and disappear, it would take no time for certain people to find out where he was, what new identity he'd assumed, and then for them to go solve a little problem. It was a chilling thought. At that moment, Wasilewski climbed back up.

'You ready?' he said to Suzy.

She got up and followed him back down the stairs.

Fraser looked over at Casey. She was groaning, about to come round again. He wanted to speak to her, to apologise for dragging her into this. But the darkness was drifting over him again, and he no longer had the strength to fight it. He felt something wet and sticky under his hand and realised that he was bleeding. He tried to reach behind him to press on the wound but he had no energy left, his arms felt heavy and useless. Breathing was hard work. His vision was going. A strange calm washed over him as he felt himself drift away.

49

Casey woke in pain. She reached up and touched her head, then cursed with the pain. She looked over and saw Fraser. He was lying in a pool of blood. She crawled over to him, each awkward movement causing a banging pain in her head. Gingerly, she looked at the wound in his back. It was oozing slowly, rather than pumping out. She hoped it was a sign that the bleeding was stopping and not an indication that his heart was. She could hear him breathing. It sounded laboured. She felt his pulse. It was faint and rapid. She had to get help.

The trap door lay open, which was fortunate; there was no way she could have lifted it by herself, in the state she was in. She crawled over to the opening and swung her legs down into the stairwell. She had to concentrate. Her vision was blurred, and her balance appeared to be non-existent. She knew she had to hurry but she couldn't go any faster, each step was an adventure in fear and pain.

Eventually, she reached the ground. She was in a garage. It was quite dark but she could see a bright sliver of light indicating the doorway. Shuffling and stumbling, she edged her way forward and pushed it open. The brightness outside was coming from a line of floodlights that shone over the driveway in front of the house. Casey no longer cared about discretion. She began to scream for help as she walked slowly along the side path, one hand flat against the wall for support. As she rounded the corner of the house, a young woman happened to look over, Casey saw her pointing, and heard her shriek. Two men rushed over and helped Casey over to the steps, where she sat down. It was then that she realised she was covered in blood.

'What on earth has happened. Do you need an ambulance?' said one of the men.

'More than one. We need a fleet,' said Casey, managing a weak smile.

As if on cue, a series of police vehicles and ambulances streamed in through the gates. With lights and sirens blaring, of course. Casey chuckled at that.

'Thank you, Fraser, you sod,' she said.

The two men looked confused. The security guards appeared in front of the house and looked in horror at Casey and then at the fast approaching squad cars. They climbed the steps together and waited by the door.

Casey watched as Notter and his posse of uniforms spilled out of the cars. Two vans at the back would be used to transport suspects and witnesses. Notter and Harry rushed over to Casey.

'What on earth...' began Notter.

'Basement,' said Casey. 'Fraser's been stabbed. Three teenagers drugged up on something. Likewise, Dod and Jamie. Send the medics in first, eh?'

'I'm on it,' said Harry. He grabbed one of the men standing nearby and barked at him. 'Show us the way to the basement' Then he waved to the ambulance crew to hurry inside. He followed them in.

'Is this all Fraser's blood?' said Notter.

'Mostly,' said Casey. 'I got a bit of a bash on the head as well.'

'Who did this?'

'Wasilewski. They're long gone.'

'They?'

'Him and his partner. Can I explain later?'

'Of course. Sorry.' Notter waved over one of the young officers.

'Help her into a car and drive to A&E. Fast as you can. Be quicker than waiting for a spare ambulance. And make sure there's someone in the back with her.'

'Yes, sir,' replied the young man, waving to a colleague to come and help.

'Thanks, sir,' said Casey. 'Some amount of paperwork with this lot.'

Notter managed a wry smile.

People had started to spill out of the club and onto the stairs. A few uniformed officers were waving them back inside. It was like trying to settle a nest of snakes. Casey felt for them, as she allowed herself to be half-carried to a car. She hoped that Fraser was continuing to breathe. It would be really annoying of him to die on her now.

50

Fraser lay back on his pillows, enjoying the coolness of crisp, white sheets against his skin. The pain had almost gone now but he couldn't be sure whether that was because his wounds were healing or on account of the welcome and regular pain relief they were pumping into him. He had to admit though, that he would be glad to get home, and have his privacy back again. Enforced company was his idea of hell, even if the company here was fairly congenial. He heard footsteps approaching and looked over, hoping it might be Casey. It was Notter. Fraser had to concede that Notter had been remarkably attentive this last week, visiting the ward every day to check on him. He was doing a pretty reasonable impression of a decent human being.

'Hi Fraser. Brought you the pan drops you asked for. You got enough reading materials?'

'Yeah. Plenty, Eric, thanks. Might even get home today. Waiting for the dreaded ward round.'

'It's not that bad, is it?'

'A crowd of students staring down at you every day? Being discussed as if you weren't there? Having teenagers periodically experiment on you with hypodermic needles? I've had more fun, to be honest. Still... better than being dead, eh?'

'I have some good news for you. All the charges against you have been dropped. As soon as you're fit again, you can come back to work.'

'And what about you?'

'I went and spoke to the boss. Discussed my situation, what with Harrison being wanted and me guilty by association. Thanks for not dropping me in it over all this. I won't forget it.'

'Don't get all soppy on me Eric. We'll never be bosom buddies, you and I, will we?'

Notter looked solemn. He nodded, almost imperceptibly.

'You're right. I deserve that,' he said. 'You won't have to put up with me when you get back, in any case. They thought I should've had a better handle on the situation. Also said my management style wasn't the best. Been a few grumblings, apparently. So, anyway, since I was only acting up in your absence, they're putting me back down to sergeant again. Been offered a transfer. As soon as you're back, I'll be off down to the Borders. Nothing to keep me here now. Kids want to stay with their gran.'

'That must be tough.'

'To be honest, although I love my kids, I don't like them very much a lot of the time, and I will get visitation rights, I think. She might make things awkward though. Seemed to take offence at my involvement in attempts to arrest her husband. Odd that,' said Notter, smiling.

'Most unreasonable,' said Fraser. 'Has he turned up yet, by the way?'

'No. No sign of him. Could be anywhere.'

'I see.'

'Anyway, I won't stay. Just thought I'd bring you this.'

He handed Fraser a small, blue pen drive.

'God, if I never see another one of those again...'

'Sorry.'

'What's on it? Where did it come from?'

'About a year ago, I suggested divorce. My wife got angry and went running to Daddy, who threatened to release compromising photos of me with some of his prostitute friends. I didn't realise at the time of course. That was before I fully understood the sort of family I'd married into. I was stupid. Bowled over by the attentions of a pretty girl and impressed by their wealth and connections. What can I say? Anyway, I have an old friend with a private security business. He helped me bug the office. I'd almost forgotten about it. Fortunately, I remembered just before the forensic team descended on the house. Only looked at it last night. Should answer a few questions for you, anyway. I just hope you're ready for the answers.'

Fraser looked up at Notter, aware of how difficult this must have been for him.

'That's not all of it', said Notter. 'Just the bit you need. The full version will be handed into evidence. I just thought you should have the chance to look over this first, before everyone else knows about it.'

'The fire.'

Notter nodded.

Fraser could feel himself getting emotional. He wanted to know, had needed to know ever since it happened. But now it was here, in his hand, he felt nothing but terror. He swallowed hard, feeling angry with himself.

'This doesn't change anything, Eric. We still have those pictures of you at the club. One false move...'

'Understood. Anyway, I'd better go. I'm watching the girls tonight. Take care of yourself. And... thanks, Fraser.'

Fraser watched Notter walk away and wondered if the man had really changed or if it was all an act. Mind you, if that's what it was, he was wasted as a policeman.

51

Fraser took a long drink from his pint. It was a while since he last had a drink. It didn't mix well with pain killers. But he was off them now, hopefully for a very long time. Tonight was a bit of a celebration, in honour of the successful conclusion to a long and difficult investigation. Fraser also regarded it as an opportunity to express his gratitude to those who had remained his friends throughout the last painful year.

Fraser watched the door, aware that he was trembling slightly, although whether that was from nerves or the temperature in here, he couldn't be sure. The pub was almost empty. It wasn't quite six yet, but he knew they would be here shortly. He tried to read his paper but the words were making no sense to him and he gave up. Eventually, the door swung open, and in came Casey, Harry and Tony.

'So?' said Tony. 'What did the doctor say?'

'I'll be back on Monday,' said Fraser.

The three of them erupted with a roar of triumph, and Casey ran and threw her arms round him, planting a noisy kiss on his cheek. Fraser smiled.

'So, what's everyone drinking then?' said Tony, coming to Fraser's rescue.

Fraser leaned towards Casey and whispered in her ear.

'Any word on Suzy and her friend?'

'No. Found the car, eventually, but no sign of them. Must have switched vehicles. Be well away by now.'

'Maybe.'

'What do you mean, maybe?'

'They know a lot, too much in some ways. If they're still useful, they'll be kept safe. If not, well, they are replaceable.'

Fraser watched as Casey processed this idea.

'Like Harrison?'

'Exactly. The important ones, the wealthy ones, and the ones at the top... we'll never know who they are.'

'So they all get off with it?'

'Might be a couple of sacrificial lambs. Threats or bribes, that kind of thing. But I think a few of our witnesses might start developing amnesia.'

'Fuck! Sometimes I hate this job.'

'That's good. The only sometimes bit, I mean.'

They touched glasses and drank to the future.

It was almost seven when Eddie arrived. Shortly afterwards Jamie and Dod came through the door.

'Got a new part-time job,' said Jamie. 'Dog-sitting for a nice couple up the west end. Dead easy money. Think I prefer dogs to people, anyway. And I've been offered my first one-man show.'

'That's great news on both counts,' said Fraser.

'Laurie sends her apologies. She also sent you this,' said Dod, handing over a small envelope and a cardboard tube.

Fraser opened the envelope and read the short letter inside.

Dear Fraser,

I do hope you're feeling okay and will soon be back at work again. I gather from Jamie that it's looking hopeful. I knew you'd get there.

The insurance came through on the house, so I'll be able to rebuild. Whilst that's going on, I've decided to spend some time back down south. An old friend from college got in touch recently, on social media, and she's offered to put me up for a few months. I've managed to wangle a few hours a week teaching at the local college. It's not much but it's a start.

Anyway, I'll be on the train when you get this, so I won't be there to say good-bye. Do take care, and don't keep that secret of yours for too long. Take a chance. I know she feels the same way.

I'm sending a little something to remind you of that.

Fondest love as always,
Laurie xxx

Casey had been reading it over his shoulder. They pulled faces at each other and laughed.

'Oh, dear,' said Casey, imbuing those two small words with more amusement than she truly felt.

Fraser picked up the cardboard tube. Inside, he could see a sheet of paper. He drew it out and unrolled it. He and Casey gasped in unison. It was a perfectly realised pastel drawing of the two of them. Dod and Jamie peered over at it.

'Wow,' said Casey. 'She is such a good draughtswoman.'

'Amazing visual memory,' said Fraser.

'Oh, is that what it is?' said Jamie, giggling.

'You think it's a premonition them?' said Fraser, laughing as a blush stole over Casey's face. She thumped his arm.

'Nah,' said Dod. 'That could never happen.'

'Yeah. Horrible idea,' said Jamie. She grinned over at the pair of them.

Fraser looked over at Casey. She was looking beautiful tonight. He got to his feet.

'My round, I think,' he said. It earned him an ironic round of applause.

The fire was lit and the small sitting room at Fraser's cottage was warming up nicely. Fraser handed a glass of wine to Casey, who was curled up like a cat, in the small armchair by the fire. In her hand, she held the flash drive that Notter had given him.

'You haven't listened to it yet?' asked Casey.

'I'm just worried that … that I won't be able to handle what's on it.'

'Did he actually say it was about the fire?'

Fraser nodded.

'I'm here now. We'll listen to it together,' said Casey.

She plugged the little device into the laptop and pressed play. Then she went and sat down on the floor next to Fraser. He draped an arm around her shoulders and drew her towards him, as Harrison's voice boomed from the speakers. A blurry video showed the interior of Harrison's study. His three hired thugs stood in a line in front of him as he paced up and down, clearly in a rage.

'What the bloody hell did you think you were doing? A warning, I said, not a bloody cremation!'

'We thought they were all out,' said one of the men. 'Cars were gone and no lights on anywhere...'

'And you didn't think to check? Of course there were no bloody lights on. It was an old woman and a child. It was eleven o'clock at night. They were sleeping. Bloody cretins! This'll bring the whole fucking force down on us; do you realise that? What is it with you guys and fire? Could you not have sprayed a message in paint, shoved dog shit through the letterbox, burned a sodding cross in the garden even...? Right, you can go and do some work for me down the road. If they come looking, I'll say you went down last week. Now bugger off, the lot of you. Get your stuff packed up. Two weeks on the Costa del Govan.'

'Switch it off, Case,' said Fraser, his voice thick with emotion.

Casey got up and shut it all down. Fraser stood, walked up behind her and wrapped his arms around her'

'So it wasn't that someone was trying to kill me, or kill anyone. Just a cock-up.'

Casey turned around so she could hug him.

'At least now you know.'

'So why don't I feel any better?'

'Maybe not yet, but you will.'

They stood quietly for a few minutes, wrapped around one another, listening to the distant whispers of the sea.

'And when are you going to tell me your story, Case?'

'There's plenty of time for that,' she said.

Fraser really hoped she was right.

THE END

27741878R00218

Printed in Great Britain
by Amazon